I0700951

HIS CAPTIVE MISTRESS

FILTHY BILLIONAIRES

Evelyn Austin

SILVER GRIFFON ASSOCIATES
ORANGE, CA, USA

Silver Griffon Associates
P.O. Box 7383
Orange, CA 92863

Book Layout ©2023 BookDesignTemplates.com
Cover Art ©2023 Kristie Vanilla Lilly Designs Co.

Accidental Mistress / Evelyn Austin. – 1st ed.
ISBN 979-8-88908-014-5

www.EvelynAustin.com

Chapter 1
Dark Domain

Present

EVERYONE, AT LEAST ONCE IN THEIR LIFE, HAS WONDERED how it's going to end. Me? At this point, I'm certain of the *when*, if not exactly the *how*.

I know I'll be dead very soon, probably in the next few hours, if there's any mercy.

No, I can't think like that. There might still be a chance for me to get out of this. For me to get away.

I try to suck in a deep breath, but the air is too thick to draw into my lungs. It feels like I'm suffocating. Like the walls of the car trunk are closing in on me. My mind swirls, but I work hard to stave off the panic. I can feel it crawling up my throat, icy and bitter.

Breathe.

In. Out. In. Out. One. Two. Three...

I don't even stop to consider why this happened, because I already know. I'm a journalist, working on what may have become my breakthrough story. In my research, I uncovered some dark secrets. Secrets that powerful people would rather keep hidden.

And now I've paid the price for it. Maybe the *ultimate* price.

No. As bleak as things look right now, I have to believe I'll find a way out of this *somehow...* some way.

***

Several Weeks Ago

I'm so *unbelievably* excited that I feel like I'm going to throw up.

My college housemate, Lexi, and I are standing in front of one of the most exclusive sex clubs in Los Angeles, *Obscura*. It's connected to the high-end club, Exeter House, and it's invite-only. Thankfully, Lexi knows someone who was able to get our names on the list for tonight.

Securing my black feather mask around my head, I glance over at Lexi. Her anxious gaze is fixed on the large glossy black doors in front of us. I recognize the look—she's seconds away from bolting in terror. Of course, this is a *huge* departure from our usual scene. We're Caltech students and spend so much of our time studying. We barely ever go to regular nightclubs, let alone a *sex* club.

But I've got a story to write, and before I can write it, I need research. I need an angle. And tonight, I'm exhilarated at the prospects in front of me. It's why I became a journalist, to explore life's dark, gritty corners—the things people want to keep hidden. My goal is to bring that darkness into the light, give it a voice. It's my duty as a would-be reporter.

With this new project, I hope to lend that voice to women who are being victimized by wealthy, powerful men. I mean…*allegedly.* I don't have any proof that it's happening here, just yet. But there have been rumors for years, whispers of dark doings at these ultra, high-end sex clubs. Tonight, I'm starting my deep dive.

When my editor assigned me this story, *The Dark Underbelly of Sex Clubs in Los Angeles,* I was hesitant at first. I'm not exactly a sex expert. I've *had* sex, of course, but I've never done anything too terribly adventurous.

But you don't have to be an expert on something in order to write about it, right? That's what research is for. If I can pull this off, then this story will open up opportunities for me. A story like this, when done right, will attract attention. With a lot of work and some luck, my career will skyrocket.

One glossy black door opens, and the club hostess smiles placidly as Lexi and I step up to the entrance. The impeccably dressed woman, masked, of course, greets us and introduces herself as Ms. Lawrence. We give her our names, and she glances down at the list in her hand. Seconds later, she nods. "There are no phones allowed inside the club. Please check them into the first room before the main entrance. Also, you must keep your masks on at all times. Anonymity is important and for the protection of all patrons," Ms. Lawrence says. "No blood play, and if you wish to make use of the fetish rooms, just give the concierge your names."

Blood play? Fetish? What the fuck?

Ms. Lawrence turns to my roommate, Lexi. "Ms. Anderson. Will Mr. Grayson be joining you tonight?"

There's a tense pause, and Lexi looks like a deer in the headlights. *Mr. Grayson* must be Ash, and she's supposed to be meeting that idiot, David, here instead.

Lexi shakes her head quickly. "No, no, I won't be with him tonight," she says, confirming my suspicion.

We check our phones at the designated area, then step farther into the club. We move down a darkened hallway with exotic saltwater fish tanks providing the only lighting. Then, another thick pair of double doors that provide a great deal of soundproofing because we don't hear the music until we crack them open.

The club is all glamor and glitz. Gold and glossy black with intimate lighting and expensive fixtures and furnishings. It reeks of luxury, wealth and sleek modernism.

From the entrance, we stand on a large mezzanine that leads down into what looks like a typical nightclub, except for the fact that everyone is masked, including the servers and bartenders. And many are barely wearing any clothes.

In front of us, there's a sweeping staircase, leading down into the depths of the club itself. As we descend, my gaze is drawn to the dance floor. A catchy rhythm pulses as masked men and women dance, hips swaying to the beat. When Lexi and I reach the bottom floor, a masked waitress immediately hands each of us a drink.

I take a sip. Vodka and cranberry juice. *Gross.*

There's no obvious place for me to put my drink down, so I guess I'll just have to hold it. I shift my focus back to the club. It's obviously high-end. Gold chrome. Dark marble. Low tables, black velvet sofas, and a grand piano. Definitely not your run-of-the-mill establishment. It's dark, elegant, with an air of wicked decadence that sends a chill down my spine.

Obscura. In my research, I discovered the name of the place means *dark* in Latin. What dark deeds are happening here?

I'm determined to find the answer to that question.

I clear my throat and pull a notepad out from my small purse. "Good thing I brought this," I tell Lexi, who's staring around with her mouth agape. "I suspected they'd take our phones. Now that we're in, we just need to find someone who will talk to us."

Lexi's brows furrow under her mask—I think. It's hard to tell in this light. "You aren't seriously going to *interview* these people, are you?"

I lift my hands. Is that a serious question? "Why else would we be here?"

"I don't know, to observe?" she says. "First things first, no taking notes at a sex club. That's just weird. Let's just…look around and get the lay of the land. You take the lounge area. And I'll have a look at the fetish rooms."

"Okay, good plan." I pause when a realization hits me. "Wait, we're separating?"

"Yes," she hisses. "Just…keep your clothes on and you'll be fine. Meet back here in an hour."

Before I can say anything, Lexi is gone, disappearing confidently into the crowd.

Okay, no problem. I can do this. I just need to act naturally, so people will talk to me. Smoothing a hand down my skimpy dress, I go in search of my first unwitting interviewee. My first stop, though, is the bar. The vodka and cranberry juice is far too strong. I need something light and fruity.

I set my drink down on the bar and try to wave down the bartender. He's so busy, he doesn't even see me. With a huff of frustration, I take in the scene around me. The people sitting around the bar are already engaged in conversation. With the masks on, it's difficult, but I try to take special note of everyone's ages. They *look* twenty-one or over, but without asking, it's really hard to tell.

As I continue my perusal, I notice a man at the end of the bar. He's clad in a chic, bespoke suit and wearing a devil mask. He leans forward, one hand curled around his drink. He looks relaxed, confident, like a lord surveying his domain. Even with his mask on, I can tell he's beautiful. He just has that energy about him. And he's staring right at *me*.

I swallow and turn my body away. I'm here for the story, not to pick up a fuck buddy.

Although...

No. I shake myself. *Stay focused.*

A few seconds later, I'm still trying to flag down the bartender when I feel a presence behind me. I half-turn to see it's the mysterious stranger. Looming over me, he signals the bartender, who comes over immediately, leaning in to take the stranger's order.

"What will you have?" the Devil asks me, a posh British accent rolling off his tongue.

"Oh, um, an appletini, please," I say to the bartender.

When I turn around to thank the stranger, he's already gone. I glance around, but he's already disappeared into the crowd of people.

Uh, okay. Well, that was weird.

I was half-hoping the Devil would say something flirty, but I obviously read him wrong. *Damn.* He might have been my first interview.

My appletini appears in front of me in short order, and I sip on it idly as I take in my surroundings. Like me, everyone around me is masked. That alone is cause for deeper investigation. Obscura relies heavily on discretion. It's club policy that everyone wears a mask at all times. I can only imagine why. There are powerful people here, and they're *allegedly* participating in some pretty twisted shit. Twisted shit that they don't want the public to know about. Otherwise, why the masks? Why confiscate patrons' phones? Could something here be illegal? I'd say it's highly likely. Everything's all a little suspicious if you ask me.

I try to pay the bartender for my drink, but he waves me off and darts off to help someone else. Did the Devil pay for my drink? Or did Lexi and I manage to stumble in during a ladies-drink-free hour? Well, whatever.

With my drink in hand, I head toward the dance floor. The music is so loud in this area that the deep bass vibrates the floor, the rhythm wending its way through my body. The dance floor is swollen with people, all half-naked, rubbing against each other. Beautiful women sway atop raised platforms on the perimeter of the dance floor and holographic projections of people in compromising positions flicker along the walls, adding to the sinful ambiance. Nothing untoward is happening out here. But that doesn't mean anything, really.

"Care to join?" a voice asks right next to my ear.

It's that rich, cultured accent from the bar. Heat floods me as I turn to see the handsome Devil standing next to me. "I'm only here to observe," I answer, standing on tiptoe and speaking loudly so that he can hear me.

He chuckles, the sound deep and sinful. "What fun is that?"

I shrug one shoulder and take a sip of my appletini. "My editor sent me here for a story. This isn't my usual scene."

My usual scene is me in my butter-soft leggings and fleece socks, huddled under my covers, with my laptop perched on my knees, watching Netflix maybe while sipping hot chocolate. *That's* my idea of a wild night. And if I'm feeling *really* sinful, I'll throw in some marshmallows.

The stranger shifts beside me. He's close now, so I can get a better look at him. Tall, broad-shouldered, dark hair. He has pale gray eyes that are as cold and hard as a polar winter. They give me chills whenever his gaze holds mine. And he smells *amazing*. Sandalwood and spice. He peers down at me as though he's stripping every layer of my clothing down to my skin, wanting to bore still deeper.

"You're working on a story?" he asks neutrally and I have no way of judging his expression behind the snarling red devil mask.

"I'm—I'm a journalist." I lift my chin, raising my gaze to meet his. "I'm investigating clubs of, um, a certain nature."

"A *certain nature*? You mean *sex*. It's not a dirty word, Angel." Those gray eyes lick every surface of my skin, as if reaching under my clothing, and I shiver.

"Yes, that's right. Sex clubs." I shrug, but it doesn't come off as nonchalantly as I'd like.

I glance up at him, but he's looking away, exposing an angry two-inch scar, just below his ear. It's jagged, like the peak of a mountain, and disappears into his hairline. I wonder how he got it?

"But," I say loudly, trying to recapture his attention. "Obscura seems like it's just a sexier version of a nightclub, from what I can see. Nothing really extraordinary."

That icy gaze shifts back to me. "These are the public-only rooms. Everyone here is by invitation only but…what you see here is not the half of what Obscura offers." He laughs then. Dry, sexy. The sound has an effect on me, drilling down to my bones, thrumming something deep inside me, chords strumming and vibrating, like an instrument. "Allow me to educate you."

I glance behind me, toward the exit. "Ummm."

"For the sake of your…*news story*," he clarifies.

I glance back at him. Does he not believe me that I'm here for research? He's right, though. I do need material. Once I leave Obscura, I most likely will never get another invite. I'm here by total fluke, so I have to make this visit count. And besides, I can't ditch Lexi. I need to stay here for another forty-five minutes, at least, so I can meet her when she's back from the fetish area.

I lick my lips, suddenly nervous. But I push past the butterflies in my stomach and nod. "Okay."

Reaching out, he smooths the tips of his fingers down my arm. Heat and goosebumps swirl in the wake of his touch. Then, he takes my hand and leads me toward another staircase. A concierge sits at the top of the stairs, allowing us to pass with a slight, deferential nod to my handsome stranger.

At that very moment, we step into another world.

There's a central seating area with cream sofas and pale marble flecked with gold. Three dark hallways stretch out in different directions, and I wonder where they lead. Each hallway has half a dozen closed doors. Private rooms, most likely. But what's happening behind those glossy black doors? It's the journalistic curiosity that drives me to wonder.

It's gorgeous up here—elaborate chandeliers giving off dim light over the taffeta wallpaper, wainscot and exquisite furniture. The decor absolutely *screams* wealth and privilege.

And it's definitely more private here, though there are still quite a few people up, sipping drinks, entwined and making out on the sofas. There's a half-naked man, crawling on his hands and knees, being led on a dog leash, but nothing blatantly salacious. My critical gaze sweeps over everyone's masked faces. Everyone looks of age, thankfully, and completely compliant.

So far so good.

"Where are we?" I ask, making a mental note of the layout.

"These are the founder's rooms," the stranger says.

"Founder rooms," I repeat. "What does that mean?"

"The founders of Exeter House," he says. "We get exclusive privileges, of course."

Hm. So he's a *founder*. A clue to his identity. Useful information that I could possibly use to narrow down who he is.

As we move deeper into the space, the crowd of people parts, watching us pass, as though this guy is some biblical prophet parting the waters. Eyes continue to follow us, follow *him*.

He guides me down the hallway on the right to one of the select back rooms. It's clear he has a specific room in mind. He stops before a lacquered black door, turning to me. "Are you certain you want to see this?"

I swallow. The fact that he needs to ask me—like it's a warning, or a point of no return—that makes me anxious. What's on the other side of that door?

I push out a little chuckle to cover my awkwardness. "Yeah, of course. It's why I'm here, isn't it?"

With a deeply satisfied smile just below the bottom edge of his mask, he twists the handle and pushes the door open. "Welcome to my dark domain."

CHAPTER 2
DOM

THE DEVIL—I STILL HAVEN'T CAUGHT AN ACTUAL NAME yet—opens the door and gestures to me. When we step into the room, I suck in a sharp breath. I don't consider myself a prude, but this is fucking crazy. The room looks very minimalist. There are large mattresses on the floor covered in black silk sheets and accented with dozens of throw pillows. Several lengths of bamboo hang suspended from metal hooks in the ceiling. None of that is shocking. What's shocking are the half dozen people tied up in intricate knots, suspended from the ceiling, or tied to a table.

"What the actual...?" I breathe, taking it all in.

Honestly, it looks like a high-end torture room. Maybe that's exactly what it is.

"This is shibari. Artistic rope bondage," the Devil explains, locking the door, then stepping up next to me. "Beautiful, isn't it?"

My gaze drifts to a woman tied up on the table, her legs spread wide. The ropes are so tight, they bite into her flesh, making her skin look red and swollen. There's a man—masked and naked—at the foot of the table, teasing the woman's entrance with a large dildo.

"It looks painful." I swallow.

Does that woman want this? Has she given her consent before being tied to this table in front of everyone else? How could someone get pleasure from this kind of thing? I find it really hard to believe possible.

With a fiendish glint in his eye, the stranger takes in my reaction and reaches for my hand, pulling me toward the woman on the table. When we're within a couple feet, he releases my hand and circles the table as though inspecting something truly wondrous. "Look at the ecstasy on her face." He's openly admiring the woman. "Look at the pure, undiluted pleasure in her eyes."

I swallow and follow the line of his vision. Like everyone here, the woman is masked, but her dewy mouth is open in an expression of pleasure, head tilted back, and a loud, guttural moan escapes her throat as the man at her feet slowly feeds the dildo past her intimate folds.

The Devil reaches out and swirls the tip of his finger around the woman's nipple. She arches her back, offering more of herself to him. But he doesn't indulge. Removing his hand, he glances up at me. "Do you see it?"

I'm mesmerized by the scene in front of me, but the sound of his voice jolts me back to reality. I lick my lips. "Y-yes."

Another man approaches the table and holds the tip of his erect cock to her mouth. her tongue darts out to taste him as the other man pushes the dildo deeper inside her. Her body moves slightly as he thrusts the dildo, simulating sex, while at the same time, she takes the other man's cock into her mouth.

As she sucks him, the other man reaches out and gently strokes her jaw, encouraging her to take him deeper. When she does, the man at her feet responds by pushing the dildo in deeper as well, matching the pace of her sucking. It's like a well-orchestrated ballet, and I'm fucking transfixed by it.

I bring my fingers up to my lips as the scene in front of me picks up tempo. I'm so fascinated by this and shocked by that reaction in and of itself. It's such a strange mixture of emotions, and I'm not quite sure what to do with it.

Someone pounds on the door. "Dom, open up."

Dom? Who the fuck…?

Before I can even ask what's happening, my host walks over to the door and wrenches it open. On the other side is Lexi, and she's with a tall man I don't recognize. I'm assuming it's the guy she's been seeing, Ash—or Mr. Grayson as the receptionist called him.

Lexi pushes past the two men and makes a beeline for me. Her brows are furrowed and she's breathing heavily, and I detect cues of deep concern behind her mask.

"Gwen, are you okay? Why aren't you downstairs?" She takes me by the shoulders.

I blink, still stunned by what I've just witnessed. "Sorry. Yeah, I'm fine. We should go. I have everything I need."

Lexi glances around the room. "What is all this?"

The Devil man—*Dom*—addresses her. "It's called shibari. Want to try it, kitten? I have some rope—"

I have no idea why, but a stinging vein of jealousy snakes through me when I hear that. I've never felt so instantaneously murderous in my entire life—though whether I want to murder Lexi or the handsome stranger isn't entirely clear.

Ash is in the other man's face so quickly, I swear he flew across the room. "*You* stay the fuck away from her," he says, drawing out every word. He sounds like he's going to murder Dom.

What the actual fuck?

The Devil laughs and lifts his hands up. "*Whoa.* Sorry, brother. Didn't see the necklace. She's all yours. Got it." Necklace? What does that mean? I glance at the one Lexi wore tonight...the one with the key at her throat, the necklace that Ash gave her.

Ash turns to Lexi. "I'm taking you two home."

Lexi shakes her head, determination in her eyes. "No. We'll call a car."

She takes my hand, and we move to walk past Ash. He reaches out and grabs Lexi's elbow and pulls her to a stop.

"We're not done," he growls.

"Yes," she says. "We are. We're done." They hold each other's gaze through their masks, and tension crackles in the air between them.

His hand tightens on her upper arm before he lets her shrug it off.

I throw one last glance over my shoulder before leaving. The Devil is staring straight at me, ignoring all the goings-on behind him. There's a self-satisfied smile on that beautiful mouth. He nods his head toward me, and I read the determination in his eyes that tell me, somehow, this won't be the last time I see him.

CHAPTER 3
FLIRTEXTING

I'M STILL IN A DAZE WHEN LEXI PULLS ME OUT OF THE SHIBARI room, down the stairs and through the main part of the club. Her guy, Ash, follows us the entire way, like he's afraid of letting Lexi out of his sight. Why? Maybe my suspicions about this place are true. Otherwise, why would he be following us so protectively? Is he worried we're going to get snatched by one of these sexual deviants?

A hot ember of fear trips down my spine, and I suddenly feel an urgency to get the fuck out of here. Back near the entrance, Ms. Lawrence spots us and walks up, addressing Lexi. "Ms. Anderson. Leaving so soon?"

Ash pushes in from behind us and addresses Ms. Lawrence. "Please retrieve their phones. And call a car for Miss Anderson's companion."

What the fuck? I've been relegated to a *companion* now, and I'm going home alone? I've obviously missed something in the time I was in the shibari room with the Devil.

After what seems like too long a wait, Ms. Lawrence returns with our phones, and I immediately power mine on. A text message pops up instantly. Just two words from an unfamiliar number that make my heart race.

Hello, Angel.

It's from a contact that's been entered into my phone and labeled *Domino*, and I know, instantly, it's the Devil. How did he manage to program his contact information into my phone so quickly? Smooth move, sure. But it's a glaring reminder that I should change my passcode if it was that easy to hack. Talk about an invasion of privacy!

With my heart still thudding hard in my chest, I glance up from my phone and see Lexi walking over to me. She and Ash have been not-so-quietly arguing about whether or not she's leaving. Spoiler alert: she's totally going to give in and stay at his place tonight. She wants to deny it, but I've known her long enough to know that she's already fallen hard for this guy.

"Hey, I'm going to stay with Ash for a little while," Lexi says. "We have a few things to get straight."

I laugh to myself, because I *knew* it. If only I'd put some money down on it. "Yeah, I figured. Looks like you two have quite a few things to work out."

She frowns. "Are you okay with going home on your own? I can totally ditch—"

I blow out a breath and wave my hand to cut her off. Honestly, I'm cool heading home alone. It'll give me a chance to map out my story. There's so much more to Obscura, I just know it. And Domino is someone important here. I'm betting that he's someone important out in the real world, too—he just has that alpha quality. "No, no. It's fine. Really. It'll give me time to think. The story I'm working on just got a whole lot bigger. Like, *huge.*"

Her brows shoot up. "Oh, wow, okay. So, um, what happened in that room?" Lexi asks.

I pull off my mask and glance away. I'm not really ready to talk about what happened upstairs. Even if I did, I wouldn't know how to put it into words anyway. "Nothing happened."

I glance back at Lexi. I can see the concern on her face. I should know better than to lie to her. She knows me too well. "That didn't look like nothing, Gwen."

"He's…interesting," I offer, hoping she'll drop it.

She doesn't.

"Okay, but *who* is he?"

I shrug. "I don't know. I only have guesses, and not good ones at this point. I need to cross-check a few details."

Namely, which British aristocrats between the ages of twenty-five and thirty-five are in town right now, how often they visit, and so on. Because one thing is clear, Domino is very comfortable at Obscura, which means he's here often.

She glares at me like a mother cautioning a child. "Just be careful. It looks like that dude is into some dark shit."

"Yeah, that's the weird thing. Domino—that's his pseudonym by the way—he wasn't participating. Not that *I* could see, anyway."

The conversation then turns to Lexi's current predicament with Ash and that other guy I don't really care for—David. He apparently stood her up tonight and Ash swooped in to "save" her from the sex club. I can't even follow their drama right now since my thoughts are swirling around my story.

My car pulls up and the driver comes around to open the door for me. "Miss Taylor?"

I give Lexi a quick hug, and she tells me that she'll text me later.

Once I'm alone in the back seat of the town car, I pull out my phone. The text from Domino taunts me.

Hello, Angel.

My thumbs hover over the text window. Should I reply? Or should I just ignore his obvious bid for my attention? Honestly, as of now, he's my only real source for material on Obscura. If I get to know him better, then maybe he'll be more frank with me—open me up to me about the deep, hidden secrets of his world.

That being said, however, I can't allow him to think I'm a pushover. He needs to be put in his place from the start, so I type out a terse response.

Stealing my phone and entering your contact info is really shady.

His reply comes a few seconds later, like he was waiting for my response.

If your phone were stolen, love, you wouldn't be texting me with it now.

I blow out a breath and push my back against the cushy seat. Okay, maybe he has me there. But hacking my phone and programming his number into it is still shady. Hmmm...maybe I can find out who he is by using the internet to do a reverse-search on his phone number. I copy it into a Google search but come up empty. It's probably a burner phone or something. My eyes narrow. Guys like Domino are smart, and they cover their tracks.

I enter my next volley.

Fair point. But I don't appreciate you snooping around on my phone. Privacy. It's a thing.

I expect him to reply right away, but he doesn't. As the seconds tick by, my heart hammers against my ribs. Did I offend him? He doesn't look like a guy who gets a lot of pushback. From what I could see at Obscura, he says jump and everyone around him asks, "How high?" But that's not me. No matter how hard I try, I can't just accept the status quo. That's a quality that will make me a good journalist. I go against the grain and I question everything.

Finally, his response pings on my phone.

You have no privacy from me, Angel. I will strip everything away until I'm left with the most raw and vulnerable parts of you. I will gaze into your darkness, and I will cherish that which causes others to flinch and look away.

I frown at my phone screen, re-reading the message several times to let it sink in. Wow, it's...oddly poetic and intense. So unexpected.

I swallow as I re-read the words, tingles sweeping down my spine. How would it feel to give myself *completely* to someone like Domino? If I'm honest, I can see the appeal. He carries himself with an air of confidence that's quite intoxicating.

I could fall for him all too easily.

Shaking myself, I switch off my phone and toss it onto the seat next to me. With just a few texts he's managed to rattle me, and I'm not sure how to feel about that. As a journalist, I need to remain as neutral as possible. I can't allow a source to get under my skin. And yet…all I can do is imagine myself tied up to that table in the shibari room, with Domino hovering above me, running his fingers down my naked body.

It's all I can think about during the ride home. And finally, after getting home and getting ready for bed, I fire up my phone again to re-read his last text to me.

Despite my reservations, I decide to entertain his flirtation. Better to keep him on the hook. Who knows what info I could glean from him if I play this right?

Why me? There's a club full of women at your disposal to seduce.

An agonizing string of seconds ticks by before his response pops up on my screen.

There's something about your purity that I want to touch—and corrupt.

I laugh to myself. Pure? Me? That statement couldn't be further from the truth. I've only been with one guy, but I'm definitely not *pure*.

Sorry to disappoint, but I'm not pure. Far from it, in fact.

I half-worry about possibly scaring him off. Maybe I should have pretended to be pure, to lure him in and get as much information as I can. But I don't know…there's something about Domino that compels me to be honest. I bet he has that effect on all women. That charm and bravado. It's alluring. Still, I can't help but wonder who he really is beneath the mask—and beneath all that wealth and power.

You've had sex, Angel. But I want more than your cunt. I want your heart and soul. I want your complete and unflinching surrender. I want my name on your breathless lips when you come. I want to savor everything you have to give.

Heat rushes to my sex and I swallow. Fucking-A. I've only known Domino for less than two hours, and I already feel like he's peered into my soul and seen my deepest, darkest, most secret desires. Things I've never admitted to anyone. Could it be a lucky guess? Is this something he says to all the women he encounters?

It must be.

There's no way I'm that special.

Over the next few weeks, we continue to text. Domino is always trying to lure me in, doling out information about Obscura like breadcrumbs. I pretend to be shocked by the details—I *am* a little shocked, honestly—but every word draws me in deeper. I can't help but be intrigued by the darkness he promises.

But we text about other things, too. Mainly my story. I ask him questions, learn a little more about the whole bondage-domination-submission-masochism thing, called BDSM; what patrons of sex clubs are looking to get out of the experience. Whatever holes I come across in my extensive research, I uncover by putting carefully worded questions to him. He will often reply with insightful answers.

I've also come up with some creative ways to investigate the scene itself. More than once, I find myself hanging around near the employee entrance at Exeter House, hoping to find someone to interview about Obscura. However, no one talks much and one informs me that signing an NDA is part of the job requirements. Eventually, I'm chased off the premises by security.

My editor already has a couple of the bigger newspapers, and a few online publications, interested in a first look for *possible* republishing. Nothing definite just yet, but even just for the chance they'll offer by reading it is unbelievably exciting.

It's the afternoon after the last day of finals for the semester. I'm sitting at the kitchen table at Hill House, eating a bowl of cereal, when I hear my name echo through the house.

"Gwen!"

It's my roommate, Lexi. I'd recognize her voice anywhere.

"I'm in the kitchen!" I call back, shoveling another spoonful of cereal into my face. It's the most nutritious thing I've eaten in days. I've been too busy flirtexting with Domino and working on my story to even *think* about food.

Lexi comes skidding into the kitchen. "Oh, there you are. Put on something cute. We're going to Exeter House."

I blink at her. "What?"

"Yeah, Maddy invited us for happy hour drinks at Isca, which is perfect, because I have a hot date later with Ash. I can just meet him at Exeter House and send you home in a car."

I laugh at Lexi's enthusiasm. "Okay, but why is Maddy inviting us to drinks?"

A sly smile hovers on her mouth. "I don't know. But I *suspect* that it has something to do with her wedding plans."

"Omg!" I clap my hands together. "It really *is* about being asked to be her bridesmaids, isn't it?"

She sighs and rolls her eyes. "Wasn't that the excuse you gave me to get me back to Exeter House so Ash could surprise *me* with a proposal?"

I nodded. "Yes, and as art often imitates life, the story I concocted as a gifted journalist is now going to come true! You and me in ugly bridesmaids dresses in a lavish billionaire wedding on a lush tropical island with loads of hot guys!"

She blows out a breath and gestures for me to get up. "Come on. The car's getting here in a half hour, and you look half dead."

"Wow, thanks." I throw her a dry look, threading my fingers through my greasy blonde hair. She's right, of course.

Lexi waves me off. "Oh, you know what I mean."

Thirty-one minutes later, we're sitting in the back seat of a black Exeter House town car, headed toward Malibu. I'm wearing my best conservative dress—mint-green satin with long sleeves, a high neckline, and an A skirt. It's classy, plain, and utterly unassuming. I bought it for my aunt's wedding three years ago and haven't worn it since.

I can't believe I'm headed back to Exeter House. My stomach is in knots. Obscura. Isca. They're both a part of Exeter House—albeit, on opposite sides of the property. Will I run into Domino at the restaurant? Will I even recognize him if I *do* run into him? He was wearing a full mask the whole time we were at Obscura. The only thing I have to identify him with is his posh British accent, which isn't at all uncommon at Exeter House. Almost as an afterthought, I remember spotting that wicked-looking scar on his neck. It stood out. Someone as wealthy as Domino likely is could have had something like that easily removed with cosmetic surgery. And yet he didn't.

"What's wrong?" Lexi asks, breaking the silence.

My gaze darts to Lexi. "Hm? What?"

"You look nervous." She narrows her eyes. "Are you afraid of running into that Devil guy again…what's his name? Dominic?"

"*Domino,*" I correct without thinking while staring out the window. "No, I doubt I'll see him there. Who knows if he even eats at Isca."

"Many of the members do," she supplies confidently, oblivious to how that information kicks the butterflies in my stomach into a frenzy. "That's what I've heard, at least."

I wonder if she's hoping she'll run into her own Exeter House Lothario. But they have a date later anyway, so why does it matter?

When we arrive at Isca, Maddy is already sitting at the bar waiting for us. As we approach, she pops off her stool and gives us both hugs.

"Thank you both so much for coming," she says, signaling to the bartender. "I'm so glad we could do this."

"We're just glad you could crawl out from your sex cocoon to spare a few minutes to see us," Lexi laughs.

Maddy arches a brow. "Billionaires have to work too, sometimes." And we all laugh.

We order our drinks and soon find out that there's no special ask regarding her wedding plans. Instead, she's invited us out to celebrate the end of the semester and beginning of summer.

With that out of the way, we get to drinking and gossiping about people we all know. We're halfway into our third cocktail when Lexi elbows me. "Hey, look at that tall, extremely handsome glass of water over there. Feeling thirsty?"

I swivel on my stool to see a very delicious specimen sitting at a table near the bar. Dark hair, combed back away from his pale eyes. Honestly, though, his straight nose and defined jawline make him look too perfect to be real. He could be a model, or an actor. Exeter House is full of them.

Maddy follows my gaze. "Ohhh. Yeah…that's Lord Devon Howard," she says in a low voice. "Honestly, you meet all kinds of famous people here."

I arch a brow, studying his solid physique, his cutting good looks. I'm not the only one surveying him with parched eyes. "*Lord?* He's famous? I think I'd remember a guy that hot if I'd seen him in a movie…"

"He's not an actor," Maddy corrects. "He's way more important than that. He's a British lord, a younger son of the Duke of Everleigh and—more importantly—second cousin, twice removed, to the King of England. Lord Devon is thirty or forty-something in the line of succession to the British throne, a direct descendant of King George V."

Lexi looks at Maddy like she's grown two heads. "Wow, stalker. How do you know so much about this guy?"

Maddy shrugs one shoulder and takes a sip of her whiskey sour. "I looked him up on the internet after Evan introduced me to him. He's very interesting."

Lexi turns to watch me watching that magnificent specimen—I mean, I can hardly tear my eyes away from him.

"I have a *brilliant* idea. Gwen, I double-dog dare you to walk by him." Lexi laughs as though that were the most daring plan ever.

I take a healthy gulp of my appletini. "I'm supposed to just *randomly* walk by his table? Won't that look a tad suspicious?"

Maddy giggles. She's tipsy. She always giggles when she's tipsy. "Oh, my God. That's brilliant, Lex. Look—" She points in the direction of Lord High Whatshisname. "The bathrooms are over there. You can just pretend you're going to the ladies' room, and walk right by, within inches, even."

I narrow my eyes at Lexi and Maddy. "Okay, but why? This is so dumb."

"You might catch his eye," Lexi says with a hand-waving gesture to help emphasize her point. "And then...I don't know, you could get swept off your feet, fall in love, get married, and have a gaggle of aristocratic babies with upper-crust British accents."

"Yeah," Maddy agrees, her eyes half-open. "That's a really solid plan. I like it."

"I respectfully decline." I sip defiantly from my drink. "Why don't *you* do it, Lex? Or you, Mads?"

"Because you're more single than we are. And that poor hot man over there does *not* deserve the wrath of a furious billionaire coming down hard on him for having one of us talk to him," Lexi says. "Unless...well, I guess I can approach him, and give him your number." She moves to get off her stool, but I stop her.

"*Fine,*" I hiss. "I'll walk to the bathroom, but if he doesn't notice me, then you two have to promise you'll drop it and stop teasing me."

Lexi and Maddy hold their hands over their hearts. "Promise," they say in unison, giggling.

My God. I'd forgotten why I never take these two out drinking together. As soon as their lips touch alcohol, they are absolutely ridiculous. Both cheap dates and both engaged to billionaires. And they just feed off each other. I definitely have not had enough to drink yet to find them amusing.

Popping off my stool, I straighten my skirt and grab my phone. Then with a sharp glance at my friends, I move toward the bathroom. I have to walk *right by* the man to get where I'm going, and I take the opportunity to get a closer look. As I approach, I don't flinch. I don't look away. He's talking to his associate across the table, and he doesn't even notice me walking toward him.

And…*dayum*. He. Is. Beautiful.

Like drool-worthy, movie-star handsome. I'm eating up the sight of him—dark hair, square jaw, strong physique, haunting silvery eyes… Just as I pass nearby, he turns his head away from me to signal to the waiter, and when he does, my heart seizes in my chest. *What?*

No. It's not possible.

This man has a long scar on his neck, just beneath his ear, jagged and evil-looking. Raised and white against his darker skin. It's the same scar I spied on Domino's neck that night at Obscura.

I suck in a loud gasp.

Holy shit.

CHAPTER 4
SCANDAL IN THE MAKING

I ALMOST TRIP OVER MY OWN HEELS IN SHOCK. MY BRAIN IS struggling to make sense of what I'm seeing. That scar creeping across Lord Devon Howard of Everleigh's neck is identical to the one on Domino.

The same Domino with whom I've been flirting via text for weeks. The one who's been acting as a source for my story. Resident Dom of a sex club in Obscura.

Domino is Lord Devon. Lord Devon is Domino.

Oh. My. God. *Ohmygod.*

"Domino." That pseudonym slips past my lips in shock before I can help it. I say it in a breath, disbelieving.

He turns his head, and his cold gaze catches mine, the initial confusion on his face melting immediately into recognition. A moment of pure charged energy passes between us, and I can practically feel the heat of shock and anger rolling off him.

He opens his mouth to say something to his associate, and I take that opportunity to beat a path to the bathroom like a coward. I quickly dip into the ladies' room and safety. As soon as

I'm inside the ice-cold bathroom, I find the first empty stall and shut myself inside. Leaning back against the wood partition, I struggle to catch my breath.

Lord. What the fuck am I going to do? He knows I saw him, recognized him as his Obscura persona. But that's no big deal, right?

Except, it *is* a big deal. If the anger in his eyes was any indication, I was never meant to know his true identity. And no wonder. He's a member of the fucking British Royal Family who has practically been outed as the operator—or officiator—or whatever the hell he is—of an exclusive sex club. All of that is a scandal in the making.

A scandal that I, a journalist, have sudden and exciting exclusivity to cover, should I so choose. My mind starts whirring with the story possibilities. This takes my angle in a new and extremely explosive direction.

Of course I have to check and recheck my facts, but...*this is huge.*

A text notification chimes on my phone, and I practically jump out of my skin. I half-expect it to be Domino—or rather, Lord Devon, cousin of the King—texting me. But no, it's Maddy.

Are you okay in there? Did you fall in?

Shit. I must have been in here for longer than I'd thought. I hear the door open, and footsteps approach the bank of stalls. It's probably Lexi or Maddy checking up on me.

"I'm fine," I say, unlocking the stall and stepping out. "I'm coming."

But it's not Lexi or Maddy.

I freeze, sucking in a sharp breath. My heart begins to race to an unsteady but frenetic pace.

Domino stands in front of me, looking like a mafia boss. Black tailored suit, perfectly coiffed dark hair, and gray eyes that push past every sensible thought I have. His feet are planted at shoulder width, arms folded across a broad chest, and there's a take-n0-prisoners expression on his face. I take a step back, my knees like jelly. I reach out and press my hand against the cold wallpapered wall, steadying myself.

I swallow. "Domino."

His lips twist up into an unexpected grin, and I'm struck by the realization that he has me cornered in a place he doesn't belong, if such a location even exists here at Exeter House.

"This-this is the ladies' room," I stammer, opening with the obvious. I don't know why I'm nervous. I've been texting him for weeks. We know each other pretty well by now. Except...that was all virtual. And now, here he is, in the flesh. Sexy as *fuck* flesh, by the way. With his mask, he's incredibly handsome. Powerful. Intimidating. *Without* his mask, his beauty is arresting. I have to remind myself to breathe.

Domino reaches over and throws the bolt, locking the main bathroom door, preventing anyone from entering. And me from easily escaping, by the way. Thank god no one else is already in here with us. Or maybe that's not a good thing?

Domino—Devon—*whoever*—turns his attention back to me, and God help me, the breath catches in my throat. As he slowly approaches, I find my voice somehow. "You shouldn't be here."

His lips quirk up into a half smile, like he's amused by my resistance. "No one tells me where I should or should not be," he states in that crisp, sophisticated accent. "Especially inside Exeter House."

I square my shoulders, fists clenched at my sides in defiance. I drum up every ounce of confidence I can possibly gather. "Ah, yes. Your *dark domain*, right? Or is that just Obscura?"

He stops just a couple inches away from me. "Obscura is merely a playground."

I narrow my eyes at him. "From what I saw, there wasn't much playing. You mostly observe. Like a Lord overseeing his domain. Why don't you partake?"

His hot gaze flicks over me, from head to toe, and I shift on my feet, suddenly self-conscious. "Always the journalist, asking questions." He reaches out and brushes the tip of his finger along the line of my jaw. "Such a curious mind."

My tongue darts out to wet my bottom lip. "This new knowledge obviously changes the direction of my story."

That's when everything shifts. He stiffens, his face going blank. Even the air around us seems colder somehow. "You will mention nothing of me, or Obscura, in your article."

A laugh bursts out of me. "Are you kidding? You *are* my article."

The second the words leave my lips, I regret them. Why did I tell him that? Transparency is important, sure, but did I have to blurt it out like *that?* God, I'm such an idiot.

He moves so quickly, I don't have a chance to react. In one fluid motion, he has me up against the wall, his huge body pinning me there. His hand finds my throat, and he squeezes. Not hard. Just enough to show me who is in control.

With his face nearly pressed against mine, he inhales deeply. "You are so naive about the world, Angel. If you publish such an article, you will destroy everything I've worked so hard to create." There's a long, thick pause where he holds my gaze to his steely gray one. The only sounds in here are the drip of a faucet and our own heavy breathing. My heart hammers a harsh staccato but whether from fear or from his nearness, I don't know. He swallows visibly, as if trying to regain control of himself. "I can't let that happen."

Even with his hand around my throat, I know, somehow, that he won't hurt me. Maybe that proves just how naive I am. He's a stranger. We've been texting regularly pretty much every day for a few weeks, but I didn't even know his real name until ten minutes ago. What else is he hiding? A dark and deviant past? Secret obsessions—something that goes deeper than what happens at Obscura?

"It's one story," I say. "You've had hundreds written about you. Thousands about your family. What's one more?"

I can feel the hard ridge of his erection resting against my hip. Heat instantly pulses through my body, to my very fingertips. The connection is every bit as powerful as when we met at Obscura weeks ago...stronger, even as his beautiful features aren't hidden behind a mask. I *hate* that he has this effect on my body. My brain is screaming for me to reach up and scratch his eyes out, while my body is practically purring with need. My hips tilt up and forward, forcing his cock to dig deeper into me.

"Oh, you like that, do you?" he whispers in my ear, his lips brushing along my lobe. Fear and desire war inside me, the tension pulling me so tight, I'm afraid I may snap in two. "Perhaps you're not as innocent as you've led me to believe. Perhaps this is all a game to you. It wouldn't be the first time the media has manipulated their way into my life."

I swallow and shake my head—as much as his hand on my throat will allow. "I've told you the truth since the beginning. You knew I was working on a story and you cooperated with me, via text. You know everything about what I'm up to." My eyes flick back up to his and then away, almost as quickly. The strong fingers on my throat stroke along my skin, making me shiver. "I can't say the same for you."

His hand on my throat doesn't tighten, but his lower half shifts, pushing harder against me. The heat of anger flashes in his eyes. "Everything I've done, every omission, was to protect something larger than myself."

I'd laugh if he didn't have me by the throat and pinned against the wall. That bigger thing he's protecting…yeah, I'm not an idiot. I'm sure he wants me to believe his deception was altruistic. But if my suspicions are true, then what he's protecting is the truth of the depravity at Obscura. He really is the Devil, the mask, his persona, a perfect reflection of the darkness inside of him. I just know it.

Slowly, he opens his hand, releasing my throat—but his body is still pressed against mine, creating a heat that engulfs me. His lips hover above mine, and *again* the breath catches in my lungs. I shouldn't be turned on by this beautiful monster, but I am. I can't help but imagine his hands exploring my naked body, his tongue devouring every drop of moisture…

God, I'm fucked up.

Truth be told, I've always had a soft spot for bad boys, but this is next level insane. Domino is far more dangerous than your run-of-the-mill motorcycle-riding, tatted-up bad boy. He has unfathomable power, influence and connections. And he's one of the richest men alive.

Clenching my jaw, I resist the urge to spit in his face. One of the most detestable creatures to ever walk this planet, in my opinion, are handsome, wealthy men. They walk all over the rest of us like we're nothing, taking what they want, destroying everything in their path, then walking away, leaving everyone else to deal with the consequences.

I lift my chin and look him square in the eye. "If nothing depraved is happening at Obscura, then you have nothing to worry about from what I might research and put in my story, right?"

He takes my chin between his fingers, lifting my head just a fraction more. "We're all depraved at Obscura, Angel. That's the appeal."

Yeah, exactly as I thought. My breath freezes in my lungs, fear and arousal swirling in an unsavory stew that heats and chills my core at once.

"What do you want from me?" I ask, a little too breathlessly, I think.

A tick pulses in his jaw. "You will shelve the story."

I blink up at him. "I could do that." My eyes flick involuntarily to his mouth and back to meet his gaze just as quickly. "But I *won't*. My conscience won't let me."

If I walk away from what Obscura might be, and what Domino's role in that is, then I'll never forgive myself. If I allow myself to be intimidated, then why be a journalist at all? No, I need to lend my voice to this—as small as my voice might be now. Sometime in the near future, it will be a roar. And I have to know I've done everything in my power to expose the dark truth of what I suspect is happening at Obscura.

He inches even closer, his lips touching mine. It's a feather-light touch that makes my nipples tighten. "Then you'll forgive me for doing everything in my power to stop it. Because that's what *I* must do."

Then, all at once, he pulls away from me, turns to unlock the bathroom door and disappears out of it.

I heave out a breath as if it's been physically pushed out of me...then sink to the floor.

What the actual fuck just happened?

Long minutes later, after splashing a little water on my face and taking some slow, deep breaths, I walk out of the bathroom. My gaze immediately darts to Domino's table, but he and his associates are gone, thank God. Maddy and Lexi are still at the bar, drinks in hand, giggling over something. When they see me, they practically jump off their stools.

"Oh, thank God," Maddy says. "We were just about to call in a search party."

Lexi's gaze flicks over my face. "You look flushed. Are you okay?"

They seem to have forgotten all about Domino—Lord Devon Whatshisface, rather—and their stupid-ass dare that seems to have gotten me into some hot water and broken my story wide open all at once.

I flash her a tight smile and nod a little too vigorously. "Yeah, I'm fine. The drinks upset my stomach a bit."

I should probably tell them about what just happened in the bathroom, but I really don't want them mixed up in all of this, especially with a close associate of their significant others. Besides, I don't have any actual proof—*yet*—that Domino is involved in any shady crap. It's all conjecture, at this point.

Given the way he acted in the bathroom, though, I'm quite sure I'm onto something.

Maddy flags down the bartender. "Can we get a ginger ale, please?"

We spend the rest of the evening laughing and gossiping—all the while, I'm looking over my shoulder to see if Domino is waiting, watching me from the shadows. But he's gone. No texts, nothing. Maybe I'm rid of him for good. That makes me frown. I'm not even sure how I feel about that.

"Oh!" Lexi glances up from her phone, a smile spreading across her face. "Ash is headed down here to grab me."

"Yeah…grab you and whisk you away for hot sexytimes to celebrate the semester being over and finals done!" Maddy laughs.

Then she promptly hops off her stool after throwing back the dregs of her martini. "I should get back upstairs. Are you headed back home, Gwen? Can I ask the front desk to order you a car?"

I glance at my phone. It's only eight-thirty. "The evening is young. I think I'm going to hang around for a bit and work on my story."

I end up ordering another drink and typing notes into my phone. Domino. Lord Devon Howard. The scar. His exalted station at Obscura. My suspicions. It all comes flowing out of me like a stream of consciousness. Then I proceed to run some preliminary Google searches. One guy actually tries to hit on me and I rebuff him but he good-naturedly sends me a drink from the bar anyway.

As I'm starting to feel a bit woozy, I order a bruschetta appetizer and hoover it up while reading everything I can get my hands on about Lord Devon Howard, son of the Duke of Everleigh.

Oddly, according the internet, he's squeaky clean—a ridiculously wealthy, philanthropic do-gooder and one of the world's most sought-after eligible bachelors. What a bunch of horse shit.

If only the internet knew the real story of sadistic sex clubs and rope bondage, shady tactics, degrading behaviors, sexual deviancy and whatever other dirt I can scrape up about his "dark domain," Obscura...

I type notes and questions into my phone and open our chat window, re-reading the texts several times over, copying relevant ones into my document.

When my phone is at seven-percent power—and I discover that I stupidly didn't slip a charge cord into my purse, I take that as my cue to head home. Once I'm snug in bed with my laptop, the real strategizing can begin for my new angle on the story.

I have just enough battery power to grab an Uber home, so I find my way out to Isca's ocean-front-patio. Despite it almost being summer, it's a little chilly out here with a breeze and I didn't think to bring a sweater.

As I pull my phone out to summon the ride, however, I get the feeling that I'm being watched. It starts with prickles on the back of my neck and a distinct uneasy feeling. I scan around me and catch a glimpse of some random stranger giving me the most intense stare.

I can't tell...was it the guy who tried to pick me up earlier? Best not hang around to find out. I can call my Uber from the next block so I head out onto the beach, picking up my pumps to carry instead of trying to attempt the sand in them.

I can make it over to the next block and the chic neighborhood with the quiet street to make my call.

But it's not too many minutes later that I realize…that's never going to happen.

And I might just never make it home.

CHAPTER 5
IMPRISONED

Present

THE MINUTE I WAS GRABBED RIGHT OFF THE BEACH BY two hulking goons and tossed into this fucking trunk, I started plotting my escape. But we've been driving around for hours now, and in the complete darkness, it's hard to focus on anything but the icy fear trickling through my veins.

After what feels like days, we come to a stop and the engine cuts off. *Oh shit.* Car doors slam, the sound echoing off cement walls. Then silence. Seconds later, footsteps and the click of the trunk. Bright lights stab my eyes, and I squint. My senses are assailed by a brief glimpse of industrial fluorescent lighting and the smell of oil, exhaust, and concrete.

We're in a parking garage.

My eyes, so long accustomed to the darkness, can barely focus. Two masked men hover over me before one of them slips a black hood over my head.

Could this be some sort of fever dream? They say that in times of deep stress and isolation, people can hallucinate. But I don't think I'd be hallucinating this, even in my own wild imagination. Maybe I've watched too much *Dateline*.

The goons flank me, each with a hand on my upper arm to guide me as we walk toward what seems like an elevator, by the sound of the doors whooshing open. I suck in a deep breath. What am I going to do? I have to be smart about this. Lashing out will probably just get me bruised and beaten. It won't change anything.

With a jolt, the elevator zooms upward, dropping my stomach toward my feet. A minute later, the door slides open. I'm shoved through it again. This flooring is different under my bare feet...polished concrete?

I reach out with my senses once again, trying to pay attention to anything I can pick up for possible clues.

After a short walk, a metallic door clanks open and I'm shoved through the doorway. Stumbling and almost falling, I'm steadied by hands. In quiet voices, they murmur to each other, wondering what they should do next.

Gruffly, I'm ordered not to take off the hood until after they've left the room, which tells me they're nervous I might be able to identify them. If they're the same guys that grabbed me on the beach, I still remember vaguely what they look like. But it was dark and I don't have a lot of details.

As soon as the door slams shut, I yank the hood off my head. Squinting, I prepare for bright lights, but there are none. I look around me, trying to figure out my surroundings. Complete darkness.

I move in the direction of the door and croak out. "I'm thirsty! I need something to drink."

"There's a bathroom opposite this door. Go there and drink out of the faucet," comes the dry reply. "Also, there'll be no banging or noise of any kind, or you will be punished."

Punished? God, I don't even want to imagine what that might entail. What could be worse than kidnapping me and locking me in a dark cell?

I rest my forehead against the cold metal door as several locks are turned and bolted. Do they really need all that to hold me in? I'm one hundred twenty-seven pounds, five-foot-six. They could overpower me easily.

Hopelessness washes over me, but the pull of my thirst is stronger. So I go in search of this mythical bathroom. My fingers trace the walls—solid cinder block with stainless-steel lining up to waist high. I circle the perimeter to get the lay of the land.

There's nothing in here except for one thin mattress on the floor, a pillow, and a blanket. I reach a doorway in the darkness and inch forward slowly. Inside, I find a tiny bathroom, as if it has been crammed inside of a closet. A toilet, a small sink, and nothing else. No mirror on the wall, no towels, no decorations. No shower or tub.

My fingers find the faucet and turn it on. I shove my face into the sink, my mouth dipping to my cupped hands. I bring the water to my lips and drink deeply. It's the most amazing water I've ever tasted. Ordinary tap water. Not even particularly cool and it tastes faintly of chlorine.

I'm also hungry, but I don't think I could eat. I'm sick with worry and the thought of what comes next. The numbness is fading and the icy fear has returned. Am I part of some human-trafficking scheme? Am I now on a container ship halfway across the ocean to be shipped overseas?

I have no idea, but there's one thing I know for absolute certain…

I've been thrown into this prison and locked away by none other than Lord Devon Howard.

The Devil himself.

I exhaust myself exploring every nook and cranny of my small cell and then collapse on the miserable pallet of a mattress on the floor. Curling up, I try to sleep, but my mind is whirring with so many questions.

What are my friends thinking?

My roommates might just be discovering that I'm missing. I'd managed to get off a few texts to my friend, Cass, about the man following me, but she probably fell asleep before realizing I never came home last night.

I wish I'd called someone or walked back toward Exeter House to alert security instead of being so stubbornly self-sufficient. I wish I'd managed to just hold on to my phone, so people could locate me. But that had been the first thing my captors had grabbed right out of my hands before shoving me into that trunk.

Domino didn't want me to write my story, and I stupidly declared I was going to do it anyway. His last words to me echo in my mind: *Then you'll forgive me for what I must do.*

Yeah, I'm not forgiving this. The fucking asshole.

This just confirms everything I thought I knew about Obscura. Stalking me, kidnapping me, and tossing me into a cell. They have this whole operation moving pretty smoothly, and I wonder how many other girls they've done this to.

I'm left to my swirling thoughts, drifting in and out of exhausted sleep in the wake of that hours-long adrenaline rush.

And I estimate that it's been about a day since I disappeared from the world when the door to my prison cell opens.

It only opens wide enough to admit an object, which slides across the floor before the door is slammed shut again. I run to the door and pound with my fists anyway, but there is no response besides the sounds of every single bolt and lock clicking home as I'm shut tight inside once more.

The object that has been left for me is a box of food. A giant bottle of chilled water, a wrapped chicken salad sandwich, and a container of various cut fruit—I taste grapes, strawberries, melons, kiwi.

Even though I'm sick with fear, I dig in heartily. Because, if I'm going to fight this, if I'm going to find a way out of this, I need my strength. And that means food, water, sleep. That means I need to try my hardest to take care of myself so that I can be ready to seize any opportunity.

After eating, I go back into the bathroom and try my best to clean up. With only cold water and no soap or towel, and my dirty, sweaty clothes, I don't accomplish much.

But not long after I finish my useless ablutions, I hear activity once more outside the prison door. The door clanks open wide, this time. I spring to my feet as I hear footsteps enter. One sole figure. But it's so dark I can't see anything beyond a vague spot where he or she is standing.

"Who are you? Why am I here?"

"I tried to prevent this." Once he speaks...that voice. I'd recognize it anywhere. British accent, cultured, highly educated, probably from the highest institution of the land. Delivered in a deep baritone.

It's him. *Domino.*

"You've tried to prevent this," I repeat in disbelief. Is he fucking joking? "Yes, when you told your goons to snatch me off the street, I'm sure you were using all of your restraint." I can't help the sarcasm, and I don't even try.

He doesn't even acknowledge my little jab. Continuing, he says, "Here, you will only get what you earn, what you *deserve.* Which is practically nothing at this point."

My hands ball into fists, so tight that my nails cut into my palms.

"You can't hold me here like this. It's illegal. I—" No need to provoke him by reminding him that I know his true identity. I've made a lot of mistakes but I'm not quite *that* stupid.

Domino stands absolutely still, but I can sense his eyes on me. I clear my throat and start again. "If—if you release me, I promise I won't tell anyone about this. I just want my freedom. That's all. *Please.* I will—"

"What will you do, Gwendolyn?"

I suck in a breath. He knows my name. But how? I never said it that night at the club, nor in any of the times we texted. He does have my phone number, and from there, I'm sure it was just a simple internet search to find out everything he needed to know.

"I demand you release me, and—"

I'm cut off by the dry, razor edge of his cruel laughter. "You aren't in a position to demand anything. You exist here. At *my* whim. *You* are now mine."

"Listen to me," I begin.

"If you behave to my expectations," he continues, ignoring me, "then your situation will improve. Until then, you will remain in the darkness. You will be given food, drink, a working bathroom, and nothing more."

He tosses something down, something heavy. It thunks against the thin mattress on the floor that stands in for a bed.

"Use that when you're ready to start earning some improvements."

I have no idea what it is. Maybe an electronic device? Would he be stupid enough to give me a phone?

He reaches out to unlatch the door and I throw myself in his direction, sprinting across the floor, straight at him. My hands connect with his arm and I grab it, holding on for dear life. He stiffens but continues to unlatch the door with his free hand. My grip tightens around the muscular forearm as if I'm going to insist he tow me out of the cell with him, clinging to him like a barnacle.

His free hand threads through my hair and he pulls…hard, peeling me off of him all too easily. His fingers curl and twist cruelly, so that my scalp stings and my breath is stolen from me.

Then, he turns me around so that my back is to his front, hand still twisting tightly in my hair. His free hand clamps around my throat firmly but not tight enough to prevent my breathing. His mouth is at my ear, lips touching my earlobe, and I shiver with fear and, to my own shame, dark arousal.

"Fret not, Angel. You will be taken care of the moment you *deserve* to be taken care of. You ring that bell I left you when you're ready. But don't forget, compliance is the key. And I anticipate your compliance." He runs his lips along the shell of my ear, as if he's tasting me. I tremble as a vein of heat slinks through me. *Fuck.* Despite everything, my body *still* responds to him—something I'll have to explore in therapy later. I struggle to pull away from him. The moment the struggle begins, he releases me.

And then he's gone. Only the echoes of the bolt locks remain in his wake.

Chapter 6
Compliance

THREE DAYS, OR WHAT I THINK ARE THREE, PASS. I CAN only measure periods of time passing by how many times I've drifted off to sleep or how many times food is brought to me. Once per day, delivered in a box. It's usually a large bottle of water, a few protein bars, a sandwich and some fruit. That's it.

The box is always delivered while I'm asleep. Which leads me to believe that they have some way of watching me in here. I've tried to look for a little red light that might indicate a camera. There has to be something.

I wish I had something to do in here, but I'm left with my thoughts and they torture me. I can't stop thinking about that dry, sandpaper laugh. That cruel lack of caring. That devastatingly gorgeous man. Such cruelty and beauty all wrapped up in one heartless devil.

He wants my silence, so he's trying to break me. But I won't give in and keep his secret. But...I *could* lie to him, make him believe I'm being compliant.

Tired of all the racing thoughts, and with no answers in sight, I decide to ring the bell. Minutes later, someone stands outside the door and calls through to me.

"What do you need?"

"I want a shower, or just some soap and a wash cloth. *Anything.* Please."

There's a pause. The next question hits me by surprise.

"Are you ready to comply? His lordship requires it."

His lordship. My thoughts turn bitter. Some lord he is, who imprisons and probably traffics women to his sick sex fetish club.

"I want to shower. I'll talk to Domino—his lordship—whoever. But please can I have a shower? And some fresh clothes."

"I'll convey your message," comes the flat reply.

An hour later, the door is unlocked. The familiar black hood with the drawstring is tossed inside before the door shuts once more. I am instructed to put it over my head and secure it around my neck.

Moments later, the door opens and two people take me by the arm and lead me out of the room and into the much cooler hallway. I sense immediately that one of my guides is female when I bump up against her body, which feels different, softer. And she's shorter than the other guy, too.

They lead me down a maze of hallways and into an echoing room, presumably a bathroom. I'm dizzy from all the walking around with a hood over my head.

"You will not take off the hood until the door closes and you must have it on when you knock on the door after your shower is done," the woman informs me coldly.

I don't say anything but wait until the door slams closed before I yank off the damn hood. And as much as I'm dying to dive into that shower, I can't help but test the door to see if I'm locked in.

I try the knob. It's been locked from the outside. Wasting no time at all—not even to wonder if there's a creepy camera in here, too—I shed my clothes and leave them in a filthy pile on the floor.

I glance at the room around me to locate the shower. The bathroom is immense—bigger than my bedroom at home, and then some—and I move to the far wall to find a window. But to my surprise, there are no windows anywhere in the bathroom. Wherever this bathroom is, it's likely located near the center of the building because the only natural lighting comes from three large skylights high above.

The décor is natural stone. A long bank of vanity counter with sinks and mirrors line one side. A free-standing white stone tub sits beside an unlit fireplace. The huge shower that stands right under one of the skylights has walls lined with plants and is furnished with natural stone as if it was a grotto.

Inside, there's a shelf with all sorts of hair and soap products and three different shower heads—one on each end and a rain-shower head from above. It takes me a minute to figure out the controls and the optimum temperature, but when I do, I stand motionless under the multiple streams of water for minutes on end, relishing the feel of the hot water sluicing over my skin.

God, it feels amazing.

Finally, I grab a fresh pink bar of rose-scented soap, get it wet and rub it over my body. It suds up immediately, and I scrub everything thoroughly. I'm determined to stay in here as long as it takes to feel clean. Hell, even longer than that. Who knows when I'll be able to have another one? Might as well make this one count.

As long as the hot water holds out, that is. I've just rinsed the second shampoo from my hair and start lathering up my body again when I get the feeling something's different. I feel eyes on me as my skin prickles with dread.

I'm no longer alone in here. With suds still all over my body, I shut off the streams of water. Whirling, I turn and confirm what I'm feeling.

The tall, dark figure is there…standing ten feet away. He's dressed more casually than when I saw him at Isca. He's wearing a white golf shirt, jeans, a leather belt and matching shoes. And, strangely, he's wearing the red devil mask from Obscura. It covers his entire face except for his mouth. The devil face is contorted into an angry grimace, black horns twisting upward over the grotesque features. Cold, gray eyes stare out at me through that shield of anonymity.

I gulp in fear and throw my hands over my body to cover myself. One arm across my breasts, a hand to shield my lower half. Even so, I know I look ridiculous, but I'm not going to give him the satisfaction of ogling my naked, still-sudsy body.

He takes a step toward me, then another, and I belatedly wonder where the towels are. I hadn't even checked before I dove in here practically head first, desperate to get clean.

There isn't a single towel hanging on any of the empty racks, however. Nor any folded on the counter or underneath.

My eyes land on a white bathrobe, folded up neatly into a square and tied by its belt, like at the spa. It's securely tucked under the Devil's arm.

"Hello, Angel," he says, and that dry, cultured voice echoes off marble and stone.

As he comes closer, I let out a whimper, much to my own chagrin, and press my back to the frigid stone of the shower wall.

He's not a good man. He's in here, closing in on me. I'm defenseless. And completely naked.

CHAPTER 7
EXPOSED

"**G**ET OUT!" I SCREAM.

I'm cornered, cold and naked in this huge shower, and there's a masked man standing, watching me through the clear glass. Every inch of me is exposed. *Vulnerable.*

Vulnerable is exactly how he wants me to feel. It's what he's tried to accomplish the entire time I've been imprisoned here.

"I said *get out,*" I repeat, calling on every ounce of calm in my body, which isn't much.

He keeps moving toward me instead, his sensuous lips upturned in a cruel smile. "You aren't in a position to demand anything. Turn on the water and rinse yourself, then come here."

"Fuck you!" I scream instead.

He laughs, then shakes his head slowly, tsking. "You do it or I will. That's your choice."

Those cold, pale gray eyes, like frozen granite, slide insolently over my body, and I grit my teeth. Without taking my eyes off of him, my hand finds the shower fixture, exposing my breasts to him while I turn on the water and rinse off the suds of my second shampoo and fourth body lathering.

I could have spent another hour in here. Happily. If I hadn't been intruded upon. I'm completely exposed but I'm also burning with rage. With short, angry jerks, I run my hands through my hair and rinse all the suds from my body. I shut off the water and turn, hoping in vain that he's left and the robe is sitting, waiting for me on the counter.

No such luck.

He's just outside the shower now and we lock gazes through the water-beaded glass door. This time, when I bring up my hand to cover my body, his lips flatten.

"Keep your hands at your sides." The voice is commanding. Regal. This is a man who is well-used to being obeyed, and he expects no less from me. My heartbeat thrums in my throat, and my hands halfway to covering myself, I freeze. Indecision grips me. Obey him and let him think he has any power over me?

Or defy him and cover up anyway? *Choose your battles, Gwen.* And there will be plenty to fight here, so I save it. He's already seen everything anyway, even while I wasn't aware. So why bother?

My hands drop to my sides, and his gorgeous mouth turns up in a wide smile revealing even, white teeth. Even behind the mask, he's an imposing, alarmingly beautiful figure. Tall, dark-haired, and a jaw so sharp and defined it could cut diamonds. Muscular build. A shirt that clings to a fit physique, hugging the muscles of his well-defined, heavily veined arms. Those hands, long fingers. Tight jeans that cling to strong thighs...

I see that he is similarly scrutinizing me, those pale eyes dropping to my beaded nipples—though whether the condition is from arousal or the cold, I honestly could not say. They linger there and he licks his lips with the tip of his red tongue before the eyes sink lower.

His hands work at his sides as if he's trying to remember to keep them to himself. Or maybe that's just me reading more noble thoughts into a man who would use his tremendous wealth to snatch a woman off the streets and make her disappear just because…because she was writing a story he didn't like.

He reaches up and slides the shower door open and now there is no barrier between us. The cold air bathes my body. Immediately goosebumps form, and I shiver.

"Come here," he commands with a deep, husky voice. And without even a thought, I step forward and drip onto the bath mat. I'm within arm's reach of him now.

"What do you want from me? Are you going to force yourself on me?" I grind out between clenched teeth, glaring at him defiantly. I'm completely naked and he could have me bent over that counter in seconds, the deed over and done with minutes after that.

My frenetic thoughts are interrupted by more of that dry laughter. "Oh, I do mean to have you, Angel. But not until you want it, too."

That familiar heat begins snaking through my body again. God *damn.* My body's treachery is infuriating. I hate that he has this effect on me. I shake my head. "Not going to happen. Give me the robe and then let me go."

He smiles. "You'll meet with me in my office so we can discuss this…business. Or…you can return to your dark room as you are. Those are your choices. There is no third option."

I blink. What a fucking asshole.

Our gazes lock and do battle for a short moment only broken by a violent shiver on my part. I stiffen my spine and tighten my fists at my side. "Fine, I'll meet with you in your office. Now give me the robe and go. I'm sure your meatheads will drag me there with a hood over my head."

He smirks. "Turn around." His fingers are undoing the knot on the belt to release the robe. I reach for it but he pulls it away.

"Just give it to me," I snap.

He undoes the knot successfully and shakes it out to its full length—not as long as I'd like, to be honest. That length will show almost all my leg. And it's thin cotton. Which will be practically see-through when damp. Oh, for fuck's sake.

"Turn around," he repeats, this time in a harder voice. A command that expects nothing but to be obeyed.

Choose your battles, Gwen.

With a sigh of frustration, I turn my back to him.

"Hold out your arms."

And I do so, putting them out as if being helped on with a coat. Slowly, I feel him slip first one sleeve and then the other over my still-wet body. The material is highly absorbent and wicks up the moisture almost immediately. It's soft and warm and feels amazing.

His fingers work quickly, scrunching the material up my wet arms when it wants to cling where it is. His fingers brush my skin as he works, and tingles shoot down my body with every unwanted touch.

"Keep your arms out, Angel. There's a good girl."

My face flushes scarlet in anger at the way he's talking to me, but I don't make a move to drop my arms. From behind, he bends over me, looking down from above. He's at least a head and shoulders taller than me, so that's easy for him to do.

Then he curtly pulls my robe closed over my front. When the material scrunches across my nipples, I almost cry out. They are so tightly erect, so sensitive that anything is making them burn with sensations. I suppress the whimper and wait while his strong hands reach around to my front and tie the belt around my waist, holding it closed.

I stare straight ahead and try not to focus on the feel of his heat near my back.

"Well done. Now put your arms down but don't turn around. That hair is still very wet."

I drop my arms and swallow. I'd protest but the droplets are still spilling down my neck from my scalp and making their way underneath my robe. If he has a towel to dry my hair, then I want it.

Sure enough, after turning away from me and then coming back, I feel the softest, microfiber towel being wrapped around the lower half of my nearly waist-length hair.

"I doubted this was your natural color...before your shower," he says in a low voice.

Heat flushes my face again. He's obviously noticed, after seeing me naked, that the carpet matches the drapes, so to speak. *Fucker.*

"I thought maybe you bleached your hair to get it this pale. It's rare to see this natural pale color on a woman. I suspect you have some Scandinavian heritage."

"I don't need to tell you anything about myself, and I most definitely won't," I say in a flat voice. I'm hating his words while loving the feel of his gentle hands drying my hair. It's a disconcerting feeling. My eyes close briefly, and I try to push that thought out of my mind, remind myself to hate him and to get myself out of this situation as soon as possible.

Talk sense into him, if possible.

"And yet, you felt it fully appropriate to probe into *my* life and identity."

"My job is to—"

He quickly twists the towel a little too tight, pinching my scalp. I let out a little yelp. "We'll talk about this in my office. You're dry enough, now."

He lays the towel on the counter and there's a tense moment where I feel like he's going to reach out and pull me to him. After a minute, I slowly turn around and meet his gaze through the demonic mask.

He opens a drawer and pulls out a new black hood like the ones that have been shoved over my head over the course of the past few days. "When you're ready, cinch this over your head and knock on the door. Someone will bring you to my office."

Without another word, he turns to leave.

"Wait—" I say to stop him, my head spinning with questions.

He places his hands on the knob, then turns back to me. "You do not give the orders here, Angel. I do. Remember that, and I promise, you will be infinitely happier."

With that, he turns the knob, pulls the door open, and is gone.

I stare after him, my mouth open, hugging myself, and with a new sense of doom dropping in my gut.

Chapter 8

Business

I USE THE TOWEL HE LEFT TO FINISH DRYING OFF MY BODY. IN the drawer, I also find a new toothbrush, a tube of toothpaste, and fresh pair of spa slippers and put them on my feet, relieved. All the contact with the stone and concrete floors was not only making my bare feet feel dirty but also making me cold.

After brushing my teeth, I re-tie the robe extra-securely around me, hoping, at some point, I'll get actual clothes to wear instead of a very short and practically see-through robe. Having cinched the hood over my head as instructed, I knock on the door.

As is the routine, now, the door opens, and after inspecting that my hood is cinched properly, two people escort me down another long hallway and up a flight of stairs.

Suddenly, we stop and my guards knock at a wooden door. I fidget beside them, and one of them shakes my shoulder as if to warn me. I can feel the two of them stiffen as if coming to attention. I'm reminded of Domino's true persona and how his station in life would command this type of respect in certain people.

They don't get much higher than his station in life without actually being royalty, I remind myself. And darkly, I remember the power he wields, too.

A voice calls out to come in, and I'm led into the room. A much bigger room, I perceive, with thick, expensive carpeting beneath my feet. My "guards" release me and I can't even hear their movements or sense where they are. I stand perfectly still, afraid that if I strike out unguided, I might crash into something and injure myself. Or disturb some priceless artifact.

But what do I care about his baubles and tchotchkes, really? Hell, maybe if I discover a kajillion-dollar Ming Dynasty vase in here, I could fling it at his head. *Asshole.*

The door clicks closed, and I strain my ears to see if I can hear the presence of another person in here. I know he's here, probably watching me from his throne.

"You may remove the hood," comes the dry voice. It's so cold in here, I start to shiver again. Slipping the hood off my face, I squint my eyes in preparation for bright lights, like I encountered in the bathroom. But here, all is subdued and dim. There are windows, but the curtains are all drawn. Wherever we are, everyone is taking great pains to make sure I don't catch a glimpse of the outside and figure out where I am.

He's at the far end of a spacious study with leather overstuffed chairs and a whole wall lined with expensive-looking books, antique lamps and other furniture. The walls are paneled in polished, decorative wood up to the chair rail level, then painted in a muted, warm beige to the ceiling, with matching wood moldings to cap them at the top.

The entire room is gorgeous. Luxurious.

And the desk he sits at. That is the crowning glory of the room. I wouldn't be surprised if some famous chunk of wood had been used to create it, like the Resolute Desk in the Oval Office or something. It's immense and solid, *powerful*. Every bit a reflection of the darkly handsome man sitting at it on a red leather buttoned wingback chair.

And he's no longer masked.

Domino is just as beautiful as the day I first saw him without his mask, when I'd been drinking with Maddy and Lexi at Isca. I remind myself that he may be beautiful, but he's dark and depraved, like so many others in his twisted, fucked-up family.

His hard gray eyes slide slowly down my body, and I know he's remembering me naked, shivering, and dripping wet. He leans back in his chair and tilts his head to the side. "You look cold.'

"It's like a refrigerator in here," I say between involuntary muscle contractions.

He presses his lips together as if to suppress a smile. "There are clothes for you on the sofa."

I glance at a pile of clothing. A cardigan sweater and what looks like a casual cotton dress. Then my eyes scan the room. "And where should I change?"

"Another choice. You can stay as you are or you can take the clothing offered, provided you put them on now. I won't repeat the offer."

I narrow my eyes at him and bite my tongue from the lashing I really want to give him. I want to hurl insults at him—pervert, degenerate, no different than that pedo-cousin of his who is all over the news.

His eyes dance with amusement as I reach out and retrieve the dress. It's of high quality, made of a soft blend of, I'd guess, cotton and linen material. It's also exactly my size in a pale pink color. Without hesitation, I drop the robe from my body and slide the dress over my naked form within seconds. Sure he got a brief glimpse of some skin, but no more. I'm satisfied with that but not so much with the annoyingly pleased look in his eye.

I snatch up the sweater and pull it on, buttoning it up to my neck. It's cashmere. So soft and deliciously warm, my shivers subside almost immediately. Scanning the couch, I check to see if I missed any—

"There aren't any undergarments. No need to bother searching for what isn't there."

I blink. He wants me still to feel vulnerable and exposed even with my clothes on. Classic intimidation tactics. Fuck him. I'm not going to let them work on me.

He indicates a chair facing his massive desk with an affable gesture. "Please sit, Gwendolyn."

My jaw tenses, and I have half a mind to tell him to go fuck himself, but after the stunt in the bathroom during my shower, he just might whip it out and do just that while I'm watching.

And...well, while the mental image of him fondling himself is admittedly hot, I have no intention of carrying out any of the lewd fantasies he might have of me watching.

I already know he's a sexual pervert who practically runs one of L.A.'s most secretive sex clubs. Secrets I mean to expose, once I find the evidence. Undoubtedly, one of those dark secrets *has* to be trafficking. It was way too easy for him to take me without having had an infrastructure already in place. Probably used many times over on innocent, underage girls from vulnerable backgrounds.

I'm bolstered by the thought that my story just might help those women. This is exactly why I opted to become a journalist, to help people and expose lies and corruption.

"Your *lordship*." I make a mocking pseudo-curtsy with flashy jazz-hand flourishes.

He's unamused, face hardening like granite. "I don't use my title here and you'd be wise not to allude to it. You may refer to me as Domino."

I blink. Why the pretense? It's clear I already know who he is. I swallow, keeping these thoughts to myself.

"We have business to discuss, Miss Taylor. Serious business." He steeples his fingers and touches them to his lips. I square my shoulders and lift my chin. Let him do his worst, then. I'm ready for it.

Except, as he lays out every piece of dirt he has on me...I discover I'm way out of my depth.

CHAPTER 9
YOLO

OMINO TAKES AN IPAD FROM A DRAWER IN HIS MASSIVE desk and slides it across to me. With it, he hands me a printed piece of paper with instructions and...what looks like a script of some kind.

My eyes slide down the page. These are explicit instructions and a "sample script" that I'm to improvise. I'm to record a brief but upbeat video to send to my family and close friends explaining my disappearance as a flighty lark and a last-minute decision to celebrate the end of the semester.

I lick my lips as my eyes glide down the page, feeling at once incensed and also relieved. The relief comes from the fact that he's going to great pains to provide a cover story for my disappearance that would allow for me to return to the world of the living again, few questions asked.

Incensed because of the presumption that I would do anything of the kind to cover for him and his hideous crimes, up to and including kidnapping and invasion of my privacy.

My eyes lift from the page, and with narrowed eyes, I glare at him. "You're kidding, right? Why would I do anything to help you cover your ass?"

He watches me with that cold, assessing stare, pale eyes drilling right through me. His expression looks like it's carved in stone…unmoving, unexpressive of any emotions he might be feeling.

"It's not my ass that needs covering, Angel."

I grit my teeth. His little pet name has become extremely irritating. I'm not beyond noting the irony of it, given his penchant for wearing devil masks.

At my continued blank stare, his eyes flit to the iPad. "Unlock it. There's no code. It's not connected to the internet, so don't bother trying to access any messaging capabilities. You won't get through. But there's a folder on the desktop with your name on it. Click to open the folder."

I blink, snatching up the device to follow his directions, opening up the folder. There are tons of files inside. Some pictures, some documents, and several videos. Many of them are labeled with my name, a date or a location. I pick one at random and click on it.

The video has no sound but from the angle, I can tell it was lifted from surveillance footage. And the angle looks like the outside of Exeter House near the service entrance closest to the nondescript exterior entrance of Obscura. My face burns with recognition. I see myself there, scoping out the place. I know exactly when this was taken. A week or so before the goons snatched me, when I'd been hanging around trying to figure out a way inside Obscura to snoop.

Biting my lip, I close that file and click on a still picture. This one shows me in an employee's server uniform in Obscura. One I'd paid off a bus boy to get for me. I click that off and find the copy of a badge I'd used my Photoshop skills to fake. Swallowing in a tight throat, I scroll through the page. There are hundreds of files in here and all of it is dirt on me and the sketchy things I did to try and get an insider's view of the operations of the sex club.

Digging for dirt and hot on the heels of a story…just like all the famous journalists do. Like Nellie Bly, stunt girl journalist and my absolute heroine of all time. All superheroes don't wear capes…

I lift my chin to the beautiful man currently scrutinizing me. "The ends justify the means—"

"And what story do you have? What proof of any wrongdoing? Please inform me of how Obscura has violated the law in any way."

I blink, hesitating. "Of course anything devious is going to be incredibly well hidden. I was still in the process of gathering evidence. Hence the tactics you see pictured here—"

"The *illegal* tactics. Trespassing, identity theft, violation of privacy, petty larceny, forgery, bribery—shall I go on? I have close contacts at the LAPD that would be very interested in hearing about these well-documented acts." I freeze, and he shakes his head as if suddenly realizing something that I'm sure he actually realized days ago. "Would be a shame for a stand-up aspiring journalist to have such black marks on her record before she's even had a chance to begin her career. And if you think you could get off on a plea deal, think again. The DA is a regular golfing partner of mine."

I blink. "Well, if it was your intention to go to the authorities, you wouldn't have gone to all the trouble to kidnap me, hold me and force me into this meeting—all *worse* violations of the law, I might add, than whatever I've done here."

His grin widens, and though it is cold, his flawless features are lit up, as if he's intrigued, amused, intensely focused on me. "So we're doing that, the playground *I know you are, but what am I* game? Because that will get you nowhere."

I worry my bottom lip, fiddle at a loose thread on my new dress, then look up at him. "Okay, so what do you want to accomplish from this meeting?"

He lifts a folder, a leather-bound folio with an old-school button-and-string closure on it. I unwind the string and pull out several sheets of paper covered with legalese. A standard but modified Non-Disclosure Agreement.

He allows me several minutes to read it. As it is legalese, I take my time to scrutinize it. Once I'm finished, I look up at him coldly.

"This says I can never write about any member of your considerably large and prominent family. Along with the fact that I can't mention your association with Obscura or even write about Obscura itself unless to refer to it only in the broadest general terms with no identifying descriptions or names associated."

He doesn't break my stare over those steepled fingers. "That is, indeed, what I wrote. So glad you're such an adept reader."

"Fuck you."

He smiles, eyes sliding down my form insolently. "Yes, please."

"And if I don't sign this?"

He doesn't speak for a moment. "If you refuse to sign this, you will be turned over to the authorities with the aforementioned evidence along with several eyewitnesses who will attest to the fact that you were caught breaking and entering in the act of theft while in possession of several grams of cocaine."

I swallow. Our staring contest continues before a massive sense of hopelessness washes over me. I have no doubt that he's crossed his *t*'s and dotted his *i*'s and has this all prepared and ready to go, should I refuse.

"My work is too important to be ruined by a busybody journalist who wants to make a name for herself."

"What work is that? Exploiting young women to feed your disturbed sexual appetites?"

He tilts his head, as if I'm some strange bug he needs to examine from a different angle. "Your perception of Obscura is horribly misconstrued, Angel. I'd very much like to straighten that out for you."

I arch my brow at him. "For what purpose? I can't write about it, ever, if I sign that."

He runs his thumb along his lower lip. "What if you could?"

I blink, feeling mildly hopeful. Perhaps he's just dangling bait out there to tease me. I had no idea what level of sadism this man truly enjoys. Maybe he gets off on offering false hope.

"Perhaps a little bit of a carrot instead of an all-stick approach might be in order." He seems to be mumbling the words to himself as he riffles through papers on his desk until he finds another file folder, flips it open and turns it so that I can read it.

My eyes catch on a list of names…names of people I don't know, but their associated institutions I immediately recognize… *New Yorker. The Observer. Atlantic. Harper's. Esquire.* And more.

"You know all these people?"

"I have connections with them, yes. My duties have allowed me to work with many different people across your fair nation and beyond." I'd only had a very short time to look him up after realizing who he was, but I did know that he was employed by the British government as an official cultural liaison with the United States as well as a joint director of several important humanitarian operations.

"So you're saying—"

"A good word from me, Miss Taylor, will get you a lot further than a hack piece aimed at an already much-beleaguered target, my family."

"This is how people like you get away with whatever you want. You're above the law."

"No, indeed. Unlike alleged others of my kin, I do not break the law. Neither does Obscura. I can afford you a fair and balanced look inside. Give you the first-person experience. And maybe we can bend the rules about how much you can write specifically, should your angle please me."

I tap the NDA that's still in front of me. "If I sign this, then what happens? I go home?"

"Not quite. Not immediately, anyway. You'll need to record the video, as instructed, and will be allowed limited contact with your friends under my direct supervision over the next thirty days—"

"*Thirty days*? A whole month?"

He arches a dark brow at me. "I'm sorry? Did you have somewhere to be? Your semester is over and your editor has given you leave to work on your story for your internship."

How does he know all that?

"There's no story if I sign that."

He shrugs. "A difficult decision you'll have to make, Angel. Life is full of them, believe me. You're young. You'll soon learn that, as I have."

He's implying that it was a difficult decision that led to him nabbing me off the street and holding me here.

"I didn't sign on to be a journalist in order to get ahead and make a name for myself. I'm in the business of exposing the dirty underbelly of exploitative operations like that sex club, to—"

"And if I offered you an inside view of that club to show you otherwise?"

I blink. "I'd like to see you try."

"Those are benefits you can earn during your stay here. But now, to the business of the NDA and the video. What is your answer?" He very pointedly checks his watch as if he has some place to be. Knowing him, he probably does.

With a sigh, I take up the pen and quickly reread the NDA. Thirty days here...in that dark room? Eating sandwiches and protein bars? Could I do it?

But he's promised me an insider's look at the club. Maybe I can dig in deep to where others haven't been able to go. Maybe I could make this into a first-person experience piece, like Gloria Steinem working as a playboy bunny. Would thirty days of captivity be worth it?

He hadn't even guaranteed me the story. Merely the opportunity to earn those inside views. So I ask him to clarify.

"You ask what you will, I'll name the price..."

"And that dark cell? I have to stay there?"

He smiles. "There's a price for everything here. But whether or not you decide to pay any of them, when you sign the NDA and walk out of here, your name will be recommended by my office to any or all of the people on that list before you. Anything else you accomplish here will be extra."

"But that won't be enough, I'll need an angle, a story."

"I'll provide that, too." He lifts the list with the names on it to show me another—a list of approved subject matters that he'll give me exclusive access to cover. Several of which list exclusive access to him and aspects of his work. While they are not extremely exciting to my particular eye, I know any or all of them could grab the attention of any of those long-form journals he's listed. Dream jobs, really, if not the actual subject that set my passion afire.

The next ten minutes pass in a blur. I sign the NDA, then make my notes to adjust his "script" of my message to my family and friends.

Then, with him sitting on the desk in front of me, beside the iPad that records, I deliver my upbeat, happy message. There's only a space of blank wall behind me. He's made sure to angle the device in that way so that no identifying aspects of this room are visible. He's missed absolutely nothing in his plan.

In the message, with a huge grin on my face and a breathless sort of tone to my voice, I tell them how I stayed at the Isca bar after Maddie and Lexi left and met an incredible man who practically swept me off my feet. We had drinks and I had quite a few. Then we went for a walk on the beach where we were having so much fun goofing around that I didn't notice dropping my shoes, or even my phone. And when he told me he was heading out on a private red-eye flight to Honolulu that night and wanted me to come along, I didn't refuse.

He's handsome, rich and absolutely obsessed with me, and it didn't occur to me, missing my phone over the past three days, that people might be worried. But I'm sending this along now from his phone.

God, what a load of bullshit all of that is. So not me. But when I finish with a bunch of giggles and a sigh and a "YOLO," I've had enough and tell him to end it.

"I tried to sell it. Quite the ridiculous story. And so very not me. I don't do YOLO, you know."

I curse inwardly. Why am I helping him?

His eyes narrow. "Maybe you should sometime…or someone should show you what you're missing out on."

He slips from his seat on the desk and is now standing just two feet from me. I look up at him, arching a brow. "Right now I'm missing out on a pitch-black prison cell and cold food delivered in a cardboard box once a day," I say dryly.

He studies me for a moment. "Well, as I said, you do have opportunities for upgrade in your circumstances as well as your access to other areas in this complex, provided…"

No longer comfortable with him standing, hovering over me, I slip out of my chair and straighten. Doesn't do me a lot of good. He still towers over me when we are standing. A formidable, intimidating presence that he has obviously honed and uses well.

"I'd be delighted to invite you to a delicious, private three-course dinner tonight, prepared by my private chef. He's excellent. We can talk about anything you like, within reason."

I blink. "Well, I'd be a fool not to accept that invitation."

His smile widens. "I haven't extended it yet, Angel. You have to earn it."

My eyes narrow. "And how do I do that?"

"Simple. It just requires one kiss."

Chapter 10
Glow Up

I STARE AT HIM IN DISBELIEF, UNSURE I EVEN HEARD HIM correctly. *A kiss?*

"But—" I begin before he cuts me off.

"It's just what I've said. I don't play games, Angel. You allow me to kiss you. One kiss and you'll be invited to dine with me tonight. And, before you ask, nothing else is on the table. It's just dinner. And, hopefully, scintillating conversation."

I swallow, suddenly imagining what it would be like to kiss him. My gaze drops to his sensuous mouth, full lips, a dusting of dark scruff along his jaw, not enough to hide his chiseled features but still enough to be interesting. What would his mouth feel like on mine? I've wondered that since the night I met him, wearing that devil mask, at Obscura weeks ago.

I straighten, squaring my shoulders as if readying for battle. "Fine. I can do one kiss to get a decent meal around here."

There's a twinkle in those cool gray eyes. "I'm glad to hear it."

And with no further comment or hesitation, he leans in to collect his kiss.

What I thought might be a quick lip-lock or maybe even a chaste sealing of a deal is anything but. Domino closes the distance between us, one hand settling against my lower back to hold me in place and the other gently pressing against the back of my head.

His lips find mine, and heat sears through me the minute they meet. Electricity crackles through me and he's seconds into breaching my defenses. His tongue sweeps along and past my lips, through the gap of my teeth to take command of my mouth, as if immediately claiming ownership of what is mine.

His invasion is thorough and determined. His tongue pushes everywhere, and his lips envelop mine in a way that only nominally allows me to think that I'm an equal partner in this contact. He does as his Obscura persona alludes to—he *dominates* me. Heat settles in my belly, and lower, stewing and boiling. My core aches with hunger, and my nipples, pressed against his shirt, bead to needy points. Even the soft texture of my dress against them makes me almost want to scream from the sensitivity.

He never stops, never relents…nor does his mouth move from mine. He takes and he takes what he wants from me with the confident assumption that my pleasure is equal to his.

It's so fucking hot, I can barely breathe—something I'm finding it hard to do regardless. He's lit a fire inside me, in those innermost places that I've neglected for so long. And even when I didn't—it had never, ever felt like this.

He stops shortly after I let out an involuntary whimper—one I hardly knew would escape until after it happened, furthering the sensation of loss of control. When he slowly pulls back from me—so slowly that I could pull him in for more, but don't—I'm shaking. There's a look in his eyes, clear surprise and also something else I can't name.

"I should have known," he whispers as if to himself, but I don't ask him what he's talking about despite my curiosity.

He steps back from me quickly, turning to make his way around the desk, as if anxious to put it between us once more. I watch him, half in shock, half in longing.

His eyes are on the desk as he reaches out to arrange some papers while avoiding my gaze. "Put the hood on, Miss Taylor. My people will take you to your room until it's time for dinner."

When he speaks, his voice sounds strange, tight—*tense.* Does he plan to go back on his bargain? Is he going to send me away? As in send me home?

At once I want to go home while also feeling like a door has just opened…a door to a room I have never seen before and am anxious to explore. I swallow and nod even though he's not looking at me. I move back toward the couch where the hood, and my damp spa robe are lying where I put them.

I pick up the hood, put it on…and wait.

A buzzer and his voice quietly informs whoever beyond that I'm ready to be taken back to my "room."

The thought of sitting there alone in the dark for hours suddenly brings me more terror than it did earlier and I start to shake again. Just before the door opens, I feel his hand on the small of my back, and I jump at the sensation.

"Until tonight, Miss Taylor."

Without a word, I turn and go with his people. They silently take me back to my dark, empty room without as much as a word. Once the hood is off and I'm able to move about my cell in the darkest dimness, I can tell that the entire place has been cleaned thoroughly. Floor swept and mopped, bathroom scrubbed and new linens on the "bed." It's still a stark, no-frills and very dark prison cell, but it's a clean one.

And inexplicably, as if it's some way to release the tension or deal with the morass of feelings stewing inside of me, I flop onto my floor mattress and sob.

I doze off, but it seems very little time goes by before others enter my room and tell me it's time to prepare for my dinner date. That's exactly how it's referred to, too—a dinner date. I'd figured this meal would have been above the pay grade of my light cotton dress. Obviously, his lordship agrees.

The same routine is repeated with the dark hood, then being led down hallways, steps, and all the twists and turns until I'm brought to a room and told to take off my hood.

I'm in a room that looks like a fancy dressing room. Along one side of the wall, there is a rack of clothing hanging along it. The other side has a counter with lit mirrors and trays of makeup. The wall adjacent has more mirrors and implements for hair styling—blow dryers, curling irons, air-wrap stylers. On the wall facing the rack of clothing, there are shelves and shelves of mannequin heads with wigs and hats on them. It's like I've walked into the backstage dressing room at the Pantages Theatre.

I sit down at the makeup counter and begin to look through what's there when someone enters the room. I turn. It's a woman wearing an obvious wig of bright pink hair, thick, chunky glasses and lots of makeup.

She grins wide. "Hi. I'm Jemma." She speaks in a British accent but it's different than Domino's. It sounds less cultured…South London, maybe?

I smile back, relieved to have someone besides Domino talk to me for the first time in three days. "I'm here to help you get ready for your dinner date. Don't worry… This is not my normal look." She blows out a breath and rolls her eyes. I realize that she's wearing a disguise, so I can't easily identify her.

Wow, talk about covering all the bases.

"Oh, great… I was just about to do—"

"Oh no, none of that. I'll do your makeup, your hair. But first, how about a mani-pedi?"

I blink. "That would be amazing."

With a wide grin, she escorts me to a nearby chair where I am pampered for the next hour while she does my toes and fingers. Such a contrast from the dark room, sleeping in my same clothes for days on end without even a shower. I blink, wondering what other things I can negotiate from the super-mysterious Lord Devon Howard.

After the mani-pedi, the bubbly Jemma—which I doubt is her real name—does my hair and makeup while regaling me with funny stories of guys hitting on her when she was out "with the blokes" at the bar last weekend. I laugh until my belly aches and can't stop smiling. Real name, disguise or no…I like Jemma.

"His Lordship wanted to make sure you had a large selection of dresses to pick from. Every color you could imagine." Then she widened her eyes. "Oh shit, it's habit you know. He doesn't like us using his title here."

My eyebrow twitches up, intrigued. "Did you know him in the UK, too?"

She shoots me a look out of the corner of her eye but doesn't answer, instead turning to the rack of dresses. "I've always thought pale pink, Tiffany blue or even lavender would look amazing with fair hair and pale skin. Red or black would wash you out."

I move up next to her, following her cue to drop the subject.

My eyes immediately gravitate to a delicate sage-green chiffon, and I pull it off the rack to hold it up against me. "All the dresses are in your size, miss," she adds helpfully.

My eyes glide along the lines of the dress. It's an A-line, full skirt with chiffon overlay, filmy and feminine with a v-neck that doesn't plunge too deeply.

"The dressing closet is right over there." Rather than a closet, it's just the corner of the room sectioned off by two floor-to-ceiling curtains. I pull them closed, thankful for the privacy since I have no underwear on. The dress fits perfectly, and as it's backless, I wouldn't be able to wear a bra even if I'd been provided with one.

When I emerge, Jemma's brows shoot up. "It's so lovely. I had my doubts but that green is gorgeous on you. It's practically the same color as your eyes."

I smile. "Green is kinda my color."

She grins. "I agree. You look lovely."

I run my hands along the chiffon skirt again, feeling every bit as lovely. Jemma pulls out a shoe rack—all my size again—and I pick out a pair of three-inch silver strappy pumps. Then, the biggest shocker of all…she pulls out some jewelry that doesn't look like it's costume.

There's a matching necklace and bracelet. They are delicate white gold. The necklace is a long strand of braided metal, worked in platinum and white gold. Each end is capped by the head of what looks like a dragon or snake with twinkling diamonds for eyes. It's exotic and very expensive looking. The bracelet matches, wrapping stiffly around my wrist and halfway up my arm. When Jemma puts the necklace on, she puts it on backward. "It's a back chain. Perfect for the cut of this dress."

The front hugs my neck like a choker and the back—I hear her click one of the snake's heads to the other strand, like a snake biting its own tail.

The cold metal lays between my shoulder blades, the tail settling just above the small of my back. For some reason, it makes me feel sexy. When I look at the full effect in the full length mirror, I'm blown away. I feel like a movie star—or maybe even royalty.

All to have a private fancy dinner with a man I hardly know—a man who kisses like Eros himself.

While I'm inspecting myself, I notice Jemma texting and then fiddling with something on the far wall. When I turn back to her, I see that she's pulled down the end of a rolled poster on the wall. Except it's just a large square of plain bright green.

I open my mouth to ask her what she's doing when another person enters. This time a man. He's wearing a turtleneck, a knit cap pulled down over his ears and a medical mask.

He looks like a burglar rather than a photographer, which is what I deduce he really is judging by the huge camera he's toting.

"Right. I'm here to snap some pictures of the young lady." Another urban British accent. I'm guessing somewhere in the north—Manchester? I have no idea. I'm crappy when it comes to placing accents, especially ones from England.

The newcomer doesn't give me his name nor does he even speak directly to me—I guess Jemma is the only exception. He instructs me to pose against the green backdrop and vary my stances, my expressions.

This is beyond weird, and I'm completely confused but follow along since it's nothing tawdry. Just unusual.

Minutes later, he ducks out of the room. Jemma wishes me a nice evening and excuses herself soon after, but not before leaving me another hood. "Try not to muss your hair, okay? You look smashing."

Once she's gone, I look at the hood in dismay, really hating the thing now. But I know I won't be allowed to leave until it's over my head, so with resignation, I put it on once again and wait for my handlers to take me wherever it is that we'll be eating.

After another long walk, where they take care to walk slower because I'm in heels, I'm left in another room. It's very quiet here.

I immediately smell the distinct scent of melting wax before I even slip off the hood to see a small and elegantly appointed room. It's oval-shaped and splendidly decorated.

And I'm not there two minutes before a door at the opposite end starts to open.

I stare across at it, gut-tightening.

What's in store for me now?

CHAPTER 11
DINNER

INTO THIS SMALL, PRIVATE DINING ROOM STEPS A BEAUTIFUL man. He's dressed formally—black tie and the cut of his tux is exquisite. As if it was made for him, which it likely was. It conforms to his broad shoulders, muscular form, tapered torso, hugging his fit physique. He oozes pure masculinity and power, even in the fluid motions of his form.

It's scary how much I'm attracted to him, and just remembering the kiss today is doing strange things to my tummy...and lower. My throat is so dry, I can barely force a swallow even though my heart is now beating in double-time.

His pale, colorless—almost silvery—gray eyes rake down my form, and he smiles.

"Good evening."

I lick my lips and avert my eyes from that probing stare. "H-hello."

I glance at the table, set with fine china, gold-limned silverware and cut crystal goblets for an intimate service of two over an elegant tablecloth of Irish lace. The chairs are deeply padded, wing back, large. He moves to the one nearest to him and pulls it away from the table, looking at me expectantly. I blink and wordlessly obey, moving to him. I can feel his eyes on me as I sink into the chair, and he pushes it to the table for me.

"You are exquisite tonight, Angel. Green is most definitely your color. My necklace..." I feel pressure where he manages to touch it without making contact with my skin. "...looks sinfully good on you."

My eyes flutter closed briefly. Even that touch, though indirect, is sending sparks through me. I think about his words from earlier today. *I do mean to have you, but not until you want it, too.* I fear that time may come all too soon. If it hasn't already arrived.

He moves to take the seat across the table from me, and as I shift in my own seat, I'm all too aware that I'm not wearing any underwear and that my nipples, currently hard, aching points, are probably clearly visible and saying their own special *hello* to him.

Tension hangs in the air between us as we exchange gazes. He presses a button on the smartwatch at his wrist, and shortly thereafter, two masked servers enter. One places a menu card before us, and the other fills our goblets with water before consulting Domino on the wine choice.

He nods. "As we discussed earlier, please."

Oh shit...wine. My weakness. I make a mental note not to drink too much. It could compromise me. He says he would never rape a woman, but he might mistake my wine-induced willingness for a *yes*.

And above all else, I've come to realize in a short period of time that when it comes to Lord Devon Howard, I need all my wits about me at all times.

As would be expected for a man of his station, his manners are impeccable. I watch with awe the elegance of his removing the napkin from his place setting and, with one smooth move, shaking it out and laying it in his lap. I try to mirror his actions but end up only looking shaky and clumsy. Oh well.

Our meal starts with a chilled cucumber soup and progresses to salad, main course, cheese plate in due time. It takes a while, with time between courses.

After a quiet soup course, I nervously rearrange my napkin in my lap and try to break the tension in the room with idle chatter. "Do you always dress up like this for dinner?"

He watches me carefully, also noting how my hands are flitting about. Perhaps he's enjoying my nervousness. "Only when I have a stunningly beautiful dinner guest to keep me company."

"That's quite often, I'm sure," I fire back quickly.

His gorgeous lips turn up in a smile. "Not as often as you are thinking, no. I'm trying to determine what shade of green your eyes are. Not quite that sage color you are wearing. They remind me of something else…celadon green, that's it. The color of a rare and ancient Chinese glaze for pottery."

I blink at him, then burst out laughing. "My eye color? Really? Isn't that a little cliché?"

And in seconds, he's laughing too. It sounds so different from that hard, sandpapery, sardonic laugh of this afternoon. "I suppose you've caught me, Angel."

My breath hitches at the way he says the nickname. There's something behind it, a charge, an emotion. My gaze flies to his and there's fire there, fire which captures me like an insect in a spider's web. Except I'm not struggling to break free, not yet.

"How do you like the wine?"

He's noticed that I only took two sips of the chilled Sauvignon blanc that was served with soup. I blink and finger the base of the elegant stemware. "It's probably the best white I've ever tasted."

An eyebrow arches. "Why not have more?"

I smile. "I'm not that cheap a date."

His brow twitches up on one side, and his mouth curls to match the movement. "I ask because it's from the vineyard on my estate in Provence."

I blink, then reach for the wine and take another tiny sip. It really is amazing…crisp, dry. Just how I like it. Instead of stroking his ego and gushing about it, I decide to deflect. "I'm not exactly a connoisseur. I've only been of legal drinking age for a little over a year, after all."

His eyes flit away for a minute, and he shifts in his seat as if my reminding him of my age has made him uncomfortable. "Tell me, Miss Taylor, why is it that you decided to pursue journalism, especially when you attend the country's top technical university? Seems like an odd choice."

"I started with a focus in mathematics. I have a knack for numbers—always have. But it's not my passion. I can't change the world if I'm good with numbers."

He blinks. "I have to disagree with that. Were it not for some really brilliant women, gifted mathematicians such as Katherine Johnson, for example, men would never have been able to get to orbit, let alone land on the moon and return safely back again."

I swirl the wine glass in my hand, contemplating that. "I want to make the world a better place for underrepresented people, give a voice to those who don't have one." My eyes leave the glass to focus back on him. "Exploited women, for example."

"Noble causes, then. I do some work in those areas as well."

I arch my brow at him, clearly in disbelief, but before I can reply, we're interrupted by the next course.

Our conversation continues, engaging, sometimes pointed. I take a jab at him and he deflects beautifully, deftly. Like he's been doing this all his life, which he likely has.

"Is it not unusual for someone of your distant relationship to the, ah, CEO of the family to be actively working as part of the firm?" I finally ask him a question that hits a little closer to home.

His brows level out as he considers his answer. "Her Late Majesty felt I had certain talents that lent themselves more easily to what she needed in this post."

"Sounds like she knew you well for a…third cousin four times removed or something?"

"We're more close knit than is often portrayed in the voluminous amounts of media that have been dedicated to the subject."

I sip again, studying him, fascinated by every tidbit and detail he allows to be dropped. He seems to know it, too, sprinkling them like breadcrumbs for me to follow or dangling like bait on a fishhook.

After the main course, Domino tells the server that we'll take dessert "in the suite." And I'm at once delighted and frightened about the change of venue. Why? What suite? And does this place have a bed in it?

And is that where he plans to try to seduce me?

I've remained judicious with the wine, but as a new glass came with every course and I needed to sample each one—all of them excellent—I've had nearly two full glasses. I'm nowhere near drunk, but the pleasant buzz at the edge of my awareness might prove dangerous. I may be just tipsy enough to get into trouble while appearing well sober enough to give consent.

It's a dangerous place to be with a tall, dark and devilishly handsome man like Lord Devon Howard in my presence. And he's made his own desires clear to me. *I mean to have you.*

Not one smidge of doubt or "what if" in those words. He spoke that as if he was certain of the future. That within the next thirty days, while captive in his opulently luxurious complex, I'd lie down on a bed and open my legs for him…

Damn, I pull my own mind away from that mental image because I'm not feeling as incensed about it as I should. In fact, it just might be turning me on a little. And that's a little too much for my liking.

He pulls out my chair, and I stand, about to ask him what's what with this "suite." Before I can, he holds up the familiar black hood.

"Where are we going?"

"It's a surprise. A good one."

I fold my arms, planting my legs apart enough to indicate that I'm not moving from the spot until I get more information.

"Let's just say I want to show you…a possibility…for your stay here."

I blink. What the hell is that supposed to mean? "No funny business…."

He smiles, obviously amused. "No, indeed. Not business and certainly not funny."

As he's guiding me to wherever we are going, he's walking slowly, and a few times, I bump into him, unused to wearing four-inch heels. His arm comes across my back, hand settling on my opposite hip as he pulls me against him and guides me with his strong, muscular—and very large—body. The feel of him rubbing up against me, even through our clothing, is making my entire body hum with desire.

Fuck.

I'm in so much trouble with this guy. This guy I'm supposed to hate for capturing me and holding me like an animal, a prisoner.

"I wanted to let you know that your video was sent to friends and family early today. They all seem very relieved and have been sending in queries. We can go over your responses to them tomorrow."

I blink under my hood and suck in a breath, thinking about what they must have gone through in the past few days, not knowing what had happened to me. And that message I sent makes me sound so flighty and insensitive. Ugh. I wonder if they'll ever forgive me.

"They're all angry."

He hesitates. "Some are, yes. But you've had a few encouraging messages, happy for you."

I can almost name who those might be. Probably my closest friends—Lexi, Cassie. Lexi has just recently found amazing and unlikely love herself with Ash. Who'd have thought such a thing could happen from crawling into bed with a complete stranger, thinking he was your boyfriend and then having the most amazing sex with him in the dark? So crazy.

And ugh, here I am thinking about hot sex again.

How long has it even been for me?

Before I can answer my own mental question, Domino stops. I hear him reach out, and the door knob emits a series of beeps. A keypad?

The lock whirs open immediately, and with his hand on the bare skin of my back, he gently guides me inside…wherever this is.

"Lights," he says, and there's a click. Then he slowly reaches out to remove my hood. His fingers brush against the base of my throat, and the touch burns. I suck in a breath, and I know he hears it. There's a low growl, almost like the sound of a big cat's purr, deep in his throat.

"So soft," he whispers, and I blink at the change in light. Then turn and look around me, stunned.

He's led me to a gorgeous suite of three rooms—a sitting room with desk, TV, bookcases, a sofa and beautiful thick rug. It's lovely. Beyond, there is a large and luxurious looking king-sized bed fully adorned with satiny bedding and loads of pillows. From the bedroom, there's a large attached bathroom with shower, tub and even a steam room. It's incredible.

And on the far side of the sitting room wall, there's another door. This one also has a keypad. I walk over to try it anyway and it's locked. My eyes find his. He's been watching me. I don't ask, and he doesn't provide an explanation to what's beyond that locked door.

"I thought we'd enjoy dessert here."

Shortly thereafter, we sit on the couch, and our white chocolate mousse and little plate of petit fours arrive. I'm so stuffed I can barely eat another bite, but it's so delicious, I can't resist.

"Your chef is incredible."

"He really is. The whole staff is. I'm a fortunate man."

"Did they follow you here from the UK?"

His cold eyes flick up at me, the color of icy granite.

I blink and spoon myself another bit of the velvety mousse. "Oh, I see, so no giving me info on the people in disguise?"

"It's for their protection, Miss Taylor. In case there's a problem with our…agreement."

"So I can't pick them out of a lineup."

Without warning, he reaches toward me with his large index finger. I draw back but the finger lands on the corner of my mouth. He holds up a dollop of mousse, and I smile awkwardly. *Oops.*

Then, he does the most startling and hottest thing. He holds his finger in front of my mouth as if I should lick the mousse off of it. I lick my lips and then open my mouth. He brings his finger to my lips and then inserts the tip between them. My lips close around his finger, and I suck the mousse off of it.

An inferno blazes up behind those silvery eyes. "The most alluring thing about you, Angel, is that you have no idea how desirable you are," he says in a hoarse whisper.

Oh god, his words, his actions, his looks—the wine—this could go in bad places very quickly. I pull my mouth away, and he lets his finger drop. Our gazes, however? They are speaking volumes to each other.

Very dirty, likely pornographic volumes.

"This is—I should—" This would be the part of the normal date where I make my excuses about having to get up in the morning. But for a very different reason than my date was boring me or I just wasn't feeling it.

"What?" he asks, as if he wants me to voice it.

"I should get back to my room."

"Would you prefer this to be your room?"

I blink, my heart speeding up hopefully. "You'd let me stay here instead of that dark cell? I'd love to."

"Not quite that easily, Angel. But there is, of course, a way to *earn* it."

My breath freezes in my chest, and I stare at him, eyes wide. He wears his persona easily for a reason. And I have a dark feeling that he's about to propose a devil's bargain.

CHAPTER 12
THE PLAYROOM

I SWALLOW, ADJUSTING IN MY SEAT BESIDE HIM ON THE now-too-small couch. "Earn this room? I can't believe I'm actually asking this but…just how do you propose I do that?"

There's an intensity in his eyes. "Spend one hour in the playroom with me."

I blink. "Your, ah, playroom?" I'm getting Christian Grey vibes right about now. I'm immediately picturing the Red Room of Pain and, like Anastasia, at least at the beginning, I'm having none of it.

The mental image is comical enough to make me laugh out loud. He watches me, unfazed.

"I have no intention of being your subservient."

"Submissive," he corrects.

"I'm not going to be your sex slave," I repeat.

He shakes his head. "That wasn't what I was asking of you. What I *was* asking is one hour with me in the playroom."

"Tied up and naked? No, thank you. I'll happily go back to the dark cell."

Without another word, he rises from the couch, re-buttons his coat and walks over to the locked door on the far wall of the sitting room. He enters a code and then gives another verbal command to turn on the lights in there.

"Come, have a look before you completely reject the idea."

He knows me well enough to know that my curiosity is a powerful thing, and just for the hell of it, I get up and stand beside him in the doorway to look into the room.

The floor plan is the mirror image of the suite—the same size bedroom and attached bathroom, right down to the mirror fireplace right behind the one in the suite where we had dessert. It kind of reminds me of the world beyond the looking glass, as if this doorway we were standing in was the portal to another world.

The entire room is decorated like a fantasy Middle-Eastern harem. The walls are painted a warm yellow-golden hue. The bed at the far end of room is low to the ground and decorated in shimmering golden satin draperies that hang down from the ceiling all around it and decorated with brightly colored pillows, as if something found inside a sheikh's luxurious tent on the desert dunes. On each side are Middle-Eastern-inspired carved armoires decorated with gold leaf details.

The fireplace is tiled with beautiful jewel-tones, as are all the accents in the room—bright pink, deep aqua, deepest purple. There are a few chairs and couches—some of them in strange shapes, U-shaped in the middle or thin, as if designed for straddling. Obviously, sex furniture. A silk hammock-like sex swing—or what I'm assuming is a sex swing—hangs in the corner. On the wall closest to me, there is a strange contraption that looks similar to an item from the *Fifty Shades* movies.

A huge step up from the garish red leather décor of the Red Room. It feels like I've stepped back in time to the royal palace in Ottoman Turkey.

Wow.

"Well, your decorator has a lot more taste than Christian Grey's, I'll give them that."

Domino says nothing and doesn't even move. I look up at him and see that he's watching me as my eyes roam over every implement in the room.

I arch a brow at him.

He gestures. "Feel free to go in and look around if you'd like."

I shake my head, instead stepping back. "No, thanks, I've seen enough."

He nods without hesitation and firmly shuts the door. "Very well."

There's a moment of tense awkwardness between us when he turns back to me. I have no idea what he'll say, and I don't even want to know.

"I'm sure you're not used to being told no by the women you take in there."

Without even changing expression, he replies. "I've never taken a woman into that room before."

I laugh, immediately taking it for a deadpan joke. But he's not laughing or smiling and there is no teasing twinkle in his eyes.

"Okay so not that room specifically but whatever other playrooms around…or at Obscura."

He looks away for a moment, hesitating before turning back to me. "Miss Taylor, I've never taken a submissive."

I blink. "You're lying."

"No, indeed."

My brows knit. "But you were at Obscura. And from the way people knew you there, you definitely are a frequent visitor—"

"A visitor, yes. An observer. In some ways, an overseer. But any one of those people who deferred to me there will tell you the same. And none of them knows my true identity."

I blink. Open my mouth to reply, then blink again. He's so earnest I can't help but believe he's telling the truth. But why volunteer that information—especially three minutes after asking me to submit to him for an hour in a sex playroom?

"You're confused," he offers.

I bust out laughing again. "What was your first clue?"

"It's simple. I've always been content to watch the goings-on at Obscura. I've had my, shall we call them, 'vanilla' relationships. I'm sure you're aware of the more high-profile ones."

"You mean the movie stars, super models and even the political figure you've dated? Oh, yeah."

"You make it sound like there were so many. Honestly, my work keeps me far too busy to build a serious relationship with anyone."

"But you have enough time to frequent a place like Obscura."

He shrugged. "George Orwell spent three years living like a homeless tramp when he had a home, career and income, just so he could fuel his art."

I blink, thinking about how my heroine reporters did similarly, lived deep undercover to have the experience to write knowledgeably about their subject matter. Is he suggesting I participate in these activities in order to be able to write about them?

Or is he looking for an excuse to get me bound and gagged and in his bed?

"Well, the offer stands, Angel. You may accept at any time and this room will become your accommodations for the rest of your stay."

I worry my bottom lip. "So I'm in the dark prison cell for the next thirty days if I don't agree?"

He smiles. "Who knows... more opportunities might crop up."

A flush of anger and frustration rises up, heating my face. "I may have willingly signed that paper and helped you with that stupid cover story behind my disappearance, but you are still a kidnapper."

His features are like stone. "I think it's time to say good night to one another before either one of us says something we'll regret."

I grit my teeth and relax them. "Fine." I stomp over to the coffee table where the stupid black hood—my one constant companion here—is lying. I grab it, shove it over my head and pull the string.

"At least let me grab one of the books on that shelf so I'll have something to do."

"You can't read in the dark, Angel. And the books stay with the room. You've made your choice."

"Very well, warden. I'm ready to be taken back to my cell and locked in, then."

A bit of that dry, humorless laughter, and a moment later, he takes my arm and silently guides me the long and winding way back to my cell himself.

Once inside, he shuts the door. I whip off my hood the second it clicks closed and whirl to flip the bird at the close door. To my shock, I feel his presence, still inside the cell with me.

"What are you doing?" I yelp, wondering if he's in here to push me on the floor pallet and have his way with me.

"I'd like to invite you to dine with me again tomorrow night."

I squint into the darkness. "You could just order me to, you know."

He doesn't reply.

"Fine. I'll go."

"As before, Angel, you need to earn the privilege."

I grit my teeth. He pisses me off so much, and the last thing I want to do is kiss him. On the other hand, I'm not looking forward to subsisting on egg salad sandwiches and protein bars, either.

"Fine. I'll kiss you."

He moves closer but doesn't touch me. When he speaks, it's in a hoarse whisper. "The price has escalated slightly."

My heart starts to hammer and my blood heats. "Two kisses?" My voice is breathless.

He laughs again. "Kiss me and find out."

He moves in then, putting a hand on each of my hips to pull me against him. His mouth lands on mine, and as before, his lips press against mine, demanding they open to him. At first I try to resist him. His hands slide up my form to rest just under my underarms while the tip of his tongue lines the seams of my lips. Seconds later, his thumbs are moving across the slick, thin chiffon material and they are circling my nipples.

When I let out a small gasp of shock and pleasure, he exploits the opportunity, pressing his mouth against mine and forcing it farther open. His tongue plunges in, exploring me thoroughly while his large hands palm my breasts, his thumb and forefingers weaving a wicked pattern over my sensitive nipples. He's teased them to aching, needy points in seconds. Overwhelmed and in the darkness, I take a step back.

He follows me. I retreat again, and he pursues without removing his mouth from mine. My back soon finds the wall, just beside the door, and he holds me firmly there, between the wall and his equally hard body.

He kisses and kisses me, thumbs never stopping their wicked teasing. My head spins, and I'm delirious with desire. It feels like tongues of flame rising up from my core, flaring and surging at his command.

I want to pull away, but I don't. It's like I'm two people. One is telling me this is the hottest thing that's ever happened to me and the other screaming that I shouldn't allow him to touch me.

Desire wins.

When he finally pulls his mouth away from mine, his body shifts and he purposely presses his very noticeable erection against my hip. I'm breathing hard. His voice is equally breathless when he murmurs to me, thick with obvious lust. "Feel what you do to me, Angel. And I know what I'm doing to you. How much we both want it." His hand drops to trace the length of the snake necklace that drops down my back. "I need to fuck you. And I will. I'll take you in ways you've never even dreamed of."

His words are like a drug, swirling around me with unrealized promise. I can barely force a swallow down my dry throat. My entire body is taut and tense, aching for release at his hands.

I'll take you in ways you never dreamed of... My mind swirls with the possibilities of what he could possibly mean by that.

My nipples are throbbing—as is my clit—in time with my heartbeat. I'm seconds away from coming just from his words, his kiss, his touch on my nipples.

"Take off your clothes, Angel," he says next.

I swallow and say nothing. I'm debating whether or not I should. How could I want so badly to fuck a man I hate?

"It wasn't a request," he says when I don't move. He steps back and reaches near the door, picking up a box that has been left there for me, apparently. "Put your dress, shoes and jewelry in this box."

"But I have nothing to wear."

"There's something here for you to wear."

I almost refuse but consider that the dress and shoes would probably be uncomfortable to sleep in anyway. So instead, I do as he says, and standing right in front of him, for the third time today, I strip down naked and put the clothes in the box. He probably can't see much in the dark.

Once the shoes, the dress, the jewelry are in the box, he hands me a small cloth bag.

"Now the hood, on your head, please."

"But—"

"Do as I say." His voice is hard, intolerant. I suck in a breath and put the hood on.

"Until tomorrow," he says tightly. Then pulls the door open and is gone.

In the bag he's left me, I notice that, along with another soft plain cotton and linen dress, there is a small jar of cold cream and a wash cloth so that I can remove my makeup. I do so, in the dark bathroom with cold water, then dress and curl onto the bed, exhausted, seething, confused.

I close my eyes, wondering if I can stand thirty days in the darkness. If I can rescind my invitation to dinner. Refuse to see him again.

Maybe I *should* refuse.

Or maybe I should accept the bargain for a nicer suite. At least it's not dark there.

Maybe, just maybe, I'll figure out a way to make him pay.

That, alone, is the thought that sustains me through the lonely night.

CHAPTER 13
CONDITIONS

I SLEEP DEEPLY—BETTER THAN I HAVE ANY NIGHT IN HERE UP until this point. Perhaps it was the wonderful, full meal. Perhaps it was my sheer exhaustion at dealing with Domino and the confusing feelings and sensations he's stirred in me.

I wake in the morning feeling refreshed, a little groggy, starving. As before, a box has appeared, but I have no appetite for the cold breakfast.

I'd kill for a cup of coffee, though. Hot and steaming. Mmm. I can practically smell it. Perhaps I could get a coffee-maker brought to that suite…

I catch myself in the middle of that thought. Am I crazy? That would mean that I'd agree to his terms—one hour in Domino's playroom, tied up, naked, made to do who knows what…

I think about that second kiss, here in the dark, when his hands had roamed my body and his kiss had ignited something deep within. Somewhere deep inside, I had to admit that the prospect of going into that room with him was looking better and better.

What if I agreed to the hour in the playroom on my terms? Would he agree? He's given me no terms so it wouldn't be a compromise…

I think again about what he said about George Orwell, who willingly lived homeless in order to write *Down and Out in Paris and London*. Some of the greatest journalists of modern times did similarly. Would it help me to write about sex clubs if I could actually participate in a BDSM scene?

But the real question was…even if I was ready to do this for research, could I trust Devon Howard to be the one to dominate me?

After sitting in the dark, hugging my knees to my chest and rocking while thinking and overthinking and rethinking every possibility, I go to the door and pound on it.

When told to put the hood on my head, I do so. The door cracks open.

"What do you want?"

"Tell *his lordship* that I'm ready to talk to him about his terms for the suite. He'll understand what that means."

"He's a busy man," comes the response. "I'll get the message to him."

A few hours later, someone comes to my door to take me to prepare for my dinner. I frown. By my calculation, it's still fairly early—mid-afternoon. I'm taken to the same bathroom as the day before.

This time I shower uninterrupted, though I keep my eye out for any interruptions. They don't come.

I discover that the dressing room where I met Jemma the day before is just adjacent to this bathroom. Robed, with dripping hair, I make my way in there to see that Jemma is waiting for me. Still those same thick-rimmed large glasses that dominate her delicate face but this time wearing a bright blue wig with pixie bangs and still that infectious grin.

"His lord—er, *he*—sent in some food. He was worried you might be hungry."

My eyes dart to a food tray, cut vegetables and a charcuterie board, and instantly my mouth waters. Someone told him I didn't touch breakfast, obviously.

"Do you think I could get some coffee, too?"

"I've got a pot of tea ready. Would that do?"

I smile. "Sure."

I serve myself up a plate from the spread while Jemma fixes us our tea and we sit in our chairs.

"How are things?" she asks as I nibble on my food and greedily sip the tea.

"Mmm, better now. I think I was in caffeine withdrawal."

She watches me and sips her own tea. "Did you have a good time last night? At dinner?"

I nodded. "I did. The meal was exquisite, and you dressed me up so pretty, I felt like I was in a fairy tale."

"Complete with your own handsome prince," she grins.

I finish chewing my bite. "Well, *grandson* of a prince…"

Our gazes meet for a split second, and then we both look away from each other. It's awkward. Does she know why I'm here? Does she know I was kidnapped? Should I ask her for help?

I blink, thinking.

What good would calling the cops do? I signed the NDA already so I have no story, and if he gets arrested, then those connections he promised me for my career are worthless.

"Can I ask, um, how long you've worked for him?"

She nods. "Little over a year."

"And how do you like living in the US?"

"I love it. Wasn't originally my choice to stay here, but I don't think I could leave now."

My eyebrows raise. "Where did you want to go?"

"Oh, don't get me wrong. I like America, but I get homesick sometimes. But things are…complicated. So I just drink my tea and find the nearest British pub in town and go with my mates and pretend."

I frown. "You—you can't go home?" My heart hurts for her, suddenly identifying all too much with her story.

She avoids my gaze and takes another sip of tea. "It's going to get cold, miss. You should drink up. Nothing worse than cold tea."

"Call me Gwen…please? I—I sure could use a friend and I can't feel like you're my friend if you're so formal with me."

When she smiles again, a cute dimple forms to the left of her mouth. "Of course, Gwen."

"Thanks. And I'll keep calling you Jemma…even though I know it isn't your real name."

After she's finished blow drying my hair, she asks, "Did you…well, we have the waxing lady here. Was wondering if you wanted to do something."

I raise my brows. "Waxing? There was a razor in the shower. I did my legs and—oh, you weren't talking about legs, were you?"

Jemma bites her lip and shakes her head.

I blink, thinking. I have no intention of giving in to Domino tonight, but I've always wanted to try a Brazilian wax. "Let me talk to her, at least. I'm curious about what she can do."

An hour later, I'm off the folding table, and I'm bald as a billiard *down there*.

Helen, the waxing lady, has given me strict instructions to avoid anything irritating and especially "None of the sexy times for twenty-four hours."

"That's not a problem," I reply dryly.

Now that I'm fully depilated, the sensation of not wearing any underwear is compounded. I feel sensitive to everything, every time I move.

Before styling my hair and doing my makeup, Jemma leads me to the clothing rack. Tonight, everything is cute mini dresses…something I might wear to a club for a girl's night out. The longest comes down to mid-thigh.

Some are more daring than others. I choose a dress with a scooped neckline, this time in pale lavender. As a fair-skinned blonde, I have to stick to my wheelhouse, which is mostly pastels. Jemma nods approvingly and then styles my hair into a gorgeous updo. It's a complex thing involving braids and leaving tendrils to spill out around my face and neck to "soften" the look. She curls them into elegant spirals and then gives me some light makeup.

The effect is lovely. I feel like I could go for a walk on the beach, holding my sandals in my hand while strolling through the sand, kicking up the sea with my bare feet. My heart drops a little at the thought. I would love to go outside. I'd love to see and feel the sunshine, for that matter.

"Are you okay, Mi—ah, Gwen?"

I bite my lip and nod. "I'm fine. Might as well let them know I'm ready to go to the suite."

Before that happens, however, the same photographer from the night before is brought in to take a new slough of pictures of me in front of the green curtain. I ask him what these are for and he doesn't even stop snapping to answer. Just proceeds as if I haven't said a word.

Afterward, Jemma grabs her phone while I find the black hood and do my thing with it.

Honestly, this is getting tedious.

And I'm ready to give Domino a piece of my mind about it.

The next time I see anything besides the black satin of the hood, I'm inside the same suite where Domino and I shared dessert the night before. But I'm alone.

There's no artificial light here so here's the chance I need to look out a window and maybe get some landmarks in view. I don't know exactly what I'd do with that information, but it would be good to know if I'd been smuggled to Mexico or was in some huge complex out in the middle of the Mojave desert or what.

But when I scan the sitting room and then the bedroom for windows, I find that every single one of them is ten feet above my head. The ceilings in these rooms are cathedral height and the windows, though they are plentiful enough to let in the direct sunlight, are all unreachable. I can't look out of them and none of them even opens to let in fresh air.

So I'd be upgrading to a cell with better lighting, clearly, and more space. And hot water, for that matter. But I still wouldn't have windows to look out of.

My shoulders sink a little at the thought. But there's no question. I need to get out of that dark cell and stay here for the next month instead.

I've finally resigned myself to inspecting the book spines on the book case, pulling one out then putting it back before pulling out a copy of *Jane Eyre,* a well-loved classic.

But I hardly have the book flipped open to page one when the door opens behind me.

Domino enters, and hard on his heels a cart is being wielded in with chafing dishes and covered plates.

The masked server sets the table for us and lays everything out like a small buffet before giving a nod of deference to Lord Devon Howard and turning to go.

As for himself, the man in question has been watching me the entire time, and I've pretended not to notice him watching me as my eyes slide down the first page of the book where I've read the first paragraph five times.

When the door shuts, I drop my pretense and shut the book. Then I turn to him and straighten my shoulders, hand working at my sides nervously. I meet his gaze. "I'm ready to talk to you about the deal to stay in this suite."

He's unsurprised. Obviously, he's already been informed. But I can't ignore that flare of interest in his eyes. He nods but doesn't speak.

"I'll go into that playroom with you for the hour you requested. But"—I jerk my chin up to meet his gaze—"I have conditions."

CHAPTER 14
VETO

DOMINO SMILES DOWN AT ME LIKE A LONG-SUFFERING parent dealing with his rebellious teenager. My face flushes with indignation, but I hold my ground. He's trying to intimidate me without so much as a word.

Finally, he deigns to speak. "I don't believe anything about conditions was mentioned in the offer."

"It was a verbal offer unless you have yet another form around here printed out in triplicate that I need to sign? No? Then it's open for negotiation, I'd say."

He folds his arms across his chest and straightens to his full height, which is well over six feet tall. He's an impressive specimen, broad, so well-built and stunningly handsome. I'm willing myself with everything in me to ignore all that and just get my point out.

"I go in there with you for an hour, but I'm not having sex with you."

"I don't believe I said—"

I keep talking right over him, which visibly irritates him. "Not only are we not having sex, but every bit of my clothing stays on."

His mouth thins. "Those are your conditions."

"I have another one. *You* can't touch me."

He blinks.

"I'll agree to those." And now it's my turn to blink, amazed at how easy that appeared to be. Until he continues talking. "But add a condition of my own. There's no safe word."

I swallow. Isn't the safe word like the basic tenet of a BDSM relationship? Like can such a dynamic even exist without it? "But—"

"Instead." Now it's his turn to cut *me* off, apparently. "You will have the power of veto three times to stop anything I try to start that you don't want."

"And after the third veto?"

"Then everything I do afterward, you must permit."

"As long as there's no sex, clothes stay on, and your hands don't touch me. One hour time limit only. Then, yes, I can do that." What could he even do with those limits placed on him, anyway?

He holds my gaze steadily, and there's a clear look of victory in his eyes. A stone drops in my stomach and I'm suddenly not so sure about this. He says, "It's a deal. I agree to all of those terms if you do."

"And after that time in there, this will be my room for the rest of the agreed stay?"

"Yes."

"And I get a coffee machine?"

He laughs. "And a tea kettle too, if you want."

I shrug. "Okay, let's do this."

He hesitates. "You didn't want to eat first?"

I shake my head. "Nah. Might as well work up the appetite, right?" My gaze holds his, darting the challenge straight at him.

I'm taking control of the situation, and I can tell he's conflicted about it.

But instead of saying anything, he moves to the door, keys in the code, angling his body purposely so I can't see what the code is.

Our dinner, waiting in its warming dishes, will keep. And afterward, this will be my room. I'll feel much better staying here tonight, because the thought of going back to that dark room all alone makes my stomach knot.

And besides, under these very protected circumstances, I'll get my first baby steps to learning what it's like to be a submissive with no fear that it will lead to something I'll regret.

I just hope I'm not about to regret the things he wants to show me.

I follow him into the room, and it's much as it was last night. It really is a lovely room. I have the distinct feeling that I've stepped into a fantasy realm.

There's even the smell of recently burned frankincense. I inspect the place, as I did the suite next door. The windows are high above our heads here as well, probably to afford privacy. Perhaps this complex of rooms was designed for just this, to house a submissive here full time and keep her near her Dom's playroom.

But if Domino has never taken a submissive before, then why is all this here? Does he even know what he's doing?

He moves to the armoires at the far wall, keying in codes to unlock them, and my eyes slide down his form again. He's wearing black trousers that hug his well-formed butt perfectly and a dark blue, long sleeve button-down shirt. Stunningly handsome. I swallow, suddenly nervous, wondering what he has in store. He opens the door to one of the armoires and pulls several items out of the drawer.

He sets down a large hourglass on the table beside the bed and next to it, an electronic timer. "An auditory reminder is always best."

"You're starting the timer now?" I say, my voice is shaky, and I'm surprised by that.

"Indeed." A beep sounds out when he presses the button, then he shows me the time starting to tick down. He then turns over the hourglass.

"First, my instructions. While we are in here, you will not speak until asked to do so or to use a veto. To do that, you simply have to say the word *veto*. Understood?"

"Yes."

He points to the contraption I noticed yesterday along the wall closest to the door to the suite. "Take off your shoes and go stand over by the Saltire Cross."

My heart starts to thump harder, but without a word, I do as he says while he watches me. Then he very pointedly unbuttons his sleeves and rolls them almost up to his elbows. After he turns back to the armoire to dig through drawers again, my gaze wanders around the room again, taking everything in. When it lands on the clock, I note that there are now fifty-five minutes left.

With my restrictions firmly in place, I'm confident I can do this.

I've got this.

When Domino turns around, he's wearing his now familiar Devil mask. Behind it, his eyes are hard but smoldering. He brings a box of items with him and stands near me, setting it aside. That's when I see a black scrap of fabric in his hands. A blindfold.

He holds it up as if he's about to tie it around my head, and before I even realize what's happening, the word "veto" escapes my lips.

He stops the moment I say it and, without a word, tosses the scrap aside. "That's one."

I swallow. Did I just waste my veto on a blindfold? But the thought of not being able to see what he's going to do next, to say nothing of how fed up I am with being led around everywhere with a bag over my head, is too much.

He approaches me and reaches out. When he's about to grasp my wrist, he stops himself, remembering the restriction about not touching me. Instead, he tells me to raise my arms above my head, and he lowers the wrist cuffs that dangle on chains from above. Then, taking care not to touch me, he clamps the cuffs around my wrists. Stepping back, he looks at me as if he expects me to protest, but I don't.

I've got two more vetoes and I'm not going to waste them.

He walks behind me, and with a firm yank, my hands are pulled up straight above my head almost to the point where I have to stand on tiptoe.

"Nod if you're comfortable."

I nod, meeting his gaze through the mask.

"Lower your eyes," he commands. I lower them to his chest, and he seems to be content with that.

Next, he pulls out a coiled length of metal. It's carved to look like a snake, and I'm reminded of the snake necklace I wore down my back last night and his reaction to it. He moves up to me and carefully winds it around my neck. It's a choker that has the head of a snake with diamond eyes on one end. On the other end, there's a tail. The choker coils tightly, cold and hard, around my neck three times. His collar of domination, ownership.

I blink and swallow, suddenly nervous. My eyes land on the nearby box, and as I shift my weight to relieve my shoulders—after only a minute or two in this position they are starting to ache—my gaze lands on the items in the box.

And that veto for the blindfold suddenly chills me inside because I only have two more.

And there are more than two things in there that I'd like to veto.

CHAPTER 15
TEARS

Domino looks me up and down with that cold, granite gaze, and as commanded, I avoid meeting his gaze directly. Which leads to my eyes settling on his tall, muscular body.

As he watches me fidget in my restraints, I become aware of the noticeable swelling just below his belt. He's clearly enjoying seeing me like this. I swallow, distinctly aware of my own heightened state of…awareness? Arousal?

The air is cool in here, and despite being clothed, my mini-dress doesn't cover much. It's sleeveless with a scoop, but not immodest, neckline. But with my arms hitched above my head, the hemline is just barely covering my hips. And, by his orders, I'm not wearing any underwear.

I swallow hard when he pulls out a really large, brightly colored and unwieldy looking dildo. The thing barely clears the edge of the box before I'm yelling. "Veto!"

That dry, sandpaper laugh and a real honest-to-goodness smile. He tosses it aside and winks at me from behind the mask. Bastard! He did it on purpose.

And I start to realize that this is a game for him. He set it up this way so he could use those vetoes to play with me. I have only one left.

And no safe word to fall back on.

Shit.

Next he pulls out a wand that looks a little like a cat toy—or a very specialized feather duster. It has a handle on one side and several long feathers on the other.

"Feathers...for an angel." I glance up before I remember not to meet his gaze, but do manage to see how he's licking his lips, savoring the thought of what he's going to do next.

That feather thingy doesn't look bad so I let him step forward with it, and when he's standing only inches away from me, he extends it, running the feathers along the length of my extended arms. When he hits my arm pit, I start giggling uncontrollably.

He moves behind me and says, with his mouth so close to my ear it's almost touching, "I love the sound of that laugh... Makes me wonder what you'll sound like in other situations. When you're aroused, when you climax. I want to hear that."

Yeah, well, fat chance he's going to hear that from me. That's for sure. His voice is sexy, husky, and he's clearly turned on. It only serves as a stark reminder for me that I need to remain in control. I swallow my throat tight. I try to ignore the enticing feel of his warm breath on my neck.

He runs the feathers over every inch of exposed skin on my back and then...starting at the base of my ankles, he slowly strokes the inside of my legs, all the way up to my very-high hemline. My eyes flutter closed, and I'm breathing hard when he brings it up the inside of my thigh and runs those feathers along my sex. He doesn't push inside—thank goodness—I'd have to veto that.

And the reminder of one last veto has me glancing at the clock. A half hour has passed.

A lot more can happen in a half hour. He's spending a lot of time tickling me at the crest of my thighs.

"Such a lucky little feather," he says from behind me still. "But I'm a patient man, and I'll be there soon enough. in the meantime, I'm savoring those delicious little sounds you're making. Such a delectable little appetizer until I can enjoy the main course."

With a streak of irritation, I'm suddenly annoyed that he's getting off on the tickle torture. But hey, I can endure another thirty minutes of this. Once that timer goes off, I never have to come in here again and he won't get anything more.

Soon enough, though, he slowly draws the feathers away, and I'm aware that nearly every inch of the surface of my skin is tingling with sensation.

My shoulders ache, and I have to shift every so often to relieve the pressure on them. He watches me for a moment, then sets aside the feathers and pulls out something weird-looking. It kind of looks like a pizza cutter—a handle with a round head on top, but instead of a circular blade, the round part is covered in wicked-looking spikes.

"This is a Wartenberg wheel," he explains in that cultured, smooth voice. "It does not break the skin, nor does it create any lasting marks."

I study it for a moment as he holds it out for my inspection. My eyes fly to the clock, and I realize there's enough time left for him to use this for my last veto, then pull a bait and switch.

I swallow but obey his command not to speak unless asked. Satisfied that I'm not going to block him using it, Domino approaches again, and standing so close he can almost touch me, he runs it over the exposed part of my front, just above the bodice line of my dress. He traces the edge of material, pressing so lightly that it tickles, like the feather. He runs it across the top of my chest, edging my collar bones, and slowly applies more pressure.

The spikes slowly dig into my skin, first a prickle, then poking deeper for more traction and a more intense sensation. I let out a little gasp but he continues, circling around behind me to apply the wheel to the back of my neck. The pain and pleasure mix is intense, and my eyes flutter closed.

I never thought that they could mix like that, pain and pleasure.

"You like that, Angel. I can tell. Your breathing response, those little delicious moans and gasps that are driving me mad for you. Is it making you wet?"

I swallow but don't answer. He hasn't told me I can speak, and I'm not going to let him trick me into disobeying so he can punish me. I've heard that Doms love to punish.

I swallow…. I've been breathing so fast that my mouth is dry. Frissons of desire travel up and down my spine with each roll of that wheel against my skin. It feels so good. I have no intention of telling him that with my words, but I have a feeling he's already put two and two together and come to that conclusion himself. It wouldn't take a brain surgeon to figure it out.

My body is alive and writhing.

"I can't wait to fuck you, Gwendolyn. To feel your heat wrapped tight around me while I push deeper. Fuck. Every single one of your sweet little angel gasps goes straight to my cock."

I'm feeling a light sort of buzz—like I've had champagne on an empty stomach, or maybe a woozy head-rush from getting out of my seat too quickly. I'm slow to notice that he's back at the box and pulling out a very heinous-looking whip with lots of tendrils and knots at the end of each one of them.

"Ve—veto," I manage breathlessly.

He turns to me. "Indeed? You're using your last veto for this?" He holds it up, and it's wicked-looking.

I nod, and he summarily tosses it aside. Again, like he was expecting it. And I've been manipulated again. His hand dips into that box, and he pulls out a stiff leather riding crop.

Fuck.

"No!" I shake my head vigorously. "Veto. *Veto.* I—"

"You used them up, Angel. You can't veto this."

"You tricked me."

He points the crop at me. "And *you* are not allowed to speak without permission."

"P-please."

"I'll hear nothing more from you, Angel. Your vetoes are gone and I have you here for another fifteen minutes."

My eyes suddenly prickle with tears, and I start to shake. I don't want that thing used on me. It'll hurt too much.

Can I endure him whipping me with it for fifteen minutes? Maybe I'll get lucky and pass out.

He approaches, seems to study the way I'm shaking, then puts the tip of the crop under my chin to lift my gaze to his. "Trust me, Angel. I'm not here to harm you. Not permanently, anyway."

A tear spills down my cheek, and he slowly moves his thumb to scoop it up. Then he licks the small bead of moisture off his thumb. "Careful. I may soon get addicted to the taste of your tears."

And the way he says it, heated, charged with something, I believe him. Without warning, he swings the crop and hits the side of my right thigh. I yell out.

"Mmm. *Yes,*" he murmurs against my hair.

A few more hits against my legs have them stinging with pain. He circles behind me where I can't see him even though I'm straining to keep him in my field of vision.

"For your disobedience, six, I think. Count them for me, Angel. And thank me after each one."

A full body shiver runs through me, but I can't tell whether it's from aroused anticipation or fear. Both, I decide as the first one lands full square on my backside.

I scream out, and he straightens. "If you don't count it, then we start again—"

"One. Thank you, sir," I cut him off with a trembling voice.

Another hit, tears spill onto my cheeks again. "Two. Th-thank y-you." I swallow.

"What was that?" he snaps.

"Thank you, sir."

"Very good, Angel. You're doing very well."

He then proceeds to hit me four more times on my ass and the back of my upper thighs. My face is soaked with tears by the time he's done, and I'm gasping from the pain.

But something else is happening, too. That high feeling that I'd been starting to feel before comes back in full force. That pleasant, buzzed feeling, like I'd just had a couple really good orgasms.

Oh, fuck, I could use a good orgasm right now. I'm so wet.

I'm hanging from my chains now, when he circles around me, inches away. He brings the crop into my line of sight. "Kiss it, Angel."

Without taking my gaze away from his, I turn and comply. He doesn't order me to lower my gaze and my eyes are locked on his when I feel the handle of the crop slide up my inner thigh, underneath my dress to trace the seam of my sex.

Soon he's using it to push it further, tracing my inner folds and quickly finding my already-pulsing clit. I moan when it connects, and he strokes it slowly in a circle. Soon I'm climbing my way to orgasm, all too easily, too.

I've never felt a sexual high like this. *Ever.*

"Climax for me, little angel. I want to hear what you sound like when I make you come."

I throw my head back…so close. So, so close.

Suddenly, he stops. At the edge of my awareness, there's a sound cutting through my haze. A persistent beeping, like an alarm.

The hour is up.

Chapter 16
Aftercare and Afterglow

ITHOUT ANOTHER WORD, DOMINO STEPS BEHIND me and hits the button to release the chains holding my arms above my head. Then, he sets aside the riding crop and walks over to turn off the alarm.

When he comes back to me, he's no longer wearing the devil mask. He says, "All done." And then he lands an affectionate peck on my forehead before releasing the cuffs that hold my wrists above my head.

When my arms come down, my knees buckle, and he lets out a hiss, catching me before I can fall or harm myself. He pulls me against his large, solid body, and then a second later, I'm scooped into his arms, held close against his broad chest while he carries me back into my new room.

"You need water." He lays me so gently on the bed, like I'm a baby. All I can do is stare up at him dazed, a stupid smile on my lips. That high is taking over, the aftermath of the pain.

He disappears for a moment into the sitting room, then returns with a bottle of water in one hand and what looks like a medicine bottle in the other.

"Take this, Angel. You need to sip slowly, but take the entire bottle of water in the next half hour. And these..." He opens the bottle and fishes out two ibuprofen pills. "For the pain and inflammation."

Wordlessly, I do as he asks, then adjust how I'm lying so that there's no pressure on my poor, sore ass. I'm sipping at the chilled water when he again leaves and returns with a several tubes. One looks like antibiotic ointment that he applies to one welt that has come close to breaking the skin—one of the first ones on the side of my leg. It's already got an angry purple bruise around it.

"Fuck," he mutters upon examining it. He gently applies the ointment. It stings, and I let out a little sob.

His hand comes up to smooth my cheek. "I'm sorry, sweet angel. I was fucking careless with that first one. I hit you too hard."

He takes the second tube—pain relief ointment—and applies it to the rest of the welts on my legs, then asks me to turn onto my stomach to get the backs of my thighs and the ones on my ass. He lifts the hem of my dress and smooths the cream over each welt. It helps with the persistent sting.

I'm still feeling that high—like he made me come five times in a row. And I still want that elusive orgasm, damn it. I feel cheated after going through all that, and at this point, I don't give a shit that I'd mentally vowed that he'd never make me come.

I want him to make me come. I want it as much as my next breath.

He dips into the bathroom to wash his hands, then out to the sitting room to pull something else out of the small fridge. He returns with a small bag of ice wrapped in a washcloth. When he sits beside me on the bed again, he gently presses the ice to that first nasty welt that he claimed as his mistake.

But I'm completely unaware of the pain right now. I need him to finish pleasuring me. I pull his hand away from the ice bag, and he turns to look at me. "Do you want some dinner now or would you prefer to wait a little? You should have something in your stomach soon."

I lick my lips. "I want you to make me come."

He hesitates and then I pick up his same hand and press it against the apex of my thighs. "*Please...*"

He takes in a deep breath, and then, decision made, he lowers his large body onto the bed beside me and gathers me against him.

I sigh with pleasure and arch my back toward him, my eyes closed.

His mouth is on mine in seconds, kissing me fiercely and his hand slides under the hem of my dress, his long fingers exploring my sex. Hot arousal seethes and roils through me. *Yes. Oh, yes.*

I'm so wet down there that his fingers are gliding easily as they probe deeper. His tongue plunges into my mouth at the same moment one finger probes my channel and pushes into my entrance. My knees fall apart, and I jut my hips toward him. He lets out a low growl.

And where he's pressed up against my hip, I feel his cock swell and harden through the layers of his clothing.

"I want to fuck this tight, wet pussy, Angel. I'm going to enjoy every inch of you underneath me, wrapped around me. I can't fucking wait to fill you up."

My hips move in time with the pumping of his hand as another finger enters me, and I tilt my head back. Suddenly, his mouth is on my breast, his lips and teeth working my nipple through the thin cotton of my dress.

I'm so close. So close. The world swirls around me in a fugue, dreamlike state. I gasp as if I can't suck in enough air. Every single inch of my body is aching for him.

"It feels so good. So good," I grind out between moans. I can already tell, the way the tension and aching ecstasy is gathering around my core that I'm climbing higher than I've ever experienced. It's surreal, and I feel like I'm about to float away as my spine arches completely off the bed and every muscle convulses in pure rapture.

My entire body shudders, and my eyes flutter. He strokes again, and the convulsions continue. I'm hardly aware of anything but the things his hand and mouth are doing to me. For these short minutes, he's become my sole focus for existing. I shudder again, his mouth returns to mine. Waves of pure, aching bliss wash over me.

He's practically lying on top of me, which is the first thing I realize when I float back to earth like a feather lilting through the air on a soft current. That delight of pure afterglow has completely enveloped me.

In all my years, I've never experienced an orgasm like that.

I lie motionless, unwilling, unable to break the spell. His fingers trail through my hair and he's kissing my neck. "That was pure heaven, to make my angel come."

I turn to him, and we kiss again on the lips. I roll on my side to face him and return the kiss vehemently, passionately. He's incredible.

He's made me feel…

I want to make him feel like that, too.

My hand wanders from his hard chest and trails across his taut, flat stomach, relishing the feel of the silky shirt sliding across his skin. As I continue to kiss him, my palm connects with his belt buckle, and I tug on it.

He pulls away to ask the question with those cloudy gray eyes. They glow, like smoldering embers, like fire set to granite.

I meet his fiery gaze. "I want to make you come."

"Yes," he murmurs hoarsely, then reaches to undo his belt buckle and open his fly. My hand slips inside, and I palm him through his underwear. We both moan at the same time.

He's fully erect and—well, there's no other way to say this—he's huge. Almost frighteningly so. At the base of his cock, my fingers barely connect around his girth. And the *length*. Shit.

Talk about the royal scepter.

If it's possible, I'm feeling aroused again just handling him.

He helps me free him from his underclothing, and soon I'm stroking his soft skin while he kisses me, his tongue thrusting forcefully into my mouth. I'm trying not to imagine what it would feel like to turn onto my back and open my legs for him, to feel him push this thick cock slowly inside of me.

My clit throbs just thinking about it. My fingers smooth and slip over his shaft, using his precum as lubricant. He thrusts his hips forward, trying to communicate the rhythm he needs.

"Sinful little angel, making the Devil come in her hand," he whispers. "But what I really want is to feel those soft thighs wrapped around me, that perfect little body writhing under me. *Fuck*, Angel. Make me come."

"Your cock feels so good," I whisper. "I want to feel your come on my skin."

Suddenly, his cock swells even bigger and stiffens like a rock. He sucks in a breath, and his cock convulses with this orgasm, his hot seed spreading across the inside of my thigh.

I'm so aroused again, I can barely breathe. Within minutes of the most brain-frying orgasm of my life…

And I'm this man's captive for the next twenty-nine days.

What the fuck have I gotten myself into?

CHAPTER 17
SURVEILLANCE

I'M SITTING SIDEWAYS IN THE LARGE STUFFED CHAIR IN MY new sitting room, nibbling on a wedge of pineapple. My hair is still wet, a soft spa robe is wrapped around my naked body, and I'm sipping some tea Domino brewed for me while I was in the shower.

He's currently showering, and I'm staring up at the ceiling, wondering what comes next.

I have no idea. But I know that if I allow things to continue as they are, we're going to end up fucking like rabbits before the night is through. My clit pulses just imagining it.

I swallow, viscerally wanting it on a level I never even knew I had while at the same time aware of the danger that would lead to. I can't have a sexual relationship with him…for so many reasons.

Not the least of which is that I have no idea what exactly his involvement is with Obscura or if there are shady dealings around the sex club or even in general. He could be a trafficker or someone who enables trafficking.

He could be up to his elbows in any sort of shady shenanigans.

He emerges from the bathroom fully dressed with towel-dried hair that, honestly, just makes him look sexier. I drop my gaze to the bowl of mixed fruit he put into my hands before going to shower with the express order to finish it.

I've finished all but the grapes.

"Don't like grapes?" he asks, taking the bowl from me.

"Only in liquid form." Speaking of which...my eyes wander to the table and the chilled bottle of wine there.

Without a word he walks over to it and begins uncorking. "Looks like some nice pasta tonight. Garlic bread, puttanesca. Smells amazing."

Watching him complete such mundane domestic chores as pouring the wine, dishing out and serving food for me is almost surreal. The man's grandfather was an HRH. His mother is a royal princess of the blood, his father one of the most esteemed dukes of the realm. He grew up in a castle. His cousins live in Buckingham Palace, for fuck's sake.

I stand from the easy chair and go to the table where he's poured two glasses of wine. Then, he begins plating the spaghetti into two dishes. I tell him to go easy on mine. I'm coming down from my high, and the soreness in my shoulders and my rear is making it so that I don't want to spend too long sitting at the table.

"Are you feeling alright?" He presses the back of his hand to my forehead.

I pull my head away from his touch. "I'm fine. Just sore."

He checks his Rolex and presses the stem as it beeps. "You can take more ibuprofen in two hours. I've set a reminder."

My stomach sinks. I was hoping he'd be gone by then. Dine and dash.

I need some alone time to process my feelings.

But I do still have a few burning questions.

My eyes dart up to the very obvious camera that's poised above the door. It matches another one in the other room that I noticed while he was in the shower.

"So you're monitoring me?" I ask, halfway through our dinner after sparse small talk. His cool gaze meets mine with a question, and I wave to the apparatus hovering above.

"Only for your safety."

"Well, there's fire sprinklers in here and an alarm so…"

Those level gray eyes study me without comment, and I narrow mine with realization.

"Oh, you're afraid I'm going to try to harm myself."

"Your privacy will be respected, Angel. I'm the only one who will see the feed from the bedroom."

"Oh, I see."

He forks in another mouthful of spaghetti. My Italian grandfather would be apoplectic to see British high manners applied to a plate of spaghetti, but I'm finding it fascinating the way he scrunches just a tiny amount of pasta onto the back of his fork.

I wait until he's just about to swallow when I ask the next question. "Will you touch yourself while you watch me in there?"

There's a satisfying choking sound in response. I did mean to be cheeky, but I can't not acknowledge that the visual turns me on more than just a little bit. Maybe I'll give him a show one of these nights.

"Don't tempt me to punish you, Angel," he says, a light warning tone distinct in his voice.

I point to the locked playroom door. "You can't punish me unless I go in there with you again. And I'm not planning on it."

"Never say never." His eyes are enigmatic, and I'm cowed in my desire to poke the bear.

When I push my plate aside, he studies it, unimpressed. "That was a small serving and you need your strength. I want you to finish that."

I bite my lip and lace my fingers together, elbows on the table—which I know is a big no-no to aristocratic British manners. "I don't want to."

"You will anyway. Or I'll feed it to you, from my bare fingers. While you kneel on the floor in front of me, your fingers laced together behind your back."

I frown at once wondering how he plans to manage that without using force but also disturbed by how arousing I find that idea, God damn it. Everything about him is turning me on. He just gave me the most mind-blowing orgasm I've ever experienced, and it's like that one taste has exposed me to an addiction, like a junkie.

He studies my defiance, then sets aside his fork pointedly and straightens his spine. "Privileges can be taken away for disobedience."

I blink. I want to argue. I want to fight but I'm also really tired and can't wait to snuggle into my new comfy bed with a blanket wrapped around me and a book in my hands.

Without a word, I pick up the bowl and begin picking at the pasta, capturing one strand at a time on my fork and swirling it. He watches me, then nods his head, satisfied.

Later, his watch alarm rings, and he gives me some more pills with another full bottle of water. He stands beside me and watches while I drink every last drop.

"You'll find some clothing in the closet in the bedroom. We will meet tomorrow to go over some responses to your family and friends. Enjoy the books. I believe some of them are your favorites."

My mouth opens to ask how he knows what my favorites are, but before I can, he turns away from me and lets himself out. Half a minute later, the automatic lock whirs closed and another bolt is closed with a key. I walk up to it and finger the thick stainless-steel disk. On my side, it's a keyhole, too. I'm well and truly locked inside. The room is much nicer, but it's still a prison cell.

And all it had cost me was an hour's indignation at the hands of the sexiest man I've ever known.

I'm itching to record my experiences in writing. To explain what I now have realized, from my rudimentary research before this, what "subspace" is and how it feels like a drug.

And despite my aches and soreness, I want more of it. And more of him.

There are a few clothes in the closet. A couple more of the cotton dresses and some long soft linen sleep shirts. I pluck up one of the shirts, slip it on and pad to the bed. There I curl up with a book—the one I'd picked up earlier, *Jane Eyre*. But my eyes glide over the words, unseeing. I can't get this evening out of my mind.

And I'm all too aware of that camera watching me. So…with the door to the bedroom shut and the light still on, I position myself in front of that camera, lie down on the bed and get myself off—loudly.

I hope he's good and frustrated. And I'm so exhausted, I soon fall into a deep sleep on the heavenly soft bed.

The bright light hits my eyes the moment a phone rings. I didn't even realize it was there. I jump out of bed. It's a hotel-style landline that displays the date and time but I suspect has no way to call the outside.

I'll have to investigate later. But right now, it's ringing practically off its hook at…is that 6:15 a.m.? Shit.

I rub my temple. "Hello?"

"An escort will be at your room to retrieve you in thirty minutes. Be dressed and ready with the hood on." The voice at the end of the line is cold, flat. Not Domino's.

I open my mouth to reply, but the line goes dead with a click.

Well, okay then. I guess the big boss wants to see me bright and early in the morning… It's stupid, but I turn to the camera and flip him the bird, like he's watching me twenty-four-seven when I know he isn't. Then I go into the bathroom, brush my teeth and hair, wash and moisturize my face before I slip on one of the ugly dresses left for me and a pair of flip-flop sandals in my size.

There's still not a stitch of underwear to be seen anywhere. I'm mentally cussing out the bastard while at the same time, my heart is pounding with anticipation to see him again, even if it is the crack-ass of dawn.

My escort is right on time, and I'm wondering if I'll be taken to see Domino or what will be coming to me. Maybe he's changed his mind and I can go free now.

Again, my escort knocks at a door. I reach out to touch it before it opens. It's made of wood, but it's plain—no polish or decorative features. Another cell, maybe?

When a phone chimes, they open the door and guide me in.

A voice from across the room thanks my escort, and they turn and leave me. It's Domino's voice.

"You may remove the hood."

I do so and fling it aside. He's sitting at his desk looking…ridiculously fucking gorgeous for this early in the morning. I mean, it's not even seven and he's fully suited up like he's about to step into an international negotiations meeting. Well, except he hasn't put his tie on yet.

On the desk in front of the chair where I sat last time, there's a large mug, and my nose tingles with delight. Coffee. *Damn.* I haven't had it for days, and the caffeine withdrawal has been causing a dull headache. With a little yelp of glee, I settle down and snatch up the mug, inhaling deeply.

"It's prepared how you like it, I believe. Extra almond milk, one sugar."

I sip it deeply, enjoying the rush of pleasure washing over me. I'd probably be guzzling it even if it was extra black, double-burnt and tasted like tar. But this coffee is absolutely delicious.

I notice he's got a half-full teacup beside a teapot. Such a Brit.

"When you return to your room, you'll find an espresso machine and coffee maker combo installed. Also hot water in case you come to your senses and desire some tea."

I sip deeply, watching him over the mug, wondering if this generosity is offered in exchange for the hand job I gave him last night.

"Is there a reason we had to meet this early? I'm half dead."

His mouth straightens, as if getting down to business. "I have a full agenda today. And I'll be traveling for the next forty-eight hours."

I blink, feeling slightly like a deflated balloon. Why does that disappoint me? I should be elated that I don't have to deal with him for two days.

We spend the next half hour going over some of the messages I've been getting from family and friends. He sits next to me and dictates what I should reply—which I then correct to make it sound like it actually came from me.

Once we're done, he rises from the chair beside me and re-takes his own across from me.

A smile hovers at the corners of his sexy mouth. "That was, ah, an interesting show you put on for me last night, Angel. I rather enjoyed it."

Heat stains my cheeks, but I keep my chin up. So I guess he *was* watching.

"Yeah, I guess you'll be missing out on tonight's show, and tomorrow's."

His mouth quirks up on one side. "Not necessarily."

My eyes narrow at him, but he offers me nothing more. He turns to some papers on his desk, and I sense that he's about to send me away. So I grip the arms of my chair. "I'd like to ask for something...I need to write. I have nothing to write with. A laptop, a tablet. Hell, even a typewriter..."

He tilts his head and looks at me, then opens one of his desk drawers and my heart speeds up with hope.

He slaps a leather-bound composition book and a steel-cased pen on the desk between us. I blink.

"Uh..."

"It's not what you had in mind, but it's better than nothing, is it not?"

I never write in longhand. I'd prefer to type with my thumbs on a tiny phone than scribble in a book.

Damn it.

He seems to be enjoying my hesitation. "Take it or leave it, Angel."

I reach for the notebook, but his hand sweeps in and pushes it aside and out of my reach before I can take it.

"But—"

"Oh, Angel, haven't you learned yet? You earn everything you get here."

I suck in a breath. "What do you want?"

His eyes slide down my form. "You know what I want."

I blink.

He opens another drawer and pulls out another hourglass. This one much smaller than the one he used in the playroom last night. Like the type of hourglass you get with a board game to time a turn. But this one isn't cheap plastic. It's made of carved wood and cut glass and it's rather beautiful.

"I touch you and put my mouth wherever I want for the duration of that timer."

I swallow thickly. "How long is it?" And who the fuck stores random hourglasses in every room of their house in the twenty-first century?

"Ten minutes."

He could do a lot in ten minutes. With his hands and his mouth. He could wreck me.

I guess the reason he hadn't eaten breakfast with his tea this morning is because *I'm* now on the menu.

CHAPTER 18
ON THE MENU

"Ten minutes of you doing whatever you want to me in exchange for a notebook and pen?" I arch my brow at the man sitting across from me. "That seems steep."

He shakes his head. "Not whatever I want. I can't fuck you, which is what I really want. But I can touch you, kiss you... for only ten minutes. It's reasonable on my end."

"Of course you'd say that. If you throw in that I get some time to chat with a real live person who isn't you every day. Jemma, maybe or someone who's worked at Obscura? I know I can't write specifically about Obscura, but I have... questions... about the scene, how all the kink things work—consent. Those type of things."

He rubs the edge of his gorgeously chiseled chin with his thumb, smirking while I talk. "You drive a hard bargain, Angel. As long as you adhere to the agreement in the NDA, I don't see a problem with you informing yourself further on how the scene works. But I will read and approve or reject anything you mean to publish on the subject. Is that clear?"

"I know better than to violate the NDA." I still have every intention of rooting out unethical and harmful practices at

Obscura and places like it, but no way am I *telling* him that. Baby steps.

I'm learning his way of things and setting a goal to always negotiate more than he offers.

"Done." His eyes dance. "*If* you concede to having your hands secured during the ten minutes."

I take in a deep breath and release it. I guess negotiations mean he has the option to up things on his end, too. But this doesn't seem like too high a concession for what I'm getting. "Okay."

He pushes back from the desk but remains seated in his chair. When he speaks, it's in that commanding voice that expects to be obeyed without question. "Come here."

My heart starts to pound so that it threatens to beat through my chest. I push to my feet and navigate my way around the massive desk to stand beside him.

"Let me see your leg. That welt from last night…" he explains.

I lift up the skirt and show him the bruise on the side of my leg and he *tsks* as if admonishing himself. "The cream I left with you. Apply it twice a day and take some ibuprofen when you return to your room."

I drop the material of my skirt. "I did worse than that back when I ran track and field in high school."

His hard gray eyes find mine, and I know there is no arguing with him. "Those bruises were not by my hand. This one is. In my absence, I'm instructing you to take charge of the aftercare."

I take a breath and release it, then nod.

"What was that?"

I arch a brow at him. "Yes, sir."

He nods in satisfaction.

"Turn around." I do so and he tells me to put my hands behind my back. He ties my wrists together with a length of rope or cloth. I can't tell what it is. All I know is that it's turning me on. Or maybe it's just his nearness.

He flips the hourglass over, and the white sand begins to trickle down through the opening.

"Sit on my lap, Angel." I turn and awkwardly lower myself onto his muscular legs. He sucks in a breath when I connect with his lap. The minute I do, I feel his cock begin to swell against my ass. "That's a good girl." He runs a hand through my long hair. "So beautiful, this hair, like a golden halo, fit for an angel."

I lick my lips as he plunges his fingers deeper into my hair and uses that grip to pull my head down to his. He wastes no time turning it into a passionate kiss, opening his mouth and plunging his tongue into mine. I open my lips to let him explore me. One large hand cups the back of my neck to hold me in place while he kisses me, the other palms my breast, roughly rubbing the soft linen of my dress against my nipple, making it swell to an aching, needy point.

The touch jolts through me to my very core. Heat and moisture gather between my thighs and I'm sure he's aware of it. There's a growl under his breath as the kiss deepens, and his hand slips inside my dress to find my bare nipple. He twists it between his thumb and forefinger while still continuing to kiss me. I gasp from the pain and pleasure his fingers evoke.

Seconds later, his mouth still fused to mine, he's pulling the top of my dress down. Due to the relaxed cut and sleeveless style, it's easy to do. There isn't even a zipper to undo. Easy access. Perhaps that's why it was in my closet in the first place.

He pulls one of my legs over his lap so that I'm straddling him and my aching mound is pressed flush against his bulging cock. The only thing separating us are the thin layer of my dress and his trousers and underwear. His hands on my hips, he grinds me against him for a moment before expelling a ragged breath and muttering some British obscenity under his breath.

Then his mouth finds my nipple and he starts to suck. Lightning shoots its heated sparks through my entire body. My mouth falls open, head dips back, and I'm lost in the feel of his tongue, the edge of his teeth gently grazing me. I let out a small whimper, and it seems to set him into overdrive.

His erection surges against me, and he's suddenly standing, propping me onto his desk. I'm half expecting him to unzip his fly and push up my skirt and start something he said he wouldn't start. I'm assessing how I will react when suddenly, he sinks back into his seat and tells me to lie back.

I can only go back to my elbows as my hands are tied together. He pushes my knees apart and flips up my skirt.

Then, that sexy mouth of his sinks to my sex, and I'm lost.

The feel of his heated mouth, the tongue that darts out to trace the seam of my sex. With the new Brazilian I had the day before, everything is extra sensitive.

But I hadn't expected him to get this far in such a short amount of time. I turn my head to get a glimpse of the hourglass. Just over half of the sand remains. And then he's sucking my clit and my eyes roll back into my head. Languid heat spreads up my belly, across the insides of my thighs. His hands are on my knees, holding them apart. I suck in a breath, so hyper-focused on what his mouth is doing that I'm forgetting everything about my surroundings. I hope he can get me to climax quickly. Pleasure and tension knot and seethe at my core.

At this rate, it looks promising. His hands slide up my thighs, and when I think he's going to slide his fingers inside me, he doesn't. It wasn't agreed upon, but I have to admit I'd really like it if he did.

I swallow. Would he do it if I asked him too?

Oh god, he increases the force of sucking and I'm moaning. In a haze of pleasure and mounting tension, my eyes focus on the trickle of sand through the hourglass. I'm seconds away from coming to climax when the sand runs out.

I don't tell him.

However moments after making that decision, he pulls his mouth away. As if he has some unnatural internal clock that has told him.

Or as if he'd planned this on purpose. Which is the most likely bet.

He straightens and gives me a heated look as I fight to come up to a sitting position.

My heart is beating, and I'm breathless and so close. Worse, my hands are tied behind my back and I can't even finish myself. He pulls my skirt back over my thighs and pushes back from the desk.

"So that's it? You're not going to—"

"The agreement was for ten minutes." He turns and meets my gaze with those granite eyes. "And I always keep to my agreements. *Always.*"

What an asshole. I sit there, shoulders slumped, staring at him as he stands up and shrugs himself back into his suit coat. Is he for real?

A buzzer sounds, and he presses a button on the phone. "Yes, I'm aware. I'll be ready for you in about five minutes. Also, please send someone to escort my guest back to her room."

My mouth is still wide open as I stare at him in disbelief. He makes a gesture with his hand, as if telling me to stand up off the desk. When I have difficulty with this, since my hands are still tied behind me, he moves to help me.

He then unties my hands from behind my back. He replaces the silk rope he used along with the hourglass into a drawer. Does he have a little BDSM compartment in there for catching women on coffee break kinks? Or if he's telling the truth and he's never taken a sub, then… what? Someone stocked that drawer for him?

He reaches over and hands me the notebook and pen. "Enjoy."

"I *was*. Until you stopped," I quip.

His eyes narrow and his mouth thins, but there's a knowing twinkle in there. As if he's amused at my annoyance. It's probably a part of his plan. Keep me hungry for it.

"I will see you in two days." When I hesitate, he nods toward the couch. "Hood on, Angel. They'll be here to collect you shortly."

I might not see him for two days but he'll be seeing much more of me. Even now, he's pitching a rather large tent in those trousers. He must be as frustrated as I am with no release but his hand.

I hope he rubs a fucking blister into it trying to satisfy himself.

With only that as a goodbye, I'm shown back to my room. Where I have books to amuse me and this blank journal. I hate writing by hand, but as it's my only choice, I start scratching away at it. The pen he gave me is expensive and of high quality but I hate it. Ball point and slender. When forced to write, I like fat pens with smooth, gliding ink.

After sighing in frustration for the fifteenth time, I toss the pen aside and go for a hot shower. Damn. The man could at least have a spa or something.

After a delicious and expertly prepared cold lunch is brought to me, another knock on the door comes. It's Jemma and she has a box.

"I was told to bring this to you. You can open it up after I leave."

We have a nice visit, and I offer her a cold soda from my fridge while we chat about more mundane things. She shies away from personal questions, and I'm learning not to go there unless she volunteers the info to me.

After she's gone for the day, I crack open the box she brought. It's a gorgeous, brand-new laptop. I gasp in excitement, bouncing up on the balls of my feet.

A laptop after all! *Yes!*

With a flick of my wrist I pick up the composition book and attempt to toss it into the trash before cracking open the beautiful machine.

Ohhh, the things I will write. The words are already flying around in my head.

I power it up immediately and wait while it goes through its boot process, happy to see it's ready for me to just dive in and go until...

Until a lock screen with a beautiful scenic picture pops up.

A lock screen with a blinking cursor and the request for the five-digit code I should enter.

What the... code?

I pick up the box and rifle through the packaging, looking for a note.

Fuck. Maybe it just automatically asks for a code but really doesn't need one?

I hit the enter key and a lock-screen pop up flashes onto the screen.

The code to unlock this screen is the same one that unlocks the door to the playroom. When you enter the playroom with me for two hours, no restrictions, no safe word and three vetoes, as before, you will then have the code to also unlock this machine.

I sit back, stunned. The playroom for two hours? No restrictions?

I swallow, staring at it, mind racing.

One way or the other, I'm fucked.

CHAPTER 19
ANTICIPATION

THE NEXT TWO DAYS STRETCH ON. I FILL UP HALF THE notebook with my disjointed scrawling, observations and even incoherent rants. I read three books—two of which are repeat reads. I pace the place. A lot.

It's a lovely, comfortable space, and I'm thrilled to have it versus the dungeon room, but I'm dying to breathe some fresh air and feel the wind on my skin, see the sunlight or starlight. Bonus points if it's somewhere pretty.

Once the card is collected with the dirty dishes, I'm on high alert, my entire body alive with the prospect of seeing him again.

And fantasizing about just what's going to happen in that room tonight.

But asking for any of that is going to come with a price and open yet another negotiation. And Domino has already laid a big juicy carrot in front of me to get me back into that playroom.

And while I'm not opposed to going… the last time ended up being not only educational but also enjoyable.

I just know that going in there is probably going to lead to sex between us.

And if that's the case, I want a whole lot more than just to be able to write on the computer.

Not that I don't want the sex for the sex itself. I'm over-the-top attracted to him. But if he's going to make it cost my complete submission with no safe word, then he's going to have to give in to my demands, too.

Perhaps he even expects it.

On the second day, I'm thrilled to see that Jemma comes in when my dinner is served. It's five-star quality, as good as the meals I've eaten in the presence of Domino.

Tonight it's mixed salad and a full assortment of charcuterie meats, foie gras, caviar, cheeses, fruits and artisan breads. And panna cotta for dessert. Cool, light and delicious.

"Oh my god, this food is so good," Jemma murmurs for the fifth time as we try out three different tapenade spreads on our thinly sliced toast and discuss the merits of each one, which one we prefer.

"I can't lie, the eats are good when I'm at work, generally."

I finish chewing my own bite, aware that I could try to manipulate the conversation to at least find out where we are. The general vicinity, anyway. She mentioned going to the pub with her "mates." Are there British-style pubs scattered throughout Southern California or are we still in Los Angeles? I have no idea.

"So, ah, have you worked in LA for long?"

She shoots me a look that tells me she's immediately onto me. She smiles and simply says, "I love California, but there's not much variety in the weather here, is there?"

Hmm. Guess I'm going to have to try harder to trick something useful out of her. I decided to take a different tack. "How did you come to work for his lordship?"

She glances out the window, then pops another cracker in her mouth and chews, as if thinking through her answer. "I was in a desperate way, and I needed help. He reached out and offered it to me when no one else would. He's a very kind man." She says this last a bit more forcefully, as if purposely trying to emphasize the point. To drive it home to me.

I blink. "He seems too good to be true."

Jemma shrugs and loads another cracker with some spreadable cheese. "He's a good man, Gwen. He helps people. Aside from all the other work he does with his diplomatic job and the charity foundation. He helps individuals."

I frown. "How does he do that?"

"Well, take Murray, for instance, the photographer."

"Lord Devon helped him too?"

She nods. "Oh, yes, big time. His story is really sad, too."

I follow her lead and load up a cracker with the same cheese and pop it into my mouth, chewing thoughtfully. It's flavorful and oh-so-creamy.

"He was here on a visit, yeah? With his mate. They were to spend the summer in LA. They crashed at a friend's flat. One night, out in Hollywood too late at night, they were attacked—robbed. His friend was shot. Dead on arrival. Murray was hurt badly and in the hospital for weeks."

I frown. "Jesus, that's terrible."

Her mouth things. "It gets worse. Not only was he left with an astronomical hospital bill—a Brit's biggest nightmare is getting caught in the American healthcare system. We don't have big bills over there. We have the NHS. But poor Murray was released with a sixty-thousand-dollar hospital bill, and he was asked to stay in the country as they worked on the case to catch his friend's killer. Which they eventually did. Then he had to stay out for all the legal stuff, too. Meanwhile, he couldn't support himself here, because, you know, he didn't have the right to work in the US as a foreigner. He was destitute. Applied to the embassy for help. The case was bumped over to his lordship, who stepped in to help."

I blinked. "That's horrible. Did Lord Devon pay the bill?"

She shook her head. "We don't know what happened, exactly. The hospital never pursued it, and his lordship offered Murray a job to work for him to help him earn his living while he was stuck here."

"I hope he gets to go home soon."

Jemma waves her hand. "Oh, he's long since paid off his debts, helped put the killer behind bars and chose to stay here working for his lordship and the foundation."

I ponder that, chewing thoughtfully on a piece of toast with foie gras and a tiny drizzle of currant jelly.

Too good to be true. I'd suspect him of putting her up to this, but she's so genuine and sincere. I make a note to see if I can get some corroborating testimony from either Murray or Lord Do-Good himself...

A person can't just hand me a story like this and expect me to turn my journalist's brain off.

But I can't deny that something rings true about it. The way Jemma speaks about him and even the few times I interacted with Murray and he mentioned "the boss."

Something in my gut told me this was the truth, but as always, that wouldn't be enough. I'd believe it for now, but only with a healthy dose of cautious skepticism.

I'm also not above noticing that Jemma had refrained from giving any details of her own story. That makes me wonder… Maybe she'll trust me enough to share it eventually.

After dinner, Jemma gives me her warm goodbyes with a wide smile and a quick hug and wishes me a good night.

For the second night in a row, I go into the bedroom, take a long, hot shower, prep for bed and then lie in front of the surveillance camera. Tonight, instead of reaching under my robe, I open my robe wide, spread my legs and quickly stroke myself to orgasm.

I have no idea if he can hear me, but I moan loudly anyway. Why not taunt him a little bit—or even a lot?

It's my way of punishment, maybe a little payback for leaving me wanting that last morning on his desk. I'd been milliseconds from climaxing under his mouth. Since he left me in that condition, I've been nonstop obsessed with the idea of sex. Like a woman in a desert fantasizing about water, I think about his hands and his mouth all over me.

Likely, he planned it that way, so that I'd spend this time getting worked up, hungry for more.

The next morning, when breakfast is quietly brought into the sitting room, I'm still groggy, half sleeping. As always, the servers wear masks and don't speak to me and leave quickly after laying out the food. With a long, drawn out sigh, I sit down to serve myself from a selection of breakfast options. Today, it's eggs Benedict, yogurt fruit and a small basket of pastries.

And there's an envelope. The label simply reads "Angel."

My stomach twists as I scoop it up, tear it open and there is a card inside. It's plain, not monogrammed, but on expensive, high-quality cardstock. His writing is elegant, neat, masculine.

Angel,

I shall be visiting you in the late afternoon, and we'll have dinner afterward. Have you agreed to my proposal regarding the laptop? You may send your reply on the reverse, tuck it into the envelope and it will be brought to me.

See you soon,

~D

I stare at large, stylized D as his signature. Whether it stands for Domino or Lord Devon—or maybe both? I have no idea. I wonder at that…and the fact that he wears the mask in the playroom. Is Domino a separate persona he effects? All these questions further stir my curiosity, and the world knows that there is no force that can long withstand the curiosity of a serious journalist.

I pull out my crappy ballpoint pen and answer him on the back. In it, I state flat out my negotiations for more in exchange for the two hours in the playroom. I also state that I won't limit how far it can go.

I ask for time out of doors, to stretch my legs, fresh air, change of scenery. I also want to interview him, off the record, about the kink scene, both privately and within the sex clubs and his insights as a supposedly new Dom.

I admit only to myself that I'm more than just professionally curious about that.

Lastly, I add that I won't allow the vetoes to be used as they were last time, to manipulate me by pulling out things he knew I'd object to. That if I were only allowed three vetoes and no safe word, then he can't use that against me as he did before.

With that, I send the card off with my dirty breakfast dishes. When my lunch arrives, a shopping bag is delivered along with it. I dive in and find a card with that same elegant hand.

Shower and use the included products.

Hydrate with the water and fruit juice in your refrigerator. At least three full bottles.

Pretty yourself, then put on the collar and the slip and be waiting for me at 3 p.m.

On your knees, hands behind your back, eyes on the floor.

~D

I blink at the specific demands but realize that since he hasn't responded to the negotiated terms, he must agree to them. I'll definitely make note to clarify that before stepping foot anywhere near that playroom door.

Because as much as I want it…I'm not going in there without my own form of empowerment.

I blink again at the realization as I use the brand-new razor and enclosed shaving cream to shave every bit of hair from my body. I condition the area affected by the Brazilian wax which is smooth as can be and leaves me feeling sexy. Then, I fully moisturize with the lightly scented bath lotion—*Angel* by Mugler. It smells sweet, like cotton candy and lemon drops.

Who knew that being a submissive could ultimately be empowering?

By the time that I'm scrubbed, shaved, polished and primped, I apply some light makeup and style my hair simply with some loose blond curls around my face. Anticipation and arousal coils in my belly. I'm taking hours to prepare myself for him. But what else do I have to do in here, really?

This isn't even a real date, and yet I've never even taken half this long to prep before.

Finally, there are only two things left in the bag—for me to wear. A translucent white lace and silk slip that hits high on my thigh and leaves nothing to the imagination. And the collar.

The collar...the golden coiled snake with the diamond eyes and the scales, each marked by a tiny shimmering green gem—emeralds, perhaps? It goes on my neck by coiling around it tightly, three times.

Just putting it on me, feeling the cold metal against my skin, the stiffness and the snug way it hugs my neck is an instant reminder of what I'm really doing.

I'm giving myself to him for the next two hours.

To him.

To possess. To own.

At 3 p.m., just as I was instructed, I kneel in front of the door, hands behind my back, eyes downward, waiting.

My heartbeat thuds in my throat and my throat is dry when I try to swallow. I'm shaking where I'm kneeling, but whether it's from fear or excitement, I couldn't say.

CHAPTER 20
IT'S JUST BEGUN

NEARLY A HALF HOUR LATER, I'M STILL KNEELING, STILL waiting for the door to open to my suite. I've been here, unmoving, and now my knees are biting into the carpet and my neck and shoulders are sore from looking at the floor and keeping my fingers laced together behind me. On top of this, the fucking collar is starting to dig into the skin on my neck.

And he's late.

I'm about to give up, and just when I start to push to my feet, I hear the beeping as someone keys in a combo on the magnetic lock. Thus, as the door swings open, Domino catches me in a weird sort of half-kneel where one of my feet is planted on the ground as if I'm about to push to my feet. My hands are at my sides, and I'm looking straight at him.

Once he turns back from closing the door, he halts where he stands, looking me over. By this time, I'm so irritated that I don't drop my gaze nor do I put my hands behind my back. My heart, however, is racing, wondering what his reaction will be.

A muscle twitches along his jaw and he doesn't look pleased, but at this point, I don't care. I haven't gone into that room with him yet. He hasn't conceded to my demands, as far as I know.

A brow twitches up and he sets aside the package he was carrying on the nearby table. "Did you not understand the directions?" he says in a quiet voice but with a firm tone I'd imagine him using to dress down a servant in one of his family's massive palaces.

"Can you not read a clock?" I shoot right back at him, and I can see he's fighting a smile at my reply.

Without waiting for him to say so, I push to my feet, bend and rub my sore knees.

He blinks, watching me. "I was delayed. I apologize."

"My knees may take some time to forgive you."

One corner of his mouth quirks up. "I'll make sure to make it up to them. And soon." His voice is full of innuendo and promises.

His eyes scan my form again, taking in my sheer slip, the collar coiled around my throat. I might as well be naked. He's wearing a blue dress shirt with an open neck, shirtsleeves rolled up to his elbows, black jeans and polished leather loafers. Casual elegance.

He's striking—remarkably handsome—with more than just beautiful, chiseled features but a manner and a presence that commands respect. Aristocratic bearing, I've heard it called before. He has it in spades.

"Come here, Angel," he says softly. His voice is even, neutral, but there's an ember smoldering in those gray eyes and my whole body tightens with anticipation and excitement, wondering where this day will take us.

I step toward him and he bends his head to land a kiss on my forehead. "I've missed you."

"You were too busy for that, I'm sure."

He takes my chin between his thumb and forefinger and lifts it, forcing me to meet his gaze. "I was indeed busy. But I assure you that I did think about you. Quite a lot. Your generous exhibitions each night on the security camera helped, though."

I blink. Those were supposed to be punishments. I wanted to frustrate him. Make him flustered about what he couldn't have but obviously wanted.

Clearly he's planning on getting what he wants today, though. I can see it in his eyes, and the obvious bulge in his jeans.

Fuck, he's beautiful. I want to feel him moving inside me. Arousal swirls down my spine, and I'm already wet. He's barely even touched me.

I swallow. "Did you receive my requests?"

"I agreed to them all."

"And the vetoes?"

He quirks a brow. "You feel I was manipulating you—"

"Because you *were*..."

"I will keep that in mind. In return, you promise me your complete obedience when we walk through that door. For two hours. None of this attitude you're showing me now."

"But if I'm too obedient, you won't have an excuse to punish me," I shoot back almost flirtatiously.

His eyes are hard as the stone from which they take their color. "Angel, in there, I don't need an excuse for anything I do. To you or otherwise."

I swallow, sudden fear tingeing my arousal. Did he go lightweight on me last time to give me a sense of false confidence? What did this mean?

"You—you're going to hurt me?" I say in a shivery whisper.

"Of course," he replies as if that was the dumbest question in the world. "But not permanently."

I hesitate.

"Do you want the combination for the lock or do you want me to leave?"

I blink, mind racing. "We can go out into the fresh air somewhere, maybe tonight?"

"As I said, I don't go back on my promises. Trust me, Angel."

I meet his gaze again, bringing my chin up. "Okay, then. Two hours it is."

His only reply is to give me a string of six numbers. I only have to hear them once and they are committed to memory—that math prodigy brain kicking in. Without another word from him, I walk over to the playroom door, key in the pass code and pull open the door once the lock whirs open.

Then, without waiting for him to say another thing, I walk through the door. The room is much as it was the last time I was here, except there is a sideboard with polished wooden boxes, covered silver bowls and plates laid out near the bed and an old school stand mirror nearby, angled toward the bed.

I take a deep breath and turn around to face the man who has just entered, shutting the door after him with a very final-sounding *click*. The smolder in his eyes has combusted info full fire now, those cold eyes, like ice aflame.

Slowly he walks toward me, and I stand my ground, remembering belatedly to drop my gaze. It lands on his broad chest instead. Since when did royal aristocrats keep themselves in such great shape? I remember reading that he's an avid horseman, plays polo regularly with his cousins and also loves pickleball, running and other sports that fill his leisure time.

And apparently lording over and observing all the goings-on at the local upscale sex club, as well. But only I know about that.

And though I'm gagged by the NDA I signed, that knowledge gives me a feeling of power.

Domino is standing inches from me, and he runs his fingers through my hair. My eyes flutter closed, relishing his touch, and then he lowers his hand to my neck and touches the collar.

"My mark on you. This means you are mine, Gwendolyn. Do you understand?"

My gaze flutters up to him and then away.

His fingers return to my hair but with a sudden jerk he's using my hair to yank my head back. "You will answer when spoken to. And only then."

"Y-yes. Yes, I understand…sir."

A look of palpable satisfaction in his eyes. "Good girl. Eyes down."

My gaze drops to his chest, which is rising and falling a little quicker now. I swallow, feeling that same aching tension thicken the air around us.

"What does this mean?" He touches my collar and expects me to answer like I'm a kindergartner.

"That I'm yours."

"And when you wear it, I own you and you will obey me. You have three vetoes that you use judiciously. And no safe word."

My heart hammers, sensing danger. I only nod.

He turns, goes to the armoire, removes the alarm clock.

"I'm setting the alarm for exactly two hours from now. All activity stops then. I don't have a two-hour glass so we'll have to stick with this modern convenience instead."

With a loud beep, he starts the time on the clock. Then he turns and moves to the bed. My heartbeat ratchets up a few notches. Does he plan to move this quickly to avoid getting caught unfinished?

Two hours is a really long time. What's the rush?

The bed is gorgeous, low to the ground, all dressed in bright silks that stream down from the ceiling around it, mimicking a sheikh's desert tent. Domino plucks a large silk cushion from among the pile atop the bed and drops it on the floor right in front of him.

"Gwendolyn. Come here."

Gingerly, I step across the plush Persian carpet to stand in front of him.

"Unbutton my shirt."

I close in on him slowly, then reach out to pluck open a random button near the middle of his broad chest. His hand closes over mine. "Start at the top, Angel."

I do as he says, slowly unbuttoning each button until I get to the part that's tucked into his jeans. He tells me to pull it out and finish. When I'm done, the shirt hangs open and his undershirt is molded against his muscular torso.

"Take it off, hang it over there." He points out a clothes rack on the other side of the room. I repeat the action when he instructs me to, remove the undershirt as well.

I get my first glimpse of the man beneath the clothing and it is…beyond impressive. His chest and torso are perfectly chiseled, six-pack abs and the crease below the hips. He looks like a Michelangelo sculpture coated in a liberal dusting of dark hair. My throat tightens with arousal. He's mouth-watering, completely shirtless.

And I want to lick him.

He watches me with burning eyes. "Touch me, Angel."

I reach out and touch his hard pecs, run a hand down his sternum. His skin trembles a little as my fingers slide lower, and I hear him suck in a quick breath. This fuels more of my excitement, that my touch is doing this to him. His arms hang at his sides, and I raise my other hand to trail after the first.

He blows out a slow breath. "I have craved your touch since the first minute I saw you, that night in Obscura. Wanted those delicate hands sliding across my body, exploring me, scratching down my back while I ride you hard and make you scream."

I suck in a breath, my core aflame at his words. They echo my own thoughts. That first night in Obscura, I'd wanted him, too. Strangely, dangerously attracted to a man whose face I couldn't see.

Without even realizing what I'm doing, my mouth moves forward and sinks to place a kiss on his chest. He stiffens, and my lips slide across those smooth, hard muscles, tasting him.

Seconds later, I'm yanked back by my hair. In shock, I gaze up at his stern face.

"Did I say you could kiss me?"

I lick my lips. "No, sir."

"Why did you do it?"

I blink. "B-because I wanted to, sir."

His jaw sets. "You don't do what you want to in here, Gwendolyn. You do what *I* want. You *obey*."

"Yes, sir. I'm sorry, sir."

He arches a fine, dark brow, eyes narrowing. "Don't tell me how sorry you are, Angel. Show me." My brow furrows in question, and he points to the cushion on the ground. "Kneel."

I sink to my knees on top of the pillow, and he lets out a breath. I'm at the level with the fly of his jeans which strains around what looks like a very swollen erection. I held his cock in my hands while I stroked him to orgasm just days ago. I'm drooling at the chance to take his length into my mouth, stroke him with my tongue, make him lose his mind while I swallow his come.

Bring. It. On.

And he does just that. First, he unbuckles his belt and whips it out of its loops in one smooth motion. Then he tosses the belt on the bed and unzips.

I lean forward in anticipation as he frees his cock from his underwear...and there it is again. Marvelously long, girthy and pointing straight up. *Ready.*

"Pleasure me, Angel, with that beautiful mouth of yours," he commands in a soft voice.

First, I lick the engorged head, and he sucks in a ragged breath. Then I open wide and angle my head to take him in, tentatively at first. I've never been around a man who was this big, and even though it's incredibly arousing, it's also a little scary. I wonder if I can take his length fully—into my throat and...elsewhere.

I'm about to find out as he juts his hips forward, and he slides into my throat, opening it up to receive him. My tongue ripples along the bottom side of his cock, and he lets go a deep growl. "Fuck."

He pulls back, then slowly repeats his thrusting action, placing one hand on top of my head to hold me steady. I reach out to encircle the base of his shaft with my fingers, to provide some control and some leverage for myself.

After a few thrusts, he orders in a tight voice. "Hands behind your back. Yes, lace the fingers together. I don't want to see your hands again."

He's still, and my tongue is now doing most of the work as I suck him and slip my tongue over and over, swirling against the tip. He throws his head back and grows even harder and bigger in my mouth.

Then he takes my head in both his hands, and with a violent jut of his hips, he sinks into my throat, my lips resting against the hilt. "Swallow my come, Angel. Drink every drop."

Two more thrusts and he's there, his cock convulsing in my mouth as hot come pours down my throat, salty and earthy. I suck him dry while his orgasm continues, and he moans, holding my head still. "Fuck," he says again, then slips himself, still hard, out of my mouth.

After a moment, he lets out a long breath as he studies me. "That mouth is sinful. Sinful enough for a devil. And how I enjoyed fucking it." He reaches out and lines my lips with his strong thumb. "Mmm. So much more to do, but as a warm up, that was fucking brilliant."

I study that glistening cock. It's still hard, and I blink. I've heard some men don't have a refractory period. Is he one of them?

I'd thought starting off with a BJ meant it would be unlikely we'd actually do the deed, but I'm wondering if, for him, that was *just a warm up.* I gulp.

Without a word, he moves to the table, takes out a warm, wet cloth from what looks like a chafing dish. It's dripping, so he wrings it out, then cleans himself off. He turns and offers me a bottle of water, and when I nod, he hands me one from the bowl of iced beverages also on the table.

Then he reaches out his hand, and wordlessly, I place my hand inside it. His fingers curl around mine and he pulls me up to a standing position, smooths my cheek with a fond smile and says, "Well, Angel, that was very good. I told you to please me and you did. But that's just the very beginning of the pleasure you'll bring me, tonight. And I'll, of course, return the favor, if you're deserving of it."

My eyes dart up to his with indignation, but when his jaw tenses, I drop my gaze again. He reaches out, and through the thin, silky fabric of my slip, he takes my nipple and twists it.

"There will be pleasure, to be certain. And also pain. Our time in this room has just begun."

And without looking at the timer, I know that we still have nearly the full two hours, yet. What could he possibly have in store for the rest of our time?

CHAPTER 21
PAIN

*T*HERE WILL BE PLEASURE…AND ALSO PAIN.

Those words echo through my mind as he moves behind me, and back to the table, I turn to watch him, but without turning to me, he says in a clipped voice, "Lie on the bed and put my belt across your stomach."

My eyes dart to the low bed where the belt is lying where he flung it a short time before. Does he mean to use it on me? How?

As if sensing my hesitation but still without turning to me, he says, "I don't believe my instructions were complicated. Further hesitation to this or any of my other orders will be punished. Be warned, Angel. Unless that's what your angling for? My punishment."

Without a word, I step forward to the bed, lowering myself to it. It's as soft and as lush as it looks. I lie back against the mound of cushions. My eyes wander to the standing mirror nearby. It's angled so that I'll see everything happening. And he will, too.

When he turns back to me, he's got the blindfold in his hands again. I stare at the scrap of silk fabric as it dangles there. I do still have all three of my vetoes. I'm tempted to use it, even though I haven't been escorted around here with a sack over my head lately. Only holed up inside my suite, instead.

I take a deep breath, and he moves forward with it. He waves it again. "No veto this time?"

I shake my head.

He kneels beside me and ties the blindfold around my head, tightly enough that it won't slip.

He grabs one of my wrists and ties it back against the headboard of the bed with what feels like one of the satin sashes that hangs down from the ceiling, then repeats the action with the other wrist. My hands are now suspended in the air behind my head. Then he asks me if I want to veto this.

I shake my head, nervous about what lies ahead. He said he wouldn't manipulate me, but I'm saving them for whatever he has in store.

He can do a lot in two hours and appears to have the stamina to do so.

He returns me to my back and then plucks up the belt and pulls my legs together, cinching the belt tightly around my knees. I frown, confused.

But it doesn't take me long to realize how completely helpless I am. It would be impossible to wiggle out of this. He strokes his fingers across my belly.

Then there's a tug on the slip I'm wearing, a hard jerk. I suck in a breath, and he orders me to hold still.

With his bare hands, he rips the slip I'm wearing down my front all the way to my waist, exposing my breasts to him.

"Mmm. Such beautiful tits. They look delicious." I feel his hot breath against my skin moments before he sucks my nipple into his mouth, tugging fiercely with his suction. "Mmm. Every inch of you is delicious, Gwendolyn. I've been dreaming of tasting you everywhere for days. I couldn't stop thinking about making you moan for me again, making you *writhe.*" His mouth moves over to the other nipple, and he sucks that one too, just as fiercely, tearing his head back and tugging it with him.

"Oh!" I let out a gasp.

He presses his mouth to my ear, and his voice is husky, low, full of arousal. "Yes, just like that. But most of all, I've been dreaming of your tears, Angel. Of how hard they make me when they stream down your cheeks, the way your lip trembles. Their salty taste. I crave your tears."

Pain pierces my nipple as he pinches it hard, and I cry out. I suck in a breath and gasp.

"We'll see if this does the trick." Something cold is pressed to the nipple he's twisting and suddenly the pain increases tenfold.

I arch my back. "Fuck!"

"You do not speak. And you do not move. Hold still, Gwendolyn."

"It hurts! What are you doing?"

"It's a nipple clamp."

Oh, fuck no. What's next, piercing? Before I can open my mouth to veto, he's attaching another one to my other nipple, and I feel some tension between them, a fine, thin chain of cool metal. The clamps are connected to each other.

My mind spins for a moment, and I know he's waiting to see if I'll veto. The pain is bad, but there's also a sharp, intense pressure building in my core—faster than ever before. I take a deep breath.

I can stand this, I think.

Nevertheless, a tear slips down from under my blindfold, and he makes a satisfied sound. "The setting is at its lowest." He bends down, pressing his face close to mine. His hot tongue darts out to scoop up my tear, and in frustration, I turn my face away from him.

He seizes my chin and pulls me back. "Don't pull away from me, Angel. Ever. You open yourself to me, and you take what I give you. Or you veto. Those are your choices."

My mind swirls in a haze of dull pain, and in frustration, more tears form. And I'm now pissed that making me cry is turning him on.

He leans away, and I feel his hand moving near my hip. There's a low growl in his throat, and suddenly I realize that he's stroking himself while watching me cry. When he reaches out to adjust the clamp, I yelp.

"No! No. Veto. Take them off."

A warm gush of air as he expels a long and obviously disappointed sigh. "Fair warning. They hurt more coming off than going on."

I tremble and bite my lip, considering, then repeat my plea. "Take them off."

"Mmm." He does as he's told, and as promised, the pain intensifies as the blood returns to my nipples. I shudder and cry some more, and he tosses the clamps aside somewhere and gently strokes my wet cheeks. "There, there, Angel. They're gone."

My nipples feel raw and sore, and the thought of him touching them again in the near future makes me cry harder. Sure enough, he straddles me and gently strokes them both at the same time with his thumbs. They sting, and I gasp.

I can feel the firmness of his erect cock pressed along my breastbone, and he places a hand on the outside of each of my breasts, pushing them together to cradle his cock. Then he slowly slides his cock back and forth along my chest, titty-fucking me.

My entire being is wrapped around him thrusting his cock against me. Everything is wrapped up in the motions of our bodies, sexual arousal drenches my consciousness. My pussy is wet and heavy with the need for release, the need to feel him inside me, stroking me to orgasm.

"I just came down your throat, and I want to come again, like this. But I'm getting greedy. I wanted your tight pussy around me next. Do you want that, Angel? Do you want me to pull your legs open so I can take you?"

I lick my lips and then release a strangled, "Yes."

"How much do you want it?"

"Please," I gasp as he continues to rub himself between my breasts, his rhythm steady.

"Answer me."

"I want your cock. I want it inside me. Please, Domino…" Then I take a deep breath and expel before uttering what I've been dying to the entire time, his real name. "Devon."

There's a strangled noise in his throat, and he lifts a leg away from me. Then he quickly removes the belt from around my knees, pushing them apart. What he does next surprises me, he reaches up and yanks off the blindfold.

His large body hovers over me, and I'm stunned by it. Sometime after he'd put on the blindfold, he had shucked the rest of his clothes. Just inside his right hip, where his underwear likely covered it, there's a tattoo of a coiled snake. I swallow, considering the resemblance between the image in the tattoo and the metal snake coiled around my throat. The connection, the claim of it. He stated as much. His mark of ownership.

For the remainder of our time in the playroom, he does own me. And I have only two vetoes left.

From a nearby silver bowl he must have brought to the bed earlier, he removes an ice cube. I suck in a breath as cold droplets fall from it and land on my hot skin. I don't even want to know where—

He lays the ice against first one sore nipple, then, dripping liberally, the other. After an initial renewal of pain, they go numb—until he moves his mouth to suck them again.

I shudder against him. It hurts, but I'm so close to coming. The tension in me is twisted so tightly that the orgasm promises to be the most intense I've ever experienced. Tiny contractions shiver through me, promising a build to something mind-blowing. I can barely catch my breath until—until...

Domino plucks up a fresh ice cube from the bowl and trails it against my skin downward from my sternum to my belly button, circling it. I shiver and writhe under him.

Then he pushes it lower, across my bare, waxed pussy and between my folds.

I jerk up against the constraints holding my hands immobile. "Fuck!"

"Silence," he barks, then presses the ice cube firmly against my clit. I struggle against it, gasping in pain. He scolds me with a shake of his head. "Remain still."

But he doesn't pull the ice cube away, watching me as more tears prickle my eyes. "Damn it!"

"What did I say, Gwendolyn?"

"It hurts! Fuck."

"That's the idea. Your pain is bringing me pleasure. Don't you want to please me?"

I shake my head and thrust my hips, but his hold pinning me down is too firm.

"Veto!" I scream out. "Fuck, get it off of me!"

And he pulls it away immediately, but the pain doesn't subside. I'm sobbing and trying to pull my legs together, but he pins me down and moves his shoulders there. His mouth moves over my chilled flesh, and he gently sucks, taking the worst of the sting of the cold away.

He sucks and he sucks, and as the feeling returns to my clit, my legs begin to shake involuntarily. My world is spiraling and turning upon itself, and I can't catch my next breath. Pleasure tightens in a dangerous coil around my center.

And I explode, shattering into a million tiny pieces, pulverized, like stinging shards of dust. The orgasm is so intense that for a moment I forget where I am, what is happening and actually become the pleasure after it washes over me, drags me under. Wave after forceful wave pulses through me and my back and hips are arched completely off the ground.

Fuck.

CHAPTER 22
THE HARD TRUTH

ONCE WE'VE BOTH CAUGHT OUR BREATH, DEVON ROLLS off me and stands. I watch his muscled backside as he moves across the room, grabs a small tube of ointment, then returns to me. After freeing my wrists, he sits on the bed next to me, takes a dollop of honey-smelling ointment and gently smooths it over my wrists and nipples. As he moves his finger over one spot, I feel a little twinge of pain and wince.

"Does that hurt?" he asks.

"A little."

Dipping his head, he touches his lips to my neck, kissing the spot. It's the single most romantic thing anyone has ever done for me. The gesture is so intimate, and it makes me feel cherished. I can't help but smile.

Lifting up again, he continues rubbing ointment into every little scrape and abrasion. There aren't many, and some I gave myself from bumping around in the dark, but he gives attention to each one—kissing them as he does.

I reach out and tug on his arm. "I'm cold."

He moves to get up. "I'll fetch a blanket."

"No," I say, stopping him. "I want you to be my blanket," I say with a playful smile.

With a quirk of his lips, he crawls onto the mattress and lies next to me, pulling me against him. I rest my head on his warm chest and listen to the steady *thud* of his heart. Lying like this, with him, is so heavenly—everything else just fades away. The time is ticking away on our two-hour timer and yet he seems more content holding me close than in continuing…and it feels good.

I brush my fingertip over his nipple, back and forth, back and forth. "Tell me something about yourself. Something I can't find on the internet."

"What do you wish to know?" His deep baritone rumbles in his chest. Fuck, he's so delicious. How am I ever going to get enough of him? I worry for my mental health once all this is over.

I raise up onto my elbow and look down at him. I brush my finger over the jagged scar just beneath his ear. "Where did you get this?"

His eyes turn dark for a second, and I have the sudden feeling that I've made the mistake of asking him something too personal. But the question is out there now, and I don't retract it. Maybe it's the curious journalist in me, but I really want to know.

There's a long stretch of silence, then, finally, he clears his throat. "Childhood accident."

What? No. He wouldn't have such a strong reaction to my question if it were just a random childhood thing, like running into a rose bush or something.

I skim my fingertip along his strong jaw, until I reach his lips. They're soft, pillowy and transport me to another world somehow. My God, the power these lips have over me. "I don't believe you," I say. "Tell me what *really* happened."

He glances away from me, and I pull my hand away. "Well, it's certainly not something you'll find out on the internet. It's been a well-kept secret. But…" He takes a deep breath and lets it go, as if it almost pains him to say what he's about to say. "When I was eleven years old, I was taken by someone close to my family."

"Wait, taken, as in *kidnapped*?" I ask, astonished. Well-kept secret indeed. I'm sure this would have been everywhere and even mentioned now in stories about him, bringing up his tragic past. I wonder how it was kept out of the tabloids? I do the quick math and realize that I wasn't even born when this happened.

"Yes," he says stiffly.

I just stare down at him, horrified. I can't even imagine how he must have felt as a ten-year-old boy, vulnerable, taken from everything he knew. "And the scar…?" I'm trying to gently pry without being too invasive about it.

He pushes out a breath and sits up. I let my hand fall away, but I'm studying him—the muscles in his shoulders are pulled tight. His breathing is deep and focused, as though every inhale and exhale is intentionally slow. There are several seconds of silence until finally, I can't take it anymore. My curiosity isn't worth the cost of him having to dredge up old, painful memories. I make a placating gesture. "It's okay. You don't have to tell me."

He glances down and twists his head, rolling his shoulders. To my relief, he ignores my offer to drop it. "I was just a kid when it happened. I'd just gotten out of school for the day, and my driver had arrived to fetch me, as usual. But this particular day, instead of taking me home, he took me deep into London—to an area I didn't recognize." He pauses and sucks in another deep breath. I reach up to stroke his back gently, encouraging him to continue. "A group of men I'd never seen before were waiting for us. They handed my driver a great deal of money, and he, in turn, handed me over to my captors."

I suck in a sharp breath—I can't help it. The image of young Devon frightened and alone, being given to complete strangers, is heartbreaking. "Why? Why would they want you?"

The second the question leaves my mouth, it occurs to me I might not want to know the answer. How many children are sex-trafficked each year? My stomach clenches, waiting for his answer.

"I was primarily kidnapped for ransom, but that didn't prevent them from being cruel when they felt my parents weren't moving fast enough." His deep baritone catches. "I was with them for one week. They starved me. Beat me. Toyed with me."

It's that last statement that makes my heart clench. He doesn't explain what he means by being "toyed" with, but I can guess. Depraved people know every form of darkness, and I'm sure the things I conjure up in my mind don't even begin to compare to what he went through.

"I got the scar from attempting to fight back," he says, finally.

I swallow back the emotion bubbling up in my throat. Reaching up, I touch his scar again. "I'm sure you were a very brave boy."

He glances at me then, and the pain I see in his eyes guts me. "Not always."

"But you got away," I say. "You survived somehow."

"Once my parents came through with the ransom, I was released. My captors dropped me off alone on a street corner in Camden."

I blink and lean back against the pillows. "God, you must have felt so helpless. It's no wonder you crave control."

He turns to look down at me, and there's a darkness in his eyes that makes me gulp. "The control they wielded over me, a *child,* was cruel, and depraved. Are you seriously comparing me to those monsters?"

I swallow. "N-no. I'm saying that it's clear control is important to you. After all, you kidnapped *me*, didn't you?"

He launches off the bed so quickly, I jolt, scrambling backward, slamming my back against the cushions.

"Is that what you think this is?" He glares down at me. "Some fucking bid for *control?*"

I'm genuinely confused by his sudden anger. "Of course," I say defensively. "What else could it possibly be? You don't like my story, fine. Someone else might have sent high-powered lawyers after me. But you chose to *kidnap* me, instead. Why? Because that's the ultimate control you can have over someone—taking away their freedom."

His eyes narrow, and he turns to me. Before I can even move, he reaches out and pulls my upper arm, dragging me to the center of the bed. With one knee on the mattress, he looms over me, pressing me down with his lower half. His swollen cock is pressed lengthwise against my pussy. Then his hand snakes up and curls around my throat. "That's where you're wrong. Taking ultimate control is something much darker, Angel. You think *that* was depraved? Should I show you just how depraved I *can* be? Is that what you want?"

I shake my head, panic and excitement warring inside me. God, I'm so fucked up. How can this *excite* me? "No," I finally choke out.

"Ah-ah," he says, shifting his hips. "I can see the way your eyes light up when I take control of your body. You enjoy this, but you're too afraid to admit it. I've long suspected you aren't as pure as you let on."

His hand tightens around my throat, and he thrusts his hips forward, the hard length of his cock pushing against my clit. He's huge, and I can feel every solid inch of him. My center floods, preparing for what I know is going to happen. He's going to fuck me...

"I have one more veto," I remind him.

"Oh, yes." He laughs, like he'd almost forgotten. "The veto." His hand leaves my throat, and he grabs my face, holding it, so I'm forced to look at him. "You have what I choose to give you," he says slowly. "Let's see if I'm the cruel captor you think I am."

Harshly, he flips me onto my stomach and uses his knee to spread my legs wide. My heart is racing, and I can barely draw a breath into my lungs. I have no idea what to expect. Is he going to tease me, then walk away? I wouldn't put that kind of torture past him. The uncertainty, the not knowing what's going to happen next, is both thrilling and terrifying all at once.

"Domino—"

Before I can even get two words out, he stops me. "You will only speak when spoken to."

Threading his hand through my long hair, he wraps it around his hand and tugs my head back. The pinpricks of pain along my scalp make me gasp. With his free hand, he reaches down and brushes his finger along my opening, teasing the sensitive flesh.

He lowers his head and speaks directly in my ear. "I'm going to fill your pussy so full of my cum, you'll be tasting me for days."

Yes.

My entire body hums at the thought of being owned by him. It's so fucked up, and if I took three seconds to analyze this strange desire, I might be disgusted with myself. But right now, I don't care. Right now, I *want* him to possess me in every possible way.

Pulling away, he straightens and releases my hair, but continues to stroke me. When his finger slides farther up, slipping between my ass cheeks, I immediately stiffen. Then he pushes his finger inside me—just barely. It's so unexpected, I nearly jump out of my skin. He uses his knee to pin me down and prevent me from squirming away.

"Whoa." He laughs. "Care to use your veto?"

I force my muscles to relax, and I allow my body to melt into the mattress. "No."

He laughs under his breath like he enjoys messing with me, but thankfully, his hand continues moving upward, toward my tailbone, then along my spine. Then his large hand flares over my rib cage and the warmth of his skin relaxes me even more.

I love the feel of his hands on me. His touch is powerful, and it fills me with a deep sense of contentment. It's nothing I've ever felt before. No man has ever made me feel this way, and if I'm being honest with myself, it scares me a little.

Suddenly I feel his lips on my back—gentle, feather-light kisses that send tingles throughout my body. I squirm a little under his mouth, hungry for something more. This careful seduction would be wonderful...some other time. But my body is wound so tight from our earlier session that I just can't stand it.

I need him inside me.

I need him *now*.

With a moan, I lift my ass off the mattress in a silent bid for him to fuck me.

One large hand smooths over the globe of my ass, and I moan again. Yes. It's working.

Lifting his hand, he brings it down with a hard slap, and I jolt. Pinpricks of pain radiate through me, and I gasp. He leans over me, whispering again in my ear. "You like that, do you, Angel?" Then his hand moves down my body again, and he slips a finger into my wet channel. "You're drenched," he growls. "So ready to take my cock."

Yes, please.

I don't dare say the words out loud for fear he'll pull away and deny me the orgasm my body so desperately needs. I let out another moan and push my face into the mattress. *My God.* This is the worst kind of torture. Heat floods my clit, and the small bud begins pulsing in tandem with my heartbeat.

Then all of a sudden, he's off the bed. I try to get a peek at what he's up to, but he hasn't given me permission to move or change my position. Besides, he's got his back to me, blocking anything I might be able to see.

I could never have imagined what he had in store for me next...

Chapter 23
Beg For It

I HEAR HIM OPEN A DRAWER, THEN RETURN. THE MATTRESS dips as he kneels between my open legs. I hear him open a cap, then seconds later, there's a tad bit of pressure on my asshole. Whatever it is, it's hard and metal—though not cold at all. He must have warmed it in his hand. He applies more pressure, and I must have flinched, because he places a large hand on the small of my back, holding me in place.

"Just relax," he says, his voice rich and smooth, like whiskey. "Trust me with your pleasure, Angel."

Swallowing, I force my muscles to relax again. It's so hard because everything in me screams to keep whatever it is *out* of my ass. I've never ventured into this realm before, and I don't really know what to expect.

As I melt back into the mattress, I can hear in his voice that I've pleased him. "Good girl."

Then he slides the metal item into me slowly. In my limited research about sex toys, I did see examples of butt plugs, and that's what this must be. Thankfully, it's small, and it doesn't stretch me too much. Once it's fully seated inside me, all I feel is a little discomfort—the odd sensation of something being there that isn't usually there. A heaviness, but no pain at all.

His hand moves up, one finger sliding between my wet folds. I moan a little as he pushes one finger deeper inside me, then another and another, until I'm stretched wide. Together with the gentle pressure of the butt plug, the sensation is more intense. But it's still not nearly enough.

"Tell me what you need, Gwendolyn."

His fingers move in and out of me slowly, and my channel clenches around his fingers in response. A shudder of pleasure ripples through me.

My God.

"*Tell me*," he demands again.

I try to find my voice. When I do, it comes out strained. "I want…" I suck in a breath. "I want your cock inside me. I want you to fuck me."

He chuckles under his breath, amused by my answer. "So eager."

Pulling his fingers out of me, he circles his fingertips around my slick entrance, teasing my clit again. A jolt of electricity zips through me, and I arch my back, silently encouraging him to continue.

When he removes his hand, I feel him position himself behind me. He threads his fingers through my hair and pulls my head back. I twist my head to the side, and he leans over to kiss me, pulling my head back even more, his mouth completely devouring mine.

The swollen tip of his cock pushes against my entrance, and I rock back, trying desperately to deepen his thrust. He responds by tightening his grip on my hair, reining me in. "I'll set the pace, Angel."

I whimper and wiggle my ass, trying to urge him on. I'm punished with a sharp slap that jolts my entire body. My skin stings where his hand made contact. "If you're not going to listen…" He starts moving away, and I whimper again.

"I'm sorry, sir," I say quickly.

"Good girl."

He releases my hair and takes his cock in hand, guiding it to my slick entrance. He teases me with the head, before pushing into me. My entire body melts as he settles himself deep inside me, his shaft stroking my inner walls. He's so big, it literally hurts but feels really good at the same time. He holds still for a minute as if giving me time to adjust. I take a deep breath, swallowing, relishing this feeling of pain and pleasure mingling.

"So fucking wet," he groans.

Pulling back, he slams into me, and I gasp.

"Do you feel that?" he asks, taking me impossibly deep. "Do you feel how fucking hard you make me? All day long, all I can think about is you, and this beautiful pussy. I can't stop thinking about all the different ways I want to *fuck* you and make you come."

I swallow hard and press my face against the mattress. He's so big, he stretches me to capacity and coupled with the butt plug, it's almost too much. But soon pain bleeds into pleasure until I'm completely lost in sensation.

"My God, yes," I moan as he retreats, almost pulling out of me completely, before pushing back in again. He does that over and over before reaching down, and rubbing my clit with the tip of his finger—a feather-light touch, just enough to tease.

"Do you want my come in your pussy, Angel?" he asks, his breath coming hard and fast.

"Yes," I breathe, so desperate for it that I can barely speak.

"Beg for it," he says, his thrust becoming more focused, more shallow.

My God. He wants me to form a coherent thought.

"*Please*," I whisper. "I want your come. I want it so badly."

With a deep chuckle, he quickens his pace again, driving into me harder, and deeper with every thrust. Fisting the comforter in my hands, I moan, pushing my ass farther up into the air, giving him a better angle. Every nerve in my body is lit up like a Christmas tree, glowing and pulsing, as he moves within me.

I can't take much more of this. I'm *desperate* for release.

"Fuck me harder," I beg. "*Please.*"

Applying more pressure to my clit, he gives me what I need, thrusting deeper, harder somehow. "God, I'm so fucking addicted to you," he says. "I don't think I'm ever going to get enough of this."

Then all of a sudden, he pulls out of me and flips me over, so I'm on my back. We're both panting, both sweating, as he re-positions himself between my thighs and pushes into me again. This time, his thrusts are agonizingly slow. I'm so fucking keyed up, I can't think straight. I smooth my hands over his back, to his hard, muscular ass. I dig my fingernails into his skin and arch upward, silently begging for him to quicken his pace.

He holds my gaze, pale gray eyes burning into my own. I half expect him to tell me to lower my gaze, but he doesn't. Instead, he continues to hold my gaze with his even as he's moving inside of me. I swallow and continue to watch him as he takes command of my body and wrings every ounce of pleasure from it—for himself and for me. He's almost daring me to look away or close my eyes. But I don't. I *can't.*

He reaches under me and grabs the globes of my ass, then begins thrusting into me hard and fast. His deep, animalistic grunts are so fucking hot, I can barely stand it. I'm so close to climax, I feel like I'm going to shatter. I've never been fucked like this. I've never felt this level of intensity, and if I don't come soon, I'll go completely feral.

His pelvis slams against my clit as his cock hammers into me. And then I feel it, that exquisite pressure as it melts into a cascade of warmth—centered around my clit at first, then radiating out to every cell of my body.

"Oh, yes," I breathe. "Oh, my God. I'm coming."

"Fuck, *yes*," he growls, plunging into me even harder, pushing into me impossibly deep. "Fuck, you're so tight. I'm going to fill your pussy with my come."

Suddenly, he stills, thrusting deep and holding there. I can feel him swell bigger inside of me, and I let out a little gasp of pleasure and pain. His grip on me tightens, and suddenly he's coming inside me. I feel every surge and pulse of his cock as he lets out a fierce growl, going absolutely rigid for long moments.

When he finally relaxes, he's coated with sweat, skin glistening and sticking where it touches mine. He collapses his full weight on me while he pulls my mouth to his, planting passionate kisses on my mouth and neck.

"Perfect," he breathes. "Just as I'd imagined it would be." He pulls back to look at me, gently smoothing the hair away from my face. "I've wanted to make you mine since the first moment I saw you…at the bar in Obscura, wearing that little black dress and sipping a martini. This bright hair was the first thing I noticed. But it only took me minutes talking to you to realize there were brains behind the beauty. A rare treasure, Angel. That's what you are."

I swallow, feeling chill as the air hits my sweaty body, but his body covers me, warming me. And his words…well, they aren't just kind. They're said with feeling, honest, authentic. He might have that high-society stiff-upper-lipness to his mannerisms, but the words are said so openly, honestly. I can't think he's lying or flattering me.

He really means what he's saying. A *rare treasure*…me?

After gently rolling me over to remove the butt plug, he's up again. He goes to the cabinet and returns with a soft spa robe. He holds out his hand to pull me off the low bed and brings me up to my feet. I blink, suddenly realizing how I'm simultaneously starving and dying of thirst.

He slips the robe on my shoulders and guides my arms down the sleeves like I'm a little girl. Then he hands me a bottle of chilled water. It's like he's read my mind. Before stepping back, he kisses my hair affectionately, and that gesture…does something to me. I blink and turn to him with a question.

"I'll order us dinner while you shower. Then I can shower and we'll eat."

I nod. "Or…you could shower with me."

His dark eyebrow arches up, but he clearly likes that idea. He grabs a robe for himself, and we walk back into the suite. He shuts the door to the playroom with a firm click. I wonder whose job it is to go in there and clean up after? I stare at the door for a moment while I sip deeply from the water bottle, wondering about the playroom. And wondering if that's the only place where he'll touch me.

I don't want it to be. Suddenly, I'm tired of ceding control of my body in exchange for privileges. I want something more.

He looks up from his phone after having sent off a few texts, and when he does, I drop my robe to the ground. As if he hadn't just had me completely naked in the other room for two hours, he appreciates me anew. Not only does he look at me like he's never seen me naked before but almost as if he's never seen *any* woman naked before.

I lift my chin up and give him my best come-hither gesture before turning to strut toward the bathroom.

My bathroom is lovely with a large shower with multiple heads for sprays from all directions. Once the water is on, he steps in after me. I turn and smile at him, then reach for the soap on the ledge. But he gently nudges my hand away and takes the soap in his large hand, instead.

He gets his hands really sudsy and then runs them over my body, coating me in soap, sliding across my skin, exploring every nook and cranny, his hands glide across my hips, my stomach, circle around to come up under my breasts, then takes each one in his grip, holding them while he runs his thumbs over my tender, beaded nipples. The contact stings a little, given the earlier activities in the playroom, but mostly I'm basking in the glow of both the aftereffects of two mind-blowing orgasms and a new, steady climb to arousal. As he touches me, I feel him grow hard again against my hip. His breath comes fast as he presses his mouth against my ear.

He's ready for more? Really? After a blowjob and vigorous sex right after that? I fall back against his hard, broad body, resting against his chest, exhausted and yet impossibly hungry for more myself. I lick my lips then, before he can continue to frustrate me, I coat my hands in soap and glide them over his strong shoulders, down his muscular arms.

Seriously, this guy works out. He's in such good shape. My hands smooth over his pecs and lower, across the washboard bumps of his firm abs, and even lower still. My hand finds his very ready cock and my fingers close around it. I begin to pump his cock in my tight fist.

His eyes fixed on mine, he satisfies me with a sharp expulsion of breath, and the next thing I know, I'm pinned to the cold marble wall of the shower and he's pulling one of my legs up to hook around his hips.

"Gwendolyn, you've swiftly become my addiction. And a dangerous one at that." With nothing further to say, he slides his thick cock inside me and positions me higher on the wall between us by holding my hips firmly in place.

"Look at me, Gwendolyn, while I'm inside you, don't pull your eyes away. You still wear my symbol. You're still mine, even here, outside the playroom. And this sweet, tight pussy, it's mine too. It feels so good. *You* feel so good."

Swiftly, ferociously, he crushes my pelvis between his own and the cold slab of white marble behind us. Soon I'm moaning and gasping his name—his real name—and begging him to make me come again. My other leg comes up to hook around his hips, and he pumps his pelvis harder, hitting me deeper. Around that stone, ungiving hardness of his cock, I come undone, gripping him over and over with my inner muscles while my orgasm plays out in heady, ecstatic convulsions. I blow out a breath, barely able to gasp my next one.

He's still while I come, but I know he's not done. He presses his mouth against my temple. "Fuck, that feels so good, when your tight little pussy grips me like that. Christ, you are perfect."

Then he moves again, pumping into me violently over and over until, with a strangled gasp, he comes again, his cock convulsing inside of me. We stay like that for several long minutes under the hot spray while he kisses my temple, my ear. "I knew it would be good. I knew it would be amazing, really. I never knew it would be like this," he says in a low voice.

Shortly thereafter, when he pulls out, we finish washing and end the shower. While we dry off, he tells me dinner is coming. And he hopes I'm not too tired because he has a "surprise" for me.

I know better than to pry and realize he'll reveal all in his own time. But I hope it means we're going out somewhere. I'm clued in a little while later when, just after the food arrives, I go to take off the winding snake collar around my neck and he tells me not to.

His smoldering eyes meet me across the table. "Where we're going, you're going to need that. Leave it on, Angel."

CHAPTER 24
OBSCURA

As soon as we're done eating, there's a knock on the door. The timing is impeccable, just another sign that this place is a well-oiled machine.

Devon walks over to open the door. He has a short conversation with whoever it is, and when he shuts the door and turns around, he has two large garment-sized boxes in his arms—with a smaller box perched on top.

"What are those?" I ask.

His lips twist into a mischievous smile. "It's your costume for this evening' s adventure." I frown at him, puzzled. What kind of adventure would require a costume?

Then it hits me. Obscura. Excitement bubbles up inside me. The second he sets the boxes down, I rip into them. In the first box, under two tons of tissue paper is what looks like a ballerina dancer's dress—a snow-white bodysuit, inlaid with tons of glimmering crystals, and a short skirt made of white tulle and faux feathers. I notice it's a bit more conservative than the other costumes I've seen at Obscura, and I wonder if that's because Devon doesn't want me showing too much skin or having other men look at me.

"It's beautiful." I hold it up to my body. It looks like it's going to fit perfectly, like with every other article of clothing I've been given here.

"I'm keen to see you in it." His eyes light up.

I reach for the second box, and again, beneath miles of tissue paper, I see a bed of more white feathers, these ones long and very real, as if from a goose or some other large bird. Also pure white…it's a gorgeous pair of wings. Angel wings attached to a golden-filigree yoke to hold them on my body. With them is a white and gold jewel-encrusted mask complete with glittery, golden halo.

"I'm sensing a theme here." I laugh.

There are a pair of white open-toed Louis Vuitton heels in the third box—and they're my size, of course. Whoever bought all this has impeccable taste. The entire outfit is perfection.

Devon leans in and places his finger beneath my chin, kissing me lightly on the lips. The simple, intimate gesture makes my heart melt a little more toward him—if that's even possible.

"Get dressed," he says. "I'll do the same and return shortly."

Just as Devon leaves, Jemma comes in after him to help me get ready. I'm sitting at the vanity and she's curling my hair when she smiles and says, "I've never seen him so happy. I think we all have you to thank for that."

My eyebrows knit together, confused. "*Me?* No. There's nothing special about me, I assure you."

Devon is a member of the royal family. I'm certain he's been with many women—models, socialites, actresses, prominent women, beautiful, sophisticated…*rich.* I'm none of those things. How could someone like me make someone like Devon happy? It doesn't even compute.

Jemma shrugs, a knowing smile on her lips. "I'm just telling you what I see. I've known His Lordship for quite a while now, and I'm telling you, I have never seen him smile so much." She holds her hands up. "Make of that that you will."

Once Jemma is done with my hair and makeup, she helps me slip the costume on. I twirl in front of the mirror, admiring the way the costume fits my frame perfectly. The feather skirt is short on my long legs but still manages to cover me completely. And with the wings, it looks truly magical.

"Did you pick this costume out?" I ask Jemma.

She shakes her head. "His Lordship was very particular about what he wanted. He had it tailor-made and delivered this morning."

I press my lips together and wonder what that means. Has he always known he was going to take me to Obscura? It would have taken a few days, at least, to tailor a costume like this.

Exactly thirty minutes later, Devon returns in his devil mask. I swallow hard at the sight of him. He's wearing a crisp tailored white button-down shirt, rolled up at the sleeves, black trousers, and a pair of polished black shoes. *Damn,* he's hot. A shiver of awareness trips down my spine, and I consider tearing those clothes off him and dragging him back to bed.

If this weren't my *one* opportunity to leave the penthouse, then I might consider it. But I want to see Obscura again, and I'm not going to risk him changing his mind.

He leans against the wall, hands in his pockets, a smile on those wicked lips. "You look gorgeous," he says, his gaze licking my exposed flesh. I can tell he's thinking the same thing I am—ditch the costumes and crawl back into bed.

"Thank you," I say. "Judging by the costumes, I'm guessing we're going to Obscura tonight."

He laughs a little, pushes off the wall, and advances on me. "Smart girl." He reaches out and brushes a fingertip down my shoulder. Whenever he's near me, I've noticed he *has* to touch me. Honestly, I can't keep my hands off him either.

I've never been in such an intense relationship, and it feels exhilarating. But more than that, it feels *right*. Like I'm exactly where I should be—which is so fucked up, considering *how* I got here. Kidnapped and tossed in a trunk isn't exactly a fairy-tale beginning.

"A few rules before we leave," he says.

I nod, so eager to leave the confines of my suite that I'd agree to almost anything at this point. "Okay."

"No one can know who you are. You speak to no one. You touch no one. And more importantly, no one touches *you*."

I reach up unconsciously and touch the snake choker necklace wound around my throat. "I doubt anyone would be dumb enough to touch me with the Devil hovering nearby.."

He curls his hands around my arms and lowers his head, his lips hovering above mine. "You'd be surprised how idiotic men can be around a beautiful woman."

Touché.

I smile. "Men *are* idiots, it's true."

He brushes his lips across mine. "Present company excluded, I assume?"

"Nope," I whisper, my breath held, anticipating his kiss.

He inhales deeply, like he's trying to calm an onslaught of desire. "I should punish you for such impertinence."

"Yes, please, and thank you." I tilt my chin up and try to kiss him, but he quickly moves out of my reach. *Damn.*

"Later, perhaps." He holds his hand out, his long fingers reaching for me. "Shall we?"

I reach out and take his hand. "I'm ready."

He moves to the door, and before turning the knob to allow us to leave, he turns to me, almost as if it's just occurring to him, and pulls out a silky bit of black fabric from his pocket. A blindfold.

Seriously?

I open my mouth to protest but he holds it up. "I insist, Angel."

Afraid that if I protest too much, he'll change his mind about allowing me to go out, I turn and allow him to tie it around my head, cloaking my eyes in darkness. I'm once again treated to a blind walk down long halls, this time guided by him, and down yet another long elevator ride, into a parking garage and then into a waiting car.

We ride in silence for a while until about ten minutes in, he pulls me against him and starts to kiss my ear, my neck. "If I didn't have more exciting plans for us in there, I wouldn't be able to stop myself now, Angel. You are more beautiful than I envisioned you would be, all dressed in pure, innocent white. But we both know you aren't that innocent, are you?"

His voice is thick with arousal, deep and seductive, and I feel the beginning stirrings of the cycle we just traveled several times together today. This man has already had sex with me three times and he wants more?

I swallow, aware of the thready pulse at my throat. His touch is no more invasive than running warm fingers up the inside of my thigh and kisses on my neck and ear. After another ten minutes, he pulls off the blindfold tied around my eyes just as I note we are exiting the freeway in Malibu.

My pulse races with anticipation. What delights will Obscura hold for us tonight? The last time I was here sealed our fate together as the night we met, the night this mutual obsession between us began with just a spark.

I doubted either one of us anticipated what it would become. He's been the one with all the power and all the control, but I feel the beginnings of a switch…since the moment we went into that playroom and sealed this connection with hot, animal sex.

As we approach the golden-lit twin towers of Exeter House, wreathed in palm trees and sedate evening lighting, Devon hands me my mask and reaches for his own. I take it, then I run my hand up his thigh and settle it firmly on his very hard cock. I have power over this man, whatever he may think about being the one who dominates.

Yes, I have power over him, and I'm not afraid to use it.

We're both masked and back in the dimly lit reception foyer of the club. Here, we're greeted once again by the perennially elegant Miss Lawrence, her long legs accentuated by a form-fitting golden cocktail dress and matching mask.

"Sir, so good to have you again. We've been wondering where you'd gotten off to."

He nods his head to her elegantly. "I've brought my guest that I messaged you about. Here, she's called Angel."

"Very good, sir," she replies with a wide smile. Then turns to me. "Welcome, Angel. You've been here before?"

"Once, yes."

She nods. "Good. And I'm sure Domino won't hesitate to make sure you understand the rules. You'll be in good hands." She smiles at him fondly, and he reaches out and touches her arm with affection. Suddenly, a spark of white-hot jealousy flares inside me. What is the relationship between these two? On the surface, it seems professional, but there's an undercurrent of something more.

My eyes narrow, taking them in even as Devon's hand settles possessively on the small of my back. Do they have a past of some kind? Maybe not, but she'd like it to be more?

I make a note to ask him later, and I hope he'll tell me the truth. In the meantime, there's a lot to see, learn and absorb here at Exeter House. A good journalist worth her salt is never off the job and never *not* asking questions.

As before, Obscura is an extremely upscale, elegantly lit and decorated night club. Beautiful, scantily clad people surround us. Devon's possessive hand guides me toward the bar, and he's not there more than twenty seconds before two drinks appear in front of us. A whiskey neat for him and an appletini for me. He remembered even that small detail.

Wow. Impressive.

I sip at my drink and take in my surroundings from behind my mask when beside me, he shifts.

"Domino! It's been, what, a week? More than that? Where have you been?" It's a woman's voice, and she's wearing a black server's uniform, a wide smile and not much else. And she's practically leaning against him.

Devon positions himself behind me and pulls me flush against his hard body. "Now, now, Violet. I have a guest with me tonight. Meet my Angel." His hand curls around my hip, and I lean back against him as I watch Violet from behind my mask. She turns to me and politely smiles. "Nice to meet you, Angel. Domino's a regular here. We all know him quite well so I'm sure you'll be seeing a lot of people welcoming him back tonight."

"You've really been gone for a while?" I ask him later after Violet has left.

"I do that sometimes. It's been a few weeks." I count back in my head. That would put his last appearance here some time around when we met or shortly thereafter. I frown, wondering about that.

But I don't have long to ponder. Suddenly, I feel his warm lips claim my neck. The bartender and a few of the servers are openly watching us with what I interpret as open curiosity from behind their plain masks. I guess it's true that Domino has never brought a sub here, or maybe even a woman at all?

His mouth then moves to my ear. "I have a particular urge, Angel. To take you back to where we started this."

I tilt my head back to look into his face, even if it is masked. Our fiery gazes meet from behind our respective disguises. "Isn't that right here?"

He shakes his head. "I was thinking of the shibari room, in fact. And perhaps this time, not merely as an observer."

Oh….*ohhhh*. Visions of the women tied up with silken ropes knotted intricately in beautiful patterns, splayed out for all to see as men moved around them, pleasuring the women with their hands, mouths and toys.

My core pulses with an aching need.

"You–you want to take me there?"

A smile hovers on his sensual lips.

I swallow. "And if I say no?"

"You don't have a veto here, Angel. You do as I say. Or, we leave."

I blink. If I didn't already want to go back, I'd feel an arc of defiance rise up inside me. Maybe he's expecting that. Maybe he wants the excuse to punish me.

But as I let him lead me around the pulsing dance floor and toward the staircase that leads up to the private, founders-only rooms of the sex club above, I remember that he's told me something very important.

He doesn't need an excuse to punish me. Or do whatever else he wants.

CHAPTER 25
KNOTTY DESIRES

THREADING HIS FINGERS THROUGH MINE, DEVON LEADS me past the concierge at the top of the stairs and down the hall to what I remember is the shibari room. With his hand hovering over the doorknob, he twists his head and smiles at me—that cool, enigmatic twist of his lips that always sets my blood on fire.

"Are you ready for this, Angel?"

A ball of anxiety clenches tight in my stomach, but I swallow and nod, flashing him a tight smile.

It's for the research, I remind myself. *I can do this.*

I'm not sure why I'm so nervous. I've been inside the shibari room. I've seen what happens on the other side of this door. But then, I was just an observer, watching as other people were tied up and dominated. This time, I get the distinct feeling I'll be an *active* participant.

Devon pushes the door open, and we step inside. There are several people engaged in various sex acts. There are two women tied up—one to a table, and the other is suspended by rope from hooks that are secured in the ceiling. Half a dozen men lavish attention on either one or both women—moving between them, stroking, licking, fucking, in a beautifully orchestrated orgy.

Heat moves through me, and I swallow, forcing myself to look, instead of shying away. The knots and rope binding that secure each woman really are beautiful—twisting to form intricate patterns that bite into their skin. And the knots themselves look quite complicated as well. I can see why shibari is seen as an art form.

"It's really quite beautiful," I whisper, taking in every detail. For research, of course.

When I look over at Devon, he's watching me carefully. Intently. Like he's studying my reaction. Again. We've been here before, and he studied me then, too. I get the sense that he's waiting for me to run away in horror or something.

A lift a brow at him, then realize he can't see me behind my mask so I very decidedly place a hand on my hip and stare back—defiant. Challenging.

Shoving his hands into his pockets, his lips quirk a little just under the bottom edge of his devil mask.

Then he turns his attention back toward the others. "Give us the room, please," he says with all the command and confidence of his position here.

Everyone stops and turns toward him, as though they've just noticed us standing here. I see the shock on several of their faces—and an indication, again, that he's never brought a sub here before. Never participated in the activities himself. I imagine his asking for the room has never happened before.

But quickly, they move to untie the women while whispering discreetly among themselves. Getting the bound women out of their restraints is quite a production, as it turns out. While they do so, several room attendants move in to wipe down the tables and equipment and provide a few fresh bundles of rope. No less than twenty minutes later, they finally file out of the room. As they do, they stare at me with open curiosity. I can feel their questions as they move past me—who is this woman, and how has she managed to tempt the Devil?

The truth is, I have no idea. I have trouble believing I'm anything special, and yet, Devon makes me feel special every moment we're together. It's wild, and I can't help but wonder when this fantasy will vanish in a puff of smoke.

When the door clicks shut and we're finally alone, Devon reaches over and slides the deadbolt into place.

I clear my throat. "That was rude, asking everyone to leave."

He gestures to the room around us. "This is my domain. They're only here because I allow them to be here. If not for me, they'd still be crammed in the musty basements of Hollywood." He walks up to me, reaching below my feather skirt to cup my ass in each hand. "Besides, I want you alone for this. I can't have other men enjoying what's mine."

That makes me smile. It shouldn't, but it does. "Oh, I'm *yours* now, am I?"

"Yes," he says without hesitation.

I reach up and brush the tip of my finger along his jawline. "Does that make *you* mine, then?"

It seems almost too good to be true. How the fuck did we get here? Is this what Stockholm syndrome is? Fuck, I don't know, and honestly, right now, I don't care. I've seen a side of Devon that intrigues me, and I want more.

An amused twist of his lips is my only answer. He leans forward and places a feather-light kiss on my lips, while his hands move to the zipper along the back of my costume. Slowly, he pulls the tab down, until the silky fabric of my bodice is sagging, exposing my breasts.

He pulls off my little dancer-style dress. When I move to take off the wings, he stops me.

"No, keep those on." He glances over my shoulder, up toward the high ceiling. "You'll need your wings."

I follow his gaze to the rope that's dangling from a wooden bar swinging the hooks, and realize he's going to tie me up and suspend me, like the woman I saw when we walked in. A shiver rolls down my spine. I've never done anything like this before, but I'm intrigued, and as fucked up as it sounds, I trust him.

I'm completely naked, except for the wings, when he threads his fingers through mine and tugs me toward the center of the room. He takes up a length of shiny black rope and holds it up for me to look at.

"Touch it. It's silk. Smooth, shiny, thin rope, but deceptively strong. Raw silk is among the strongest fibers on the planet. The marks it will leave on your skin will be nothing short of exquisite."

I run a finger along the smooth, golden rope. It's pristinely clean and just as silky as it looks. "Have–have you done this before?" I'm skeptical because he's admitted to me that he's never taken a sub and doesn't participate in the activities here.

"I have. I've been instructed in knotwork and have worked on mannequins and live models."

I blink, suddenly jealous. I realize he's probably told me the truth, that he's never taken a sub. But that doesn't preclude not having participated in the BDSM scene or having had sex as a Dom. I'm at once itching to ask and yet I don't want to know. I don't want to imagine him touching another woman. Because I know there must have been many. The way women follow him with their eyes wherever he goes…. The way they looked at me as I followed him in tonight, all staring intently like they'd love nothing more than to trade places with me.

Devon begins unwinding the length of rope from its bundle while staring intently at me. "Bondage is, first and foremost, about trust. It's about connection and emotional reliance. It's about the sub trusting her Dom and about the Dom trusting that the sub will tell him what she can and cannot handle and for him to rise to the occasion to support her, physically, emotionally…sexually. Can you do that, Angel? Do you trust me?"

My heartbeat has sped up, and cold thrills have clawed up my throat, threatening to prevent me from speaking. As we hold our gazes, slowly I nod.

"That's not acceptable. You must tell me in words. Tell me that you trust me."

I lick my lips and straighten my spine. "I do. I trust you, sir."

He cups his hand around my cheek and jaw, bends and presses a long, passionate kiss to my mouth, commanding it to open and accept the invasion of his tongue. Arousal floods every inch of my body. This man has given me three orgasms today, has been inside me twice, and yet I'm aching for him like a woman starving.

He pulls away, and a smile quirks on that sexy mouth. "Mmm. Tonight the Devil will have his angel in every way that he wants. And now, that gorgeous pink flush to your glowing skin will only look better when this rope puts the marks everywhere that I bind you. Kneel."

I do as he says, and then he bends to pull my arms behind my back and lace my fingers together to hold them there. He begins knotting the rope at my wrists, after testing how tight will still allow me to be comfortable. Then he begins taking the ends of the ropes and lacing them up my arms, as if creating sleeves, looping them back and forth over each arm until they reach my elbows, where he ends with another tight knot.

His mouth is at my ear as he continues, pulling my ankles together behind me. "Shibari is not about the end result; it's the process of creating beauty out of what binds us together, no pun intended. I wrap you in my binds to express the trust between us, yes, but also the balance of power. I have the power to bind you, immobilize you, and leave you bound. And you have the power to end this when you want. Tell me *Halt*, and I will stop."

I raise my brows. He's given me a safe word for the very first time. Does that mean something? Soon, he's binding the rope that connects my wrists to my ankles, lacing and looping the rope back and forth. I lean slightly against the ropes, testing them. My ankles and wrists are bound to each other in a sort of reverse hogtie.

I don't know how long it takes—I've lost all sense of time. I'm so lost in the pleasure of watching Devon's intense focus as he slides the ropes along my skin, knotting, testing the slack, and even undoing and redoing when he's not satisfied. My gaze slides down to his crotch, and I notice a very prominent bulge there. He's getting off on this, on tying me up in this artsy way and immobilizing me, on having complete control over my body.

Devon threads the end of the rope between my legs, pulling it tight like a thong. I swallow, feeling an electric jolt when the rope rubs up against my clit. He winds the rope around my waist like a belt and pulls it tight to cinch against my skin. It pinches but isn't fully uncomfortable, and I'm quickly discovering that the pinch and friction make me so fully aware of every inch of my body and the attention he's lavishing on it that the heightened awareness is bringing on that elevated level of excitement, like when I'm with him in the playroom.

He pauses a moment to take in his work and then he looks into my eyes. He doesn't speak but waits for me to possibly protest.

Instead, I lower my gaze to his chest, then lower. The obvious bulge in his pants is all the confirmation I need that he's feeling it, too.

He finishes, winding the rope around my torso several times so that it outlines my breasts and almost imitates a bra. But it's served to give me enough structure and support that he can move to the next phase of the process.

With my heart beating frantically, I watch as he presses a button on the wall to lower the swing-like structure. Then, very carefully, he grabs the rope where it attaches my wrists to my ankles—where I now realize he's created a sort of handle for himself—and picks me up like a sack of groceries. Suddenly my head flops toward the floor, but he's got me up high enough that I'm in no danger.

I find it disorienting, but also enjoy getting to be able to fully take in his bulging crotch. Mmm. I want him to drop his clothes already. I want that gorgeous cock inside me, stretching me, making me come.

I want to scream his name.

I have to admit, being vulnerable like this, and open to his every whim, with the knots and the rope biting into my skin…is electrifying. Energy snaps in my veins and heat floods my center.

Devon ties me to the wooden bar of the swing by the wrists and ankles. "You, my angel, my pretty little ornament. Will you shine for me?"

I stare straight ahead, hearing his words through the buzz and crackle of my own thick desire. Everything swirls around me in surreality, like a dream.

"Tell me, Angel. Tell me you want this."

I lick my lips to try and work some moisture into my mouth. "I want to shine for you. I want to please you."

He lets out an almost explosive breath as if I couldn't have responded with anything more perfect. "Oh, you please me, Angel. You please me very much. And I promise very soon to return the favor."

But his words are doing just that already. Intense satisfaction and a rush of joy fill me when he says those words. The mechanism whirs to life when he presses the button, and soon, I'm slowly lifted off the ground. With a yelp, I'm yanked off my knees and slowly lifted, looking down at the floor. Now there's fear mixed in with all the rest in an intense sort of stew.

He's barely touched me, except for the knotting of the ropes, and yet I feel like I'm about to come. Fuck, how I want his hands on me.

I flick my gaze to the side, and he is there. He pulls back my hair, that's been hanging down over my face, and carefully knots the long mane in a makeshift messy bun. "There, now I can gaze into your beautiful face. Look at me, Angel. Look at your master."

My eyebrow quirks up at the change in term. So he's promoted himself. I raise my chin and look into his eyes. He's raised the swing to almost the height of his head, and I'm surprised to note that, even though I'm technically hanging from my wrists and ankles, the weight of my body is not pulling me there. In fact, the weight is so evenly distributed that I can barely feel the tension in any one place. He's tied me up perfectly.

Devon takes my chin in his hand and pulls me toward him. The swing gives, and I move. There, he lavishes my mouth with the full force of his passion. His lips claiming mine, his tongue owning me. I give a little whimper when he pulls away, and he growls, deep in his throat.

"Fuck, Angel. I've been picturing you up here like this, suspended here, ever since that first night I brought you to this room. I knew I wanted you then. I knew, one way or the other, that I'd have you. I can't count the number of ways I mean to have you. It defies description."

"Then show me, instead."

He barks out a harsh laugh, takes a step back, and then hits the wood plank from which I'm suspended with all of his force. I let out a shriek, and suddenly the world is spinning all around me. The rope above me winds tight. I remember, as a child, sitting in the playground on the swing, winding and unwinding the chains on the swing as I twirled first clockwise, then counterclockwise. I remember the giddy exhilaration I felt then.

I feel it again now. Once the swing's rope has tightened to maximum tension, it begins to unwind and I twirl in the opposite direction. Devon reaches out once the swing starts to slow down and asks me, "Are you feeling okay?"

I let out a breathy "Yes," and he bats my swing in a twirl once more, repeating the action several times until finally, when I do come to a standstill, the world feels like it's still moving. I groan, trying to regain my bearings while suspended upside down.

Devon reaches out and palms my breast. "Exquisite. You make the most stunning ornament. I knew you would. I could stare at you all day, but then I wouldn't be able to fuck you."

"Oh, yes, please."

"Mmm, not yet." His thumb scrapes against my nipple as he takes my other breast in his palm. "So much more of you to enjoy like this. Denying myself what I'm desperate for will only make it all the sweeter when I finally lay you out and open your legs for me."

I can barely breathe. My body is moving—almost of its own accord—as he fondles me just roughly enough that it's setting every nerve on fire. Then one hand slides along the silk, tracing the length of rope that runs along the seam of my sex. It's more than just a little damp from my arousal, and I can hear his breathing quicken when he notices too.

"Fuck. You are making me pay for delaying this, aren't you? So fucking irresistible. So perfect." The pressure on that rope tightens and connects with my clit again, and I jump, letting out a squeal. "Mmm. Every sound from your mouth, Angel, every breath. Let me hear them all while I make you come."

He applies pressure at just the right spot over my clit, and if I could, I would leap out of my own skin. It's like he's delivered an electric shock straight on my clit. My squeal, this time, is almost a shout. He rubs me there, over and over again, and it doesn't take me long at all before that build to climax is almost realized.

"Tell me. Tell me what you want, Angel. Do you want your orgasm?"

I lift my head and pant at him breathlessly. "I. Want. Your. Cock."

Suddenly his hand stills, and he looks me over, cups my cheek, and says, "Well, then. What the angel wants, she shall get, won't she?"

CHAPTER 26
DISPLAY

I'M SECONDS AWAY FROM COMING WHEN HE STOPS, AND MY clit is still throbbing almost painfully. I let go a wordless protest as he walks away from me, first to throw a blanket down on the ground below me and then to the controller for the lowering mechanism.

The moment I'm lowered, he helps me by laying me on my side, pushing my hair away from my face, then setting to work to unknot the rope. He says nothing, but his breathing is coming quick and his erection looks like it's about to bust through his pants. And he's less gentle than I'm sure he's even consciously aware as he tugs at the ropes to loosen the knots and unwind the ropes.

Once the ropes are off me, he turns me onto my back and runs a reverent hand over my skin. "These markings from the ropes…they're temporary, but my hold on you, the bind between us won't fade like the evidence on your skin. Do you hear me, Angel? You are exquisite and you are mine. All mine."

I look down to follow the tracings of his fingers, and I'm stunned to realize how much it heightens my own arousal to see the red marks across my skin. "Please…" I murmur. "I want you. I *need* you."

He presses a finger to my lips. "All in good time, my sweet angel. But I think…it might be kind of us to reward those we sent out of the room with a little show, what do you think?

My eyes widen, staring up at him in shock as he pulls his phone out of his pocket and texts someone. Then, he walks over to the door and unlocks it. With a quirk of his beautiful lips, he gathers me up off the floor and places me on the table that's positioned in the center of the room.

His large hands rove over my naked skin again, his fingertips following the lines created by the ropes. "So beautiful," he whispers. "So perfect."

His words thread through me, and warmth suffuses my body. He thinks I'm beautiful. I arch my back, silently begging him for more. "Please," I breathe, on the brink of completely losing it. Pleasure is coursing through me like a drug, and I need *more*. Harder, deeper. I want it all. Anything and everything he'll give me.

"Patience," he says with an edge to his tone. I can hear the raw desire in his deep baritone, and it electrifies me, feeding my own arousal.

Seconds later, the door opens, and several people file into the room—at least two dozen. Word gets around, I guess. I instantly feel shy and move to cover my breasts with my hands—but Devon grabs my wrists, stopping me.

"Don't hide yourself," he says, before easing away and releasing his grip. "Let them see your beauty. Let them see what's *mine*."

I nod slightly and swallow, letting my hands fall limp at my sides. I try to forget about the two dozen people staring at us. I have a mask on, after all, and my identity is completely hidden.

I'm safe here, cloaked in anonymity, I remind myself. And honestly, having an audience is both terrifying and enthralling all at once. What the fuck is *wrong* with me? I've clearly gone insane.

Devon leans over and places a gentle kiss on my forehead, then places a hand on my knee and spreads my legs wide. A growl emerges from somewhere deep in his chest, and he lowers his head, touching the tip of his tongue to my hard, aching nipple. Pleasure zips through my veins, and I nearly launch off the table.

"You're hungry for cock," he says. "You want my come inside you."

I wriggle beneath him, and I let out a little squeak of desperation. "Yes."

He moves to the other breast, his tongue swirling around the tight peak, then he sucks gently. *My God.* If he doesn't fuck me soon, I'm going to explode. Every cell in my body is going to spontaneously combust.

"There are several cocks in this room," he says, coming up for air. "I'm sure one or several would be more than happy to fuck your beautiful pussy. Is that what you want, Angel?"

"No!" I call out, nearly jolting off the table. "I want your cock. Only you."

His deep chuckle reverberates through me, and I realize that his statement was a test. Will any cock satisfy me, or is it *him* I want? I'm too lost in sensation to put it into words, but I have the sinking feeling that no other cock would ever satisfy me the way Devon does. In all too short of a time, I've become completely addicted to him.

"Good girl," he growls, brushing his finger along my jaw.

He moves down my body, and his mouth finds the sensitive folds between my thighs. I let my legs fall open wider as my head tilts back against the table, and I let out a groan. He strokes my clit with his tongue, hard and fast, completely devouring me, working me into an undulating frenzy of need. I want him so badly that I honestly don't know how much more I can take.

Then just as quickly as his onslaught began, he pulls away, and I'm left desperate and gasping. "No, please don't stop," I whimper. I reach for him, but he's already several feet away.

I hear his belt as he unthreads it from his slacks, and then I hear the distinct sound of his zipper lowering. *Oh, my God.* My entire body shivers in anticipation. I need this so badly. I need *him.*

He returns to the table and grabbing my hips, pulls me forward. He folds my legs in front of me, so they're between my chest and his. I feel a bit like a pretzel, but it isn't painful, so I just go with it. I'm down for just about anything, at this point. Anything to get him inside me.

And then I feel it—the swollen tip of his cock pressed against my entrance.

"Christ," he hisses as he slowly pushes into me. I struggle to breathe as he seats himself all the way inside me, stretching me to capacity. I'm still not used to it, and I wonder if I ever will be. He's so fucking huge.

"Fuck, *yes,*" he growls, pulling back slightly, then driving back into me. "This pussy is mine now. No one will ever touch you but me."

Yes. My God. It feels so good to be owned by Devon—to be cherished and dominated by him.

"This cock," he says pulling back. Then he surges forward, sinking into me even deeper. "Only this cock will make you come."

"Yes," I breathe, my gaze meeting his through our masks. *"Please."*

His pace is tortuously slow, and every measured stroke embeds his cock deeper inside me. The sensations crashing over me are so overwhelming, I don't know how much more I can take. I pull my legs free and hook my heels on the edge of the table for leverage. My body moves in time with his, and my hands slip down under the waist of his pants to grip the globes of his bare ass—urging him on, harder and faster and *deeper.*

"Is this what you needed, Angel?" he asks, breath heaving from his lungs.

"Yes," I manage to get out.

"I'm going to fill you with my come," he says. "So you know who you belong to."

"Yes," I say again. I know what he's saying is true—I belong to him, and he belongs to me. I've never been more certain of anything in my life. "I want your come inside me. Please. Give it to me. I need it *now.*"

"Such a greedy cunt," he whispers in my ear. Then he seizes my hips in his hands and pulls my pelvis flush against his, using his grip to piston into me deeper, harder, faster.

He's moving so fast that I can't even catch my breath. Wave after wave of orgasm rips through me and he's still moving. I throw my head back and moan. Waves of sweet ecstasy wash over me, and he's not letting up. I fall slack against the table in the afterglow, and only then does he stop, only pulling out long enough to flip me over and pull me so that my legs dangle off the table.

In this position, I get a full view of our audience. Everyone is glued to us, though some are touching each other—or themselves—under their own clothing. One woman is standing, transfixed by Domino's actions, her mouth agape and sequined bikini-clad chest heaving. She's reaching out, and with her grip wrapped around the cock of the man beside her, she's pumping it up and down while he juts his hips toward her, but his eyes fastened on me. Several other women are watching me, too, and touching the women next to them. I lick my lips, and Devon's mouth is at my ear. "Watch them watching us. See how we're making them all get off, too? Do you like that, Angel? Do you like seeing how much our play is turning them all on?"

"Yes," I breathe.

From behind, he pulls my legs apart just enough to slip his huge cock back inside me from behind. He's got my hips clenched in his large hands again, squeezing tightly as his deep, baritone grunts in my ear.

"Fuck. This pussy feels so good. I fear I'll never get enough." His mouth moves near my ear again, nipping at the lobe as he pumps his cock into me, and I feel that build again, impossibly. I can't even count how many times this man has made me come today, but I'm shocked to realize that I'm greedy for more.

His mouth moves around to the back of my neck, and with a deep, guttural groan, he sinks his teeth deeply into the nape of my neck. I let out a gasp of shock and he doesn't release me even as the movements of his hips quicken and his cock swells impossibly large inside me. His teeth still hold me at my nape, and the pain of the bite brings tears to my eyes. It's just that perfect mix, like in the playroom, of pain and pleasure to heighten the entire experience. A rush of endorphins washes over me, and my awareness ratchets up. I just had an orgasm but can already tell that this next one is going to blow it out of the water in intensity. He seems to know it too as he hasn't let up with his teeth.

"Ahhh," I let out, not even sure whether I'm expressing pleasure or pain. There's a collective gasp in the crowd watching us, and I'm vaguely aware that our display has just taken everything up a level for them, too.

As my orgasm slams through me this time, his hips stop moving, but his teeth haven't relented in that deep bite on my neck. Tears flow down my cheeks even as I come apart in the most intense climax—higher than I've ever climbed and deeper than I've ever come crashing down again. Long minutes while his fingers move to my clit to draw it out until down, down, down I go, and now I'm aware of the sound of weeping.

As if from a distance, I realize that it's me. His teeth release me at my neck and his cock moves inside me again. When he speaks, it's with a breathless, hoarse voice that I hardly recognize. A dark voice. "You've been marked by me, Angel. The devil's mark on you. Now take my come. Take it all."

He thrusts deep, and I feel the pulsing of his cock inside me as, with a loud growl, he pours himself into me. His hands have gripped my hips so hard I'm sure there will be bruising there tomorrow, but I don't care. I'm so high from the experience—the exhibition, the pain, the binding, the pleasure. Everything is so new, so unexpected. So forbidden and alluring.

And he's right. He's put his mark on me, and I'm his, for good or ill. Knowing the Devil who dominates the halls of Obscura, I'm sure it is a lot of both.

CHAPTER 27
PRIVATE AFFAIRS

IS ORGASM DONE, HE COLLAPSES BRIEFLY AGAINST MY back, breath rushing hot and fast against the tender wound at my neck. Someone stands nearby us, and I see that it's a woman dressed in a silky black dress and matching feathery mask, a room attendant. She's holding a robe for me, and Domino stands, slipping it over my shoulders and whispering orders to her.

"Your personal aftercare room at once, Domino. Of course," she acquiesces with a wide smile while openly studying me like they all are. If this is Domino's first time bringing a woman here or participating, then they are as full of questions as I am. Just about different things, I suppose.

Devon helps me off the table and fits the robe over me properly while the attendant picks up my discarded costume, slips it into a black cloth bag and hands it to Devon after he zips up and has buckled his belt onto his waist.

Devon wraps a strong arm around my shoulder and pulls me flush against him. The move is decidedly possessive, almost as if he's afraid someone might deign to touch me.

He leads us out through a disguised door at the back of the room behind a hanging tapestry and some paneling. A secret doorway? I've never noticed anyone using this entrance either time that I've been in the room, but maybe it's only for founders.

On the other side is a dark hallway, dimly lit by an amber ambient glow, as if by lantern light, but there are no lanterns. The walls are painted dark and there are more doors here. Just as Devon has his hand on one of the handles, another figure emerges out of the dimness. A man dressed in fitted dark pants and a white button-down shirt left unbuttoned at the throat. Underneath that tailored shirt, I can tell he's all muscle. And he's wearing a very imposing-looking stag mask. As we move to walk past the stag, he stops to address Devon.

"Hey, Dom—who is this?" he asks, amusement in his tone. He has someone behind him—a woman wearing a bunny costume, her eyes cast to the ground. She must be his sub. "I don't think I've ever seen you here with anyone." His gaze flicks over me, a spark of heat in his eyes. "She's gorgeous."

Gorgeous, wow. I've never gotten a compliment like that before. Cute, sure. Maybe adorable. Devon has called me beautiful. But *gorgeous* is a whole new level, and I can only give full credit to the stunning costume and makeup. Honestly, Jemma could make a bridge troll look attractive. The girl has some serious talent.

Devon's strong arm snakes around my waist, his hand resting on my hip, pulling me against him possessively. "Hart, this is Angel," he answers, his tone flat and unreadable. "And you'll note the necklace, which means 'no touching.'"

I swallow, my muscles immediately tensing up, because I can't tell if Devon is joking or not.

A few tense seconds tick by before Hart's lips stretch into a smile, and he lets out a low chuckle that fills the confined space.

"I wouldn't *dream* of touching anything of yours, Dom. We all know your reputation."

I stiffen. *Reputation?* What does Hart know that I don't? I force a laugh and tilt my head to the side, attempting to appear calm and playful. "Oh, now I need to know. What reputation is that?"

Devon's hand squeezes my hip, his fingertips biting into my skin through the costume, and I remember with a jolt that I wasn't supposed to talk to anyone. It was one of the conditions of Devon bringing me to Obscura.

Whoops. But…sorry, not sorry.

Hart's enigmatic eyes shift to me. "Oh, you don't know?"

I blink and shake my head, almost imperceptibly. Maybe I shouldn't have asked. I have a feeling that whatever I'm about to hear, I'm better off *not* knowing. God, I'm such an idiot. Why am I asking questions I don't really want the answer to? I was perfectly content with the version of Devon I've come to know. Why fuck with a good thing?

Hart reaches over and slaps Devon on the shoulder. "Your man here is notorious for getting what he wants *when* he wants it. And anyone who comes between Dom and his goal…well, pray for them."

I release the breath I'd been holding. That, at least, I already knew. I mean, fuck, he was willing to kidnap me just to prevent me from running with a story he didn't like. I can only imagine the other things he's done—though I'm certain he'd never actually harm or kill anyone…I don't *think*, anyway.

Actually, no, I'm not certain about that.

A shiver rolls down my spine, and I let out an awkward little laugh.

Luckily, Devon speaks up so I don't have to, "Well, thanks for the lesson, Hart. You're an arsehole, as usual, for spilling all my secrets." The words are harsh, but I can tell Devon means them good-naturedly. Just guys tormenting each other. "If you'll excuse us, I have something I need to tend to."

Hart lets his hand drop. "Yup, no worries. Get to it, brother." His dark gaze falls to me, and I can't help but gulp. "It was nice meeting you, Angel."

My God, the stag is beautiful. I can see very little of his face, but if that jawline is any indication, his face beneath that mask is perfectly chiseled. Are all the men here at Obscura beautiful? Is it a requirement for membership or something?

Hart walks in the opposite direction with his mute bunny in tow as Devon pulls me into a small sitting room—a very *fancy* sitting room with dark filigree wallpaper and gold-plated wall sconces that let off very little light. It looks exactly like the sitting room a wealthy aristocrat from Victorian England would have, and I have the sneaking suspicion this is Devon's private domain within Obscura.

He closes the door and directs me to sit down. He takes off his mask, and I follow suit with mine as he walks over to a beautiful mahogany cabinet and takes something out. He takes a tube of something in hand and sits next to me on the leather sofa.

"Let me see your neck," he says, brushing the strands of my hair back.

I twist away from him a little, so he can get a better look at the back of my neck. He did bite down *really* hard, and even now, it stings. I'm sure he must have broken the skin.

"So, um question," I hedge.

"Yes?" He rubs a sweet-smelling ointment on my neck gently.

"Why do you have your own personal aftercare room if you never partake?" I ask.

He doesn't answer immediately. Instead, he finishes tending to the bite mark, then leans over and presses his lips to his bite mark. "I'm sorry to have injured you," he says with true regret in his tone. "I should never have allowed myself to get so out of control."

I turn to him, reaching up to cup his jaw. "You have nothing to be sorry for. I enjoyed your…*enthusiasm*."

He leans forward and places a kiss on the tip of my nose. "You're a miracle, Gwendolyn Taylor. I've never met anyone like you."

I can feel a blush rise to my cheeks, but I shake my head and laugh. "I see what you're doing. You're trying to distract me. But you haven't answered my question. If you've never partaken in what Obscura has to offer, or have never even privately taken a sub, then why do you have your own private aftercare room?"

He leans back a little, studying my face. Honestly, it's like he's never seen me before. His eyes rove over every detail, and I resist the urge to shy away.

"I created Obscura so people could explore their darkest desires without fear of judgment. And, when not in a committed relationship, I took the opportunity to explore my own." He gestures to the four walls around us. "I had this room built with the hope I would find someone I could share those dark desires with. But, until now, no one has come remotely close to catching my interest."

I laugh at the absurdity of that. "How can that possibly be true? This place is filled to bursting with gorgeous women—and any one of them would gladly submit to you, I'm sure."

The looks we get when we walk through Obscura are evidence of that. The women want him, and the men want to *be* him. Within the walls of Obscura, he's the master of the universe.

"I've been surrounded by beautiful faces my whole life," he says. "It takes more than physical beauty to tempt me. It takes a certain amount of fortitude and strength of character that I can't quite explain."

Warmth spreads through me at his words. He thinks I'm strong? That has to be the sweetest compliment anyone has ever given me. And I can see the depth of feeling in his steely gray eyes.

I lean forward, a smile tugging at my lips. "So, what you're saying is that you like me."

That makes him smile, too. And God, that smile makes my heart melt every single time. I wonder how I'll ever walk away from it. "Yes, I suppose that is exactly what I'm saying."

He takes a long moment to look over the markings the shibari rope and knots made on my skin. Already, most of them have faded but some still remain. He inspects them closely, as if to assure himself that they haven't broken the skin or they won't bruise. He takes a handful of my hair to move aside again and applies a different ointment, this one strongly smelling of mint. "Arnica cream," he says. "To minimize the bruising. I'm a little unhappy with you, Angel."

My spine stiffens, and I lift my head slightly to look at him. The tone of his voice was still light, but his expression is dead serious. "Why? What did I do?"

"It's what you didn't do. I gave you a safe word and you didn't use it. I—that is your safeguard in a situation like this. A Dom is never supposed to lose control, but you, as the sub, are the one in ultimate control. I was caught up in the moment, and that is completely on me. But you, Angel, you could have used the safe word when I did that."

"I didn't want to. I…" I shrug my shoulders. "I trusted you."

He reaches out a hand to smooth my cheek, the expression on his face one of pure appreciation. "You are brave, Gwendolyn. And trust is important. But never risk yourself like that again. We've just begun this journey, and it's likely you didn't notice my loss of control."

I frown, considering that. He'd started out dominant and progressed into overpowering, but I'd just found it incredibly arousing. He's talking as if he really feared for my safety—from him.

"This isn't a reprimand, Angel. It's a warning. Hopefully one you won't need to take heed of."

I quirk my brow, and he pulls me against him, kissing me on the forehead, the temple, the ear, the lips. His mouth lingers on mine in a steady and long affectionate kiss, even a passionate one, but one that isn't necessarily meant to incite passion. I get the sense that he's finally exhausted himself with me today. And given my own fatigue and achiness, I've done the same.

I could use a good hot soak and a comfy bed.

He gets up and goes back to the cabinet, then returns with a generic set of spa pajamas from Exeter House, a bottle of water, and some pain reliever.

"I want to keep a close eye on that. But I'll honor our boundaries. Will you come to my room tonight and sleep there?"

I arch a brow, tilting my chin up to look at him. He's seriously asking. And wait—what? His room? At *Exeter House*? Not the complex where he was holding me as captive?

Without a word, I nod. I don't want to be alone, and the thought of sleeping next to him, maybe even in his arms, is almost as alluring as having sex with him.

He smiles. "Very good. There is the matter of possible recognition from people you know when you're supposed to be in Hawaii. But there is a service elevator that will take us up to my penthouse. Naturally, you won't have free roam of the place, you understand."

I swallow and nod. I'd love to be able to write about my experiences, but my new laptop is back at the complex, wherever my holding cell is. In any case, I'm too tired so I'll write tomorrow when I get back there and have the time to do so.

Ten minutes later, he's escorted us down a very private hallway to a side entrance to his penthouse. One that opens from the outdoor patio that overlooks the darkened beach below.

I'd take a moment to admire the view and draw in the fresh ocean air, but I'm exhausted and really want to clean up and snuggle up with him.

He leads me through the luxurious rooms, asking if I'm hungry, and I shake my head. I can barely keep my eyes open as all the adrenaline that had pumped through me from the scene at Obscura is fading away.

Wordlessly, he pulls me into a steaming shower with him, and not long later, he's tucking me into his huge bed. I slide into the silky soft sheets, and when he comes around, he pulls me against him.

It takes me almost no time at all to fall asleep against his broad chest, where I'm held snug against him. Just as I'm about to fall asleep, I remember, as if from a distance, as if in a dream, that he's used a key to lock us inside the room.

Even now, he's taking no chances that I might get away.

CHAPTER 28
UP IN THE AIR

A FEATHER-LIGHT TOUCH TICKLES ME ON MY NECK AND chest. "Awake, Sleeping Beauty…or shall you only arise with a kiss?"

I crack an eye open. Devon has his head propped up on his hand and he's tickling me softly with his fingers. Just when they're about to slip under the sheets and find more intimate parts of me, I mutter, "A kiss, of course. If you can survive my morning breath, you can survive anything."

He laughs and bends over me, planting an affectionate kiss on my lips. Mmm. I roll over, wondering if I should beg a toothbrush off him before coming back to bed and demanding he actually wakes me up properly—with sex.

When I reach for him, I realize he's fully clothed. He's been up for a while, it seems. My eyes float to the huge beach-view windows. It's quite dim outside, just before or after dawn.

I frown. "What is it with you and mornings? Don't you like sleeping? What's wrong with you?"

"I have official business that requires a long flight."

I frown. He's leaving again? "Where?"

"It's Commonwealth-related business, in Belize."

I reach up to rub some sleep from my eyes. "When will you be back?"

"In three or four days. Maybe longer."

I stiffen. "What? That sucks!" I fold my hands tightly across my chest and scowl at him.

"Mmm. Yeah, it does suck…unless…" His fingers continue to idly move, tickling me across my chest.

I raise a brow. "Yes?"

"Unless you were to come with me."

I clasp my hands together in front of my face excitedly. "Really? No way!"

"Yes way," he says. In that beautiful accent, it sounds almost funny. "I already have a bag packed for you and a hot latte waiting in the car."

"Mmm, a latte sounds like heaven," I say, rolling out of bed. I stretch and rise to my feet, heading to the bathroom. To my surprise, there's a rose-gold electric toothbrush waiting for me, along with a few toiletries, and a makeup bag that Jemma must have put together for me. This man thinks of everything.

Too good to be true.

The words float through my mind, but I shove them aside. I have a habit of overthinking everything. It's what makes me a great journalist, but in life, I'm afraid it prevents me from really *living* life.

This is my opportunity to let loose, and I'm taking it. Today, I'm enjoying every second I can with Devon. Devouring every bit of happiness that I can.

Twenty minutes later, I'm dressed and ready. When I come out of the bathroom, Devon's hungry gaze flicks over my little cotton dress and sandals.

"You look delicious."

I laugh. "My one mission in life is to tempt you."

He licks his bottom lip. "Mission accomplished, then. It's too bad we don't have more time."

I push out my bottom lip, feigning sympathy. "Too bad, so sad."

Devon leads me down a service elevator to the parking garage where a blacked-out town car is waiting for us. The door is already open, and Devon presses his hand to the small of my back and guides me into the car quickly—I'm assuming so no one catches sight of me. I'm supposed to be in Hawaii, apparently.

As promised, there's a hot latte waiting for me, and I lunge for it. "Oh, bless you," I say, taking that first heavenly sip. "Can the perfect man exist? Maybe," I muse out loud.

He laughs. "So easily pleased."

I sink back against the backrest with the paper cup held between my hands. The drive to the private airport is only a half hour, and it goes by so quickly. When we arrive, there's a private jet waiting for us.

What the…?

I point at the plane we've parked in front of. "Is that for us?"

Devon is looking down at his phone, but he glances up and looks out the window. "Of course," he says matter-of-factly. "How else would we travel to Belize?"

I blink at him. "I don't know, a commercial airline?"

One side of his mouth quirks up. "At a private airport?"

I narrow my eyes at him. "I've never flown privately before."

He leans forward and takes my chin between his fingers. The heat in his gaze sends a shiver of awareness rolling down my spine. "Get used to it, Angel."

He shows me around the inside of the jet, and it is amazing—an honest-to-God fantasy. I've only seen planes like this in the movies. There are several luxurious white leather chairs and accompanying low tables, a couch lounge, a surprisingly large bathroom—complete with a shower. And in the very back of the plane, there's a full-sized *bedroom* with a king-sized bed, two comfy-looking chairs, and a huge television that's set into the wall. It's the epitome of luxury.

There are a few other people present. One woman, and two men, all dressed in business attire with laptops and various devices and notepads around them, set up like they're already at the office. Devon doesn't introduce me to them, and they barely look up at me. I wonder at that.

I noticed earlier that my prepared bag also had my new laptop in it so I might be joining them. Or...I might be napping in that giant bed after takeoff. It's fifty-fifty right now.

Unfortunately, we're instructed to strap into a chair for takeoff and Devon sits beside me. I sip from my latte, and he uncaps a water bottle. He then pulls out his phone to do some business while the flight readies for takeoff.

Less than a half hour after boarding, we're in the air, and it's only then that I realize I don't have my passport. I turn to ask Devon and he only looks up from his phone to inform me, in a quiet voice.

"I have connections with your country's passport control and expedited a copy of your valid passport for emergency travel."

I arch a brow at him. "Emergency?"

"Yes, it was an urgent case of needing you with me on this trip."

My mouth opens, and I stare openly at him as he appears slightly uncomfortable and throws a glance at his staff. I'd swoop in to give him a kiss, but it's clear he doesn't like PDA in front of his subordinates.

Not ten minutes later, he unbuckles and stands up, stretching. "Did you still want that nap? It's a six-hour flight…"

I pop up beside him, wondering if I might be too excited to take a nap. But who knows. I could use more sleep after yesterday's activities and this morning's early wake-up call.

Devon escorts me to the aft of the plane, where the bedroom is. His staff hardly seems to notice us. Or perhaps they're paid to be discreet and uncurious about their boss. Who can say?

"Wow, this plane is amazing," I squeak, kicking off my sandals and throwing myself onto the bed. I lay on my back like a starfish, before grabbing a pillow and pulling it under my head. I push out a long sigh. "This mattress feels like lying on a cloud. I could just stay right here like this for the entire flight."

Devon joins me on the bed, a satisfied smile on his beautiful mouth. "I'm glad you like it." He reaches over and brushes a strand of hair away from my face. "I've owned this plane for two years, but I've never used the bed. I think it may need a proper christening."

The fact that this bed has never been used makes me happier than I care to admit, even to myself. He's never had a submissive, but if the tabloids are to be believed, he gets a fair amount of ass. The fact that he hasn't brought them here pleases me.

I bite my bottom lip and sit up, leaning toward him. "What do you have in mind?"

He fucked me so hard yesterday, I'm still sore in places I never knew existed. But with Devon, I'm *always* game for more.

He brushes his lips along my mouth. "God damn, how did I get so lucky?"

"I don't know," I say playfully. "How *did* you get so lucky?"

There's a knock at the door, and with a groan, Devon stands up to answer. It's a flight attendant. "Champagne and strawberries, your lordship."

"Thank you, Sara." He takes the tray and closes the door, locking it behind him.

I sit up a little straighter. "Ohhhh, champagne, my favorite. Now, who's the lucky one?"

He sets the tray down on a coffee table that's situated between the two chairs. Then he straightens and turns toward me, arms crossed over his chest. "The champagne is yours," he says. "For a price."

I'm immediately intrigued. "Oh, a price? And what might that be?"

He just lifts a brow, like he's going to make me guess.

Rising up onto my knees, I find the hem of my cotton dress and pull it over my head, flinging it aside, then unhook my bra, and fling that aside as well. Now, I'm kneeling on the bed in only my panties.

His eyes skim down my face to my breasts, and I watch in real time as the bulge in his pants becomes more pronounced. He wants to tease me, does he? Well, two can play at this game. And given how things went yesterday, we seem to play together rather well.

He nods toward the door, still speaking in a low voice. "Be warned. These walls are thin and noise carries on a plane. So it goes without saying that you need to stay quiet. No matter what

I do to you. No matter how much you want to cry out. Is that understood?"

I blink my eyes, almost innocently, and feign a pout. "And what about you? Do you need to stay quiet as well?" I pause, and he seems to look puzzled. "I mean, when I do things to you?"

Something ignites behind his eyes. Intrigue, arousal. He rolls his lips into his mouth, considering. "What you do to me will be done by my command, little angel. Don't get any ideas."

I reach up and cup my breasts, my thumbs idly toying with my own nipples. His eyes gravitate to the action like iron shavings to a magnet. "What about what I do to myself? Will that be by your command, too?"

He licks his lips, and I can see that he's now fully erect. "Of course. I command, you obey. By now this should be clear to you."

I continue to stimulate my nipples, then tilt my head back and open my mouth, letting out a long sigh. Out of the corner of my eyes, I notice him sink into one of the chairs after angling it to face me.

He leans against the back cushion and stares at me with burning eyes. "Lie back on the bed, Angel, and pinch those nipples for me. Pinch them until they are red."

I swallow and stare at him in excitement tinged with shock. "You want me to hurt myself?"

His eyes narrow only slightly. "I want you to please me. And when you do what I say, you please me. No matter what it is. The trust you show me by obeying my commands brings me pleasure. Do you want to please me, Angel?"

I lie back once more against the soft faux-fur cushions. "I do."

And without another word, I pinch my own nipples hard. A burst of breath explodes from his chest, and it lights something in me. Between my own thumb and forefinger, I roll the beaded points mercilessly, opening my mouth to emit a charged breath but expelling no sound, as he commanded.

He shifts in his seat, rests his head in his chin, elbow perched on the arm of his chair. He watches me repeat the action for a few minutes, then sucks in a breath. "Spread those beautiful legs for me, Angel. Spread them wide."

Without missing a beat, I do as he says. His eyes settle on my panty-covered crotch. "Touch yourself there."

I move one of my hands to the mound between my legs, about to slip it under my panties when he tells me not to. So I rub myself over the top while continuing to stimulate my nipple. His gaze locks with mine again, and we're both breathing heavily.

His hand moves to the swelling below his belt, and he strokes himself through his pants. Shit. It's so hot I can barely contain myself.

"Keep your eyes on me, Gwendolyn. Who are you thinking of while you touch yourself?"

I blow out a breath. As if. What a question. "You."

He cocks a brow at me as if I'm supposed to elaborate on that.

"Only you, sir. I'm thinking about your hands and your mouth on my body."

He swallows, and his hand moves a little faster over the pronounced ridge in his pants. "Very good, Angel. You'll do everything I tell you to do, won't you? You'll do it even if you don't want to…because it pleases me. And you want nothing more than to bring me pleasure."

A cold stab of fear pierces me. What does he mean by that? What does he have in mind? I suck in a breath, lick my lips and nod.

"No nodding. Use words. Tell me."

"I want to pleasure you, sir. I want nothing more."

"Good." He rises up from the chair and walks to the edge of the bed. Looking down at me, I see a glint of something in his eyes—hunger. With his gaze still fixed on me, he unbuckles his belt and pulls it free with a *snap.*

I gulp at the sight of that belt he is holding loosely in his hand. I don't need to ask myself what he plans on doing with it—I already know. He's going to use it on me, and that thought terrifies me a little.

"You disobeyed me yesterday," he says. "You didn't think I would allow that to go unanswered, did you?"

I suck in a breath and search my memory. *Did* I disobey him? When? I honestly can't remember. But the denial won't form on my lips, so I just shake my head, completely mute.

"At Obscura. I explicitly told you not to speak to anyone."

Oh. Right. *Shit.* I spoke to the sexy stag, Hart.

"When I give you orders, Angel, it's for your own safety. It's vital that you do as you're told." He reaches out and touches the tip of his finger to the underside of my chin, lifting it up, so that I'm looking him directly in the eyes. "Any disobedience must be addressed; otherwise, I'm doing you a disservice."

My eyes dart to the belt in his hand, then back to his face. I lick my bottom lip. "I'm afraid."

I've never been whipped by a belt before, and I'm not quite sure what to expect. Pain, sure. But how much? And would he stop if I asked him to?

His thumb strokes my chin. "You know I would never truly harm you."

I nod.

"Do you trust me, Angel?"

I nod.

"What is the safe word?"

I swallow and recall the word he gave me last night. "Halt."

"Good. Use it this time, if you need it. My pleasure is nothing to your safety."

I nod again. "Okay."

I feel a bit easier about it knowing he's truly concerned for my safety. But anxiety is still coiled tight in my stomach. I suck in a deep breath and try hard to tamp it down.

"Turn over, on your knees," he commands.

I immediately do as I'm told. He smooths his hand down my back, his thumb applying pressure to my spine. Then he moves down to my hip, tugging the hem of my panties down—just enough to expose the cheeks of my ass.

"Five strokes. Are you ready?" he asks, dark arousal dripping from his tone.

I swallow and nod.

"Say it," he snaps.

"Y-yes. I'm ready."

"One." The belt comes down on my ass hard, and I yelp in surprise. He pauses, giving me time to adjust to the spark of fire moving across my skin. I squeeze my eyes shut and bite my bottom lip, but the pain isn't nearly as bad as I thought it would be. Maybe he's deliberately being more gentle than he normally would be.

"Two," he says a split second before the belt comes down on me again. This lash is a little sharper and a little more painful, but to my surprise, a hint of pleasure follows in its wake—a tingle of electricity that goes straight to the core of me.

"Three," he announces, but this one is so hard it rocks my entire body and brings tears to my eyes. Pain spreads across my skin like molten lava has been poured over me.

"Four." The crack of his belt fills the air and again comes down on me hard. I'm sure he's holding back for my benefit, but it's still so painful it leaves me breathless.

As he pulls his arm back to lay the final blow, I twist around and hold my arm up. "Wait," I sob. Then I remember the safe word. "Halt. *Please.*"

Chapter 29
Paradise

HE STOPS INSTANTLY, DROPPING THE BELT ONTO THE mattress, then gathering me up into his arms. The second he envelopes me with his large body, I break apart, my tears dissolving into sobs. But oddly, it's not about the belt or the pain. It's something that runs far deeper—the emotional impact of everything that's happened—the kidnapping, the sexual awakening, the freedom and vulnerability I feel with Devon…

"Shhh. Shhh," he soothes, rocking me back and forth gently. "It's okay. You did so well."

I soak him in as I lean against his chest—his warmth, the subtle scent of his cologne, the gentle beat of his heart. If I could just stay like this forever, I would be the happiest woman in the world. I feel so safe, protected…*cherished*. A feeling I've never experienced with a man.

I pull back a little to look at his face. He smiles down at me, wiping the tears away from my face with the pad of his thumb, and I suck in a stuttering breath. "I'm sorry," I say. "I didn't—"

He places his finger over my mouth, stopping me. "You did amazing."

I laugh a little under my breath. "Hardly." My gaze drops to his crotch, and I can see the very prominent ridge of his cock straining against the fabric.

I lick my lips and reach for his zipper, but he catches my wrist, stopping me. Then he brings my hand up and brushes his lips along my knuckles. "There will be plenty of time for that later. You need time to recover."

I swallow back my disappointment as his hand drops and he places a gentle kiss on the tip of my nose. I could push the issue, but I can see the resolve in his eyes. My needs come before his, apparently, and he's not going to touch me until he knows my body is ready.

The rest of the flight is the epitome of leisure. After smoothing ointment over my backside, I throw on some comfortable—and loose—clothes, and we spend the rest of the flight curled up in bed, sipping champagne and watching action movies.

We're forced to take our seats for landing a few hours later, but the excitement of seeing Belize is worth crawling out of our mile-high oasis. As soon as we land, we're swept away by a private car and taken to the resort—which, my God, is incredibly gorgeous. There are exquisitely decorated lounges, restaurants, bars, shops and beautiful swimming pools in the public areas. It's a luxury village tucked into a tropical forest.

Devon takes my hand in his as we're led to our private thatched-roof cabana. The staff is waiting for us there—a butler, a concierge, and a maid—all smiling and welcoming.

Once we're alone, I tour the small cabana, peeking into every room. There's a sitting room, a kitchenette, a gorgeous bathroom, a bedroom with french doors, and a patio perched on the cliff face, suspended over a crystal-blue ocean. Here, there's a private hot tub and infinity plunge pool and stairs that lead down to the beach.

It's perfect and so secluded it feels like we're on an island all alone.

Devon meets me in the bedroom. "Do you approve?"

I nod casually, glancing around. "It'll suffice," I say sarcastically.

He laughs and pulls me into his arms. "Good. Now for the bad news, I have an event in an hour. Will you be okay on your own?"

"Yeah, I think I'll be fine," I laugh.

He kisses the tip of my nose. I've noticed he likes doing that. "Good girl. Just a couple of rules: you're welcome to explore the resort, but do not, under any circumstances, leave the premises."

"Okay," I say, nodding. No problem, I have no interest in leaving, anyway. There's way too much to explore.

"And remember, don't tell anyone your name. Gwendolyn Taylor is back in the States."

"Okay, then what's my name while I'm here?"

"If you must give your name, tell them it's Angel," he says with a smile.

I smile at the meaning of it. He's called me Angel since we met. I raise a brow. "No last name?"

"No last name."

I shrug one shoulder. "Okay, like Beyoncé. Sure."

"Anything you want, just charge it to me. I've already informed them you have *carte blanche*."

Carte blanche. Wow. At a resort like this, that's no small thing. A bottle of water here probably costs half my rent.

"Lastly, you aren't to be photographed. I know security cameras are one thing you won't be able to control, but no optional tourist photographer, no being included in selfies, no photos."

I nod. Makes sense.

"Thank you," I say with a smile. I thread my fingers through his and pull him toward the bathroom. The giant tub is actually outside, on an open-air deck that overlooks the ocean, and I'm dying to take it for a spin. "Now, um, you probably want to take a bath. You know, to get ready for your event. So you're all squeaky clean."

He laughs, allowing me to lead him. "Dear God, I've created a monster."

I glance over my shoulder at him, batting my eyelashes. Ever since the airplane, and seeing the erection he was sporting, I've been hot and ready. My gaze darts to his crotch, and I lick my bottom lip. I can't help it. "You only have yourself to blame."

Once I fill the tub with hot water, we both strip off our clothes and climb in. I take my time washing his hard body with the sweet-smelling soap that's sitting next to the tub. Once he's completely clean, I reach under the water and take his cock in hand, slowly stroking him. He lets his head fall back onto the lip of the tub, and I smile to myself. I love this power I have over him, giving him pleasure, making his large, imposing frame tremble beneath my hand.

Just when I think he's close to the edge, I climb on top of him, riding his rigid cock. We moan in unison, and he grabs my hips, forcing me to hurry my pace. We've been craving each other since the plane, which just feeds into the urgency and desperation we both feel. In just a few seconds, we're both coming, screaming out. We're outside, and God only knows who can hear us, but we can't be seen. And honestly, I don't care.

Our week in Belize passes in a sort of dream. In the mornings, he usually wakes me up early for sex of one flavor or another. He likes waking me up by going down on me and giving me a brain-frying orgasm before fucking me hard against the headboard or pulling me onto my knees in front of him. Then he's out the door for morning meetings while I lounge around watching shows on streaming and eating breakfast in bed. Or soaking in an impossible amount of bubbles in the outdoor tub and eating there with a spectacular tray of fruits and pastries brought right to me.

He comes back for lunch and we eat together. It's all secluded and domestic. His afternoon meetings are the times when I spend either shopping in the brightly lit shops or walking along the soft white powdered beach for miles, dipping my toes in the warm Caribbean water.

The evenings are for glam. We dine at the finest restaurants on the resort—there are seven, one for every night we're to stay, and I look forward to trying them all. He's dressed semi-casually—for him, anyway—in Caribbean-style linen suits to suit the heat. I'm usually in a cocktail dress with matching shoes and always wearing the snake necklace clamped around my throat at his insistence. I like it, actually, especially the fact that it matches his tattoo of a tiny coiled snake.

When I first noticed it, I was taken aback. I didn't realize that members of the royal family could get tattoos, but then, it was rather foolish of me. How many of them had I ever seen photographed in small amounts of clothing? I guess illicit beach pictures of the Prince and Princess of Wales were as close as it got—or should get, anyway. Besides, the press seldom paid much attention to minor royals like Devon.

Which definitely put him in a very desirable position of being immensely privileged while living a luxurious life cloaked in relative anonymity. A very powerful position to be in.

After drinks, sometimes dancing, we come back to the bungalow and spend hours making love. Sometimes vanilla, but more often we start out rougher, harder while playing out some scene dictated by his desires. I'm slowly growing as addicted to the pain he inflicts as he once told me he was addicted to the taste of my tears.

At night, when he stands over me and orders me onto my knees or bent over the bed, my heart rate jumps and the shot of adrenaline through my system lifts our lovemaking to a whole new level. Multiple orgasms every night before we finally fall onto the sheets exhausted, tangled in each other's arms, our skin sweat-fused together.

Sometimes, we discuss the content of his meetings. He's here on official Commonwealth business but also has humanitarian efforts working in the country that are fully funded by his foundation.

One night, he tells me all about it as he feeds me chocolate. We're on the back deck looking out over the ocean and the shimmering small pool. He's sitting on the double lounger in his underwear, and I'm completely naked with my head in his lap. A warm breeze caresses my skin everywhere, and the incessant sound of the sea provides the backdrop to our conversation. His other hand traces the red rope marks made by his silk rope, his skillful knots and ties, binding me all over my body. Just a little while earlier, he'd spent nearly an hour using the beautiful shibari knotwork to bind my hands behind my back, my head to my knees with my legs apart. And he kept me tied the entire time that he rode me roughly with his huge cock while I came three times.

No wonder we're feeling the slight edge of fatigue. We've been wearing each other out in the most pleasurable of ways. And for now, at least, we were basking in the fresh afterglow of great sex. Until it all inevitably starts again in a half hour or so.

I swallow the sweet, juicy bite of chocolate-covered strawberry he offers me. "How long has your foundation been working to rebuild the homes?"

"The hurricane wiped out over four hundred homes last season. The relief organization has been working nonstop on the cleanup and rebuilding efforts. Our financial backing has allowed them to increase their rate of restoration by nearly sixty percent. Of course, there's a deadline. The end of the summer will bring more hurricanes, most likely."

"Let's hope not as bad as the last one."

He's staring out at the ocean, the sky dimly lit just above it from a sunset of over an hour ago. He idly runs the back of his knuckle along my cheek. "Even so, these homes will be of better quality and materials than the ones they were able to originally build, so hopefully they'll withstand the weather better."

I blink, thinking about all the details he handles, the way in which he's hands-on with his foundation's projects. It reminds me of all that Jemma told me when she sang his praises. I'd thought she'd been overdoing it, but the more I hear about his work, the more I'm inclined to believe her.

And the more I get to know him, the more I'm inclined to understand just where her admiration comes from.

I lift my head from his lap and snuggle into his side. "You are pretty damn impressive, do you know that, Lord Devon Howard?"

He chuckles. "Never call me that again. But call me *master* again."

He traces my lips with his fingers, and I turn to deliberately suck one of them deep into my mouth. I look up at him, my eyes drooping with desire.

"Master. *Lord* and Master," I breathe once he's slowly slid his finger out.

He sucks in a ragged breath. "Fuck, I'm hard again." He pulls me against him and starts to kiss me. At first, it's mere affection, but then he deepens the kiss and my heart starts to race with a raggedy rhythm, leading me to believe we're in store for more fun very soon.

"Ah, my God, Gwendolyn, you are very dangerous, do you know that? A man could very easily become addicted to these lips. Perhaps I already have."

I quirk a brow at him and then palm his rock-hard cock through the silky boxers. Mmm. It's still early, and though the first round only ended a little while ago, maybe we'll hit a triple crown tonight?

He leans in and kisses me more passionately still, his tongue and lips possessing my mouth utterly.

As I'm reaching into his underwear to pull out his cock and begin pumping it slowly in my hand, his phone rings. I grip him tightly as he groans.

"Let it go to voicemail," I say, then bend down to lick the crown of his erection.

He threads his fingers through my hair and curls them, pulling against my scalp. I moan, and the phone goes silent. My lips close in around the head of his cock, and my tongue slides down the shaft.

As I'm about to slide my head even lower, the phone rings again.

This time, maddeningly, he answers it—while his cock is still in my mouth. So I do my best to punish him for that fact by sliding even lower. Then I begin sucking, and I feel his hips flex toward me, almost automatically.

"Is this urgent?" he answers tersely into the phone. There's a long silence as I continue my work, licking him like a candy cane.

As the silence stretches, his fingers go slack in my hair, and he withdraws his hand. A moment after that, he's nudging my head away.

"Tell me everything you know." His voice is different now, darker, with an underlying level of stress.

Another beat, and he's getting up from the lounge and pacing while I sit back and watch him. A cool post-sunset breeze rises off the ocean and caresses my naked body as I watch him. He's tense and definitely not happy with whatever he's being told on the other end of the call.

I guess that means no triple crown tonight unless I get a chance to take his mind off of whatever the bad news is later.

After a few minutes, he leaves his pacing on the patio to go inside the bungalow. I can only hear scraps of conversation from here, but he's demanding answers from the other person, one after the other. When I finally give up waiting for him and go inside to find my new silky kimono-style robe, he's bent over a desk in the study scribbling notes on the notepad.

I'm contemplating either a hot steam shower or a soak in the Jacuzzi with a new book when he enters the bedroom. I turn to him, and his face is grave.

I blink. *Who died?*

"What's wrong?" I finally squeak out after a long stretch of silence between us.

He rubs his jaw and looks at me with that strange expression. It's a mixture of concern, dread and…pity?

"What's wrong?" I repeat again, this time a little bit louder.

He swallows and holds out his arm to me. "Come here, Angel. I have something to tell you."

I blink. "What?" I say almost breathlessly, cold fear clawing its way up my throat. Something's happened. Something bad.

He's at my side in an instant, instead of expecting me to come to him. He pulls me into his arms and then tight against him.

"I've made arrangements to fly us back to the States at once. There's been an accident. Your mother is in hospital."

I'm so glad he's holding me because when the news registers, my knees buckle. *Mom?* Oh my god…

I pull away and look into Devon's eyes. "Is she okay?"

God, please tell me she's okay. Instead, he just shakes his head. "I don't know. They're working on her now."

They're *working on her?* I swallow a sob and fall back against his chest. He allows me to cry for a few minutes, rubbing my back and rocking gently. Finally, I suck in a deep breath and straighten, wiping away the tears. I need to get there. I need to get to the hospital.

Pushing to my feet, I start frantically tossing things on the bed to pack up, so we can leave. Tears still streaming down my face, I dart in and out of each room, gathering all of our personal things until finally, Devon captures me in a hug. "You don't need to pack, Angel. My staff will do that. Go find some clothes to put on. We'll leave for the airport immediately."

I swallow and nod stiffly.

Somewhere in the emotional haze, I manage to throw on a pair of jeans and a T-shirt with a pair of white sneakers. I'm in a kind of haze as I move through each task—getting dressed, getting into the car, going through exit immigration, boarding Devon's private jet…

Chapter 30
Dumbfounded

I'M BACK ON DEVON'S PLANE. IT'S JUST HIM AND ME THIS time, and his pilot has registered a longer flight plan than the one we would have flown the day after tomorrow back to Los Angeles. It's the middle of the night, and we are somewhere over the Gulf of Mexico and on our way to New Brunswick, New Jersey, my hometown.

I'm staring off into space, with nothing to say, nothing I want to do. My mind keeps rolling over and over again back to that news, and I'm filled with sick, nauseating worry. The only thing anchoring me to the here and now, this moment is the large hand that's been wrapped around mine for hours. Even while he does work on his tablet, he hasn't taken that hand away from me. And every so often, it squeezes mine in silent reassurance.

In the frenzied drive to the airport from the resort in Belize, Devon had filled me in on all that he knew.

Mom, in the hospital. Hit-and-run accident while out for a leisurely walk. It's so strange that I can't picture it. Who would run over a middle-aged registered nurse during a sedate afternoon stroll? And why would they drive away after doing it?

It sounds like something freakish and unreal, like something out of a bad mafia movie. I can't even wrap my head around it. My sister is at school in Florida, and Mom has no one else.

She's fiercely independent and doesn't need anyone, she'd be the first to tell anyone, but at a time like this... My heart hasn't stopped racing. I squeeze Devon's hand and pull it into my lap and don't say a word until the plane lands and we are quickly on the way to the hospital.

When we pull up in front of the hospital doors, Devon takes my hand and brushes a kiss along my knuckles. "I'll give you time with your mom, but I'll be waiting right here."

I smile tightly. "No, I'm sure you've got a million things to do. Don't worry about me. Really. I'll probably be here for a while."

I can see the reluctance in his eyes. He wants to stay with me, and I'm sure he'd be at my side every step of the way if I asked him to be, but I need to be alone now. I can't think about anything other than Mom and getting her through whatever obstacles await.

He nods. "I'll arrange for a driver and a room for you nearby. I'll text you the details."

"Thank you," I say quietly. "You are too good to be true."

That makes him smile. He hands me a phone—which I'm guessing is a burner phone—and a manila envelope. "Your passport and ID. The phone already has my number programmed into it. Just promise me you won't reach out to your friends, as we've agreed. Our situation is still...delicate. I'm trusting you."

Delicate.

I'd ask him what he means by that, but honestly, my thoughts are on my mom and making sure she's okay. So I just nod and kiss him quickly. "I'll call you," I say.

Once I'm inside the hospital, I'm directed to the Intensive Care Unit, where Mom is hooked up to a dozen different machines. A sob catches in my throat at the sight of her. She's unconscious, and when the doctor comes in a half hour later, he explains the extensive injuries she suffered—a broken collarbone, broken pelvis, a head injury, and several internal lacerations.

"We have her sedated," the doctor says. "We'll monitor her over the next couple of days, and if she shows improvement, then we can slowly wean her off the sedatives."

The next couple of days are hell, and I spend every second I can at her side—only going to the luxury hotel Devon booked for me to sleep. My driver, Nick, is really nice, and he pretty much just sits in the hospital parking lot all day, waiting around in case I want to go anywhere. I get the distinct feeling, though, that he's not just here to drive me around—he's here to watch me and report back to Devon.

On the fourth day, the medical staff feels confident enough in mom's improvement that they bring her out of sedation.

"Hi, baby," she says with a weak smile. Then she glances around and looks genuinely confused. "Where am I? What happened?"

I explain everything, relief washing over me. It's going to be a long road to recovery, but she'll be okay...eventually.

"They caught the guy that ran you over," I say. Devon called me yesterday to tell me—and I can't help but wonder if he had something to do with the swift capture of the asshole.

That afternoon, while mom's being transferred out of the Intensive Care Unit, I ask Nick to take me back to the hotel so I can nap and wash up before heading back over to the hospital.

After my shower, I'm lying on my bed, wondering what my friends are up to. I promised Devon I wouldn't contact my friends—but I never said I wouldn't check up on them via social media. I log into my Instagram, and there are literally hundreds of messages, notifications and likes waiting for me.

Confused, I scroll through the comments.

So jealous. You're really living the life!

You look great, girl! I love Hawaii. Have a great trip!

I'm living for your glam travel posts!

My glam travel posts? I continue scrolling through the comments, and they all say pretty much the same thing. *What the fuck?*

I switch over to my profile and...holy shit. There are fifty or more posts that I *didn't* make, all with my happy, smiling face in gorgeous, exotic locations. Hawaii, according to the caption.

I sit up in bed and scroll through the fictitious posts. An entire fucking story has been created—a whole new life. Me and some random dude at dinner, at the beach, *hiking* up the side of a volcano. I've never hiked a day in my *life.*

This has to be Devon's doing. No one else could possibly pull something like this off. Now all the photo shoots in front of the green screen after my kidnapping make sense. My face and body was superimposed onto these photographs, and it is so seamless no one would ever know it's not me.

My mind is racing, and it takes several long minutes to process or even fathom…

How. Fucking. *Terrifying.*

It's obvious this isn't Devon's first time completely recreating a fictional life. And if he's willing to go to these lengths to explain my absence and cover his tracks, then what else is he capable of? Especially to cover for himself—along with his family?

My blood runs cold in my veins.

And if he's capable of these manipulations, what other, darker things is he capable of?

Over the next few days, as I oversee the beginning of Mom's recovery, and make arrangements about her house, her job, and all her follow-up appointments, I play nice with Devon over text, even faking through a few video calls.

When he asks me what's wrong, I tell him the truth—I haven't been sleeping well. And I've made sure that those calls were short.

And, knowing that Mom will be in the hospital and follow-up full-time care for at least a month and a half, I make my own arrangements to bolt back to California and get my own life in order. My *real* life.

The glam life splashed across my social media account reeks of more than just a story to explain my absence. There's a whole underlying feeling of cover-up or even set-up underneath that. As if Devon has been using this as his insurance should I ever decide I want to violate the NDA and talk about being abducted by force. By him.

Everything on here feels like it might even be an attempt to buy me off and undermine my credibility. An insurance plan, yes, but also a complete fucking re-write of my life.

With a cold determination, I begin planning my escape—from Devon's watchdog and from this entire fucking gilded trap I've been enjoying far too much.

That changes now.

As it turns out, just after midnight, I'm on a plane back to LA. It's a red-eye flight which, hopefully, will prevent the discovery that I'm missing until long after I've landed and left the airport on the other end.

The day before departing, I spend part of the morning with Mom at the hospital. She's provided me with a list of things that she would like and I have a few other errands to run for her, which include stopping by Mom's house to pick up some things.

Nick always waits politely outside in the car. It takes me a moment to gather the items she asked for. A few nightgowns, her warm house robe, some slippers, a few books, her tablet and chargers. While I'm there, I take advantage of Mom's desktop computer and, borrowing her credit card number, I buy myself a plane ticket back to LAX for late this evening.

My sister is coming up from Florida tomorrow, so Mom won't be alone. It's the perfect time for me to head back to California.

Because Devon has left me all my documents, the travel arrangements are all very easy to do, and traveling will only require me to slip by Nick, get to the airport, and get on the plane.

When visiting hours end at 9 p.m., Nick takes me back to the hotel, as usual. I head up to my room, and before we say goodnight, we agree on heading over to the hospital at 10 a.m. tomorrow. I'll be in California by then, obviously, but he doesn't need to know that.

An hour later, I slip downstairs to the lobby and ask the front desk to call me a taxi. I purposefully leave my phone upstairs, in case it has a tracker. In fact, I'm sure it does. It feels like an appendage is missing, but I can make it a few hours without a phone until I get back to California.

Then I meet the taxi at the curb to take me to the nearby train station. And as I still have my valid New Jersey transit pass, it's just a matter of hopping on the next train to the Newark airport.

I have only a shoulder bag with me and no luggage, so things go smoothly at the airport. Two hours after leaving the hotel, at nearly midnight, I'm boarding a plane to LAX. Simple as that.

By the time Nick knocks on my door to take me to the hospital in the morning, I will be safely at Hill House where I can figure out my next step.

The awkward part is arriving on my front doorstep at four-thirty in the morning, California time. I hadn't thought that far ahead and as I don't have my key—or any of my other possessions with me—I can't let myself in.

So I sit on the front step of Hill House and wait for my roommates to start stirring. I watch the sky gradually lighten and run through the craziness of these past three weeks of my life.

If it were the weekend, I could be waiting outside for hours. But it's a Tuesday, so my first roomie to pop out the door with the usual spring in her step is Avery.

I should have known. She's the early bird of the house and is usually out the door by seven, even when she doesn't have an early class.

She freezes, and her eyes widen when she notices me. "Gwen? Holy crap. You're back!"

My entire body aches. With all the anxiety of this "escape" back to my old life, I haven't slept all night. Only Sam is up thankfully, and I beg off giving them any details by telling them I'm exhausted.

I give them each a hug and promise I'll tell them more tonight.

Then I quickly sneak upstairs, take a quick shower and fall into bed between my sheets, exhausted, relieved and so uncertain about what I'm going to do next.

CHAPTER 31
THE HARD TRUTH

I SLEEP THROUGH TUESDAY ENTIRELY, WAKING UP ONLY long enough to pee and eat some of Avery's yogurt, then go back to sleep. When I finally get out of bed, it's late Wednesday morning.

My first order of business is a shower and breakfast—which Avery, again, lovingly donates. I'll have to get to the grocery store at some point.

A bit later, there's a knock on my bedroom door.

"Come in," I say, shrugging on a hoodie.

The door opens to reveal Cassie on the other side. With a tight smile, she holds up my phone—the one I lost while being kidnapped outside Exeter House all those weeks ago.

"I thought you might want this," she says. "I charged it for you."

I take it from her and sit back on the bed. "Thanks."

Cassie lowers herself onto the mattress next to me. "I should be pissed at you," she says. "When you just took off without saying anything, you really freaked us out."

I shake my head. "I'm really sorry about all that." I struggle with whether or not I should tell Cassie the truth. I mean, why not? I don't need to protect Devon anymore, do I? There's that

NDA I signed, but I'm pretty sure signing something like that under duress isn't legally binding. I guess the problem is proving I was even kidnapped in the first place.

As, apparently, was his plan. And I played right into it.

In the end, it's just too much to get into right now, so I decide on confessing everything some other time—when I'm more emotionally prepared.

Cassie narrows her eyes, suspicion and concern written all over her face. "There's one thing I don't get, though…"

I shrug and arch my brow at her. "What's that?"

"Why would you leave Exeter House, and hop on a plane to Hawaii without your shoe or your phone? That's….not exactly normal."

I suck in a breath, prepared to repeat that story about being drunk off my ass and not realizing I was missing my phone until the next morning when I woke up next to a hot guy in Hawaii. But right now, I don't have it in me to lie.

"You are such a good friend," I say. "And I appreciate you more than you know. A lot happened that night, and I can't really get into it now, but just know…I'm okay. Everything is okay."

That's not entirely true. My heart is fucking shattered, actually. Everything I thought I knew about Devon was just an illusion. The man I fell in love with is probably just a fictional character that he invented to get what he wanted—*me, my silence, my submission, and probably even more.*

"I love you, Gwen." She smiles softly. "I'm here whenever you're ready to talk."

Cassie has always been more sensitive and observant than the others. It doesn't surprise me that she was able to pick up on things that didn't quite add up.

"Thanks. Love you, too."

When Cassie leaves, I lie back on my bed and turn my phone on. It starts pinging like crazy—mostly messages from my friends, asking about my crazy, impulsive trip and wanting details about the hot guy I was with.

And then I see them—the texts from Devon.

Nick said you dodged him this morning. We found your other phone at the hotel. Where are you?

He must have been desperate if he was texting me on a phone he knew I didn't have with me.

Gwendolyn. Answer me. Now. Your sister said you were back in California. Pick up your phone.

Fuck. Did he speak to my sister? Jeezus. Does this guy even know what boundaries are? Damn, Devon really does just walk through life, taking what he wants, causing destruction to follow in his wake. Without a thought, probably even without a care.

I'm making my way through the rest of his texts when I hear someone thundering up the main staircase. Avery comes bursting into my room—without even knocking. Rude.

"Gwen," she says, breathless, hanging on the door. "Oh, my God. Get some clothes on, and come downstairs right now. Someone is here for you."

Cassie comes up behind Avery, peeking her head in. "Did you tell her?" she asks Avery.

"Of course I did," she says, exasperated. "Do you think I'm just up here for my health when there's an *actual* member of the British royal family standing awkwardly in our foyer?"

My heart leaps into my throat.

Holy shit.

He's here? *Now?*

In the back of my mind, I knew this was bound to happen. Devon isn't the kind of guy who will just walk away—especially after everything that's happened between us. I supposedly "owe" him another week, and I'm sure he's here to demand it. To lure me back into his fictional world.

Yeah, *fuck that.*

"Tell him I'm not here."

Avery purses her lips. "Haley already kinda told him you were here."

"And why wouldn't you want him to know you're here?" Cassie asks, all that sensitive intuition from earlier evaporating with one look at the high-and-mighty Lord Devon Howard. She's practically foaming at the mouth. "My God, Gwen. He's fucking hot, and he's a goddamn royal."

I consider asking them to distract him while I sneak out the back, but I know my running away isn't going to solve anything. He'll just keep coming, demanding answers.

I push out a breath and stand up. "Okay, tell him I'll be down in a second."

They rush off, and I take my time brushing out my hair, then throw some leggings on. I look like absolute shit, but whatever— this is what he gets.

I walk downstairs on semi-unstable legs to a gaggle of my housemates, all peppering Devon with questions. I hear his deep baritone before I see him, leaning against a beam in the foyer, patiently answering all their questions. But as my foot hits the bottom step, the wood creaks and Devon looks up. Our gazes collide, and I pause mid-step, my heart in my throat.

"Hey," I say, lifting my chin.

His gaze flicks over me, as though assuring himself I'm okay. I can see the concern written all over his face, and it gives my heart a little pang.

Don't get sucked back in, Gwen.

I clear my throat, which snags the attention of my housemates. "Thanks, guys. Can you give us a second?"

"Sure," a couple of them say in unison. They slowly, if reluctantly, clear the room.

Once everyone has filed out, I walk over to the front door and open it. "Outside," I say stiffly. "We won't get any privacy otherwise. They're all listening at the door."

With a stiff nod, he follows me outside, onto the porch. I cross my arms over my chest, steeling myself inwardly. Just standing within two feet of Devon is doing things to me. I have to fight the overwhelming urge to lean against him and sink into the comfort of his arms.

Damn, this is hard.

I glance down at my socked feet. "What are you doing here?"

He doesn't answer me. Instead, he asks his own question. "Why did you flee New Jersey?"

I shake my head, not daring to look up into his beautiful gray eyes. "You created a whole new life for me online. You rewrote my entire story."

He pushes out a breath, and from the corner of my eye, I can see him shift on his feet. "Christ, I knew this would happen. This is precisely why I told you not to contact your friends. Things would get twisted before I had a chance to explain."

I look up at him then. "I didn't contact my friends," I say defensively. "I logged onto my social media feed and saw my face plastered all over it—laughing, having fun in Hawaii with"—I lift my arm in exasperation—"some random guy I've never seen before in my life."

"We needed to explain your absence—"

"*We?*" I interrupt, fury in my tone. "We? Oh, no. *You.* You needed to explain my absence, so shit didn't get complicated for you."

"Angel—"

"No, you don't get to call me that," I say, finding my voice. I swallow back a sob. "I thought what we had was real. But now I know, it was all just fucked up—a twisted little sick little fairy tale, designed by you to keep me quiet."

Devon takes a step toward me. "Gwendolyn, *no.* That's not what this is." He reaches out for me, but I lift my arm and take another step back, evading his grasp.

I narrow my eyes at him. "Oh, no? Then let me ask you something—you had my signed NDA. You had this very elaborate and thorough explanation for my absence. Why did you keep me captive? Why didn't you tell me everything, then give me the choice to stay or leave?"

He sinks back, and his eyes soften in defeat.

"Yeah," I say. "That's what I thought. You didn't have to hold me prisoner past the first few days until I signed the papers. But you did anyway, regardless of what it was going to cost me."

"You enjoyed yourself..." he says.

I shake my head. "Devon, we're done. This whole fictional recreation of my life just opened my eyes to the fact that you will stop at nothing to get what you want. Kidnapping. Threats. Manipulation. And I don't want to be a part of it. I'm a journalist because I believe in the truth. I believe in transparency." He opens his mouth to speak, but I interrupt. "So let me be transparent with you now. You and me, we're not a thing. I want you to leave me alone."

"Gwen—"

I hold my hand up as I open the door and slip inside, shutting the door behind me and throwing the lock. I lean against the thick plank of wood, sucking in several sharp breaths, trying to keep the tears at bay.

Avery and Sam come out of the kitchen, their faces full of questions. I just shake my head. "If he comes to the door again, send him away, I will not see him. Ever again." Then I dart up the staircase.

The next few days are rough. I get regular updates from New Jersey. Mom is doing better, thank God. I'm stressed but happy to hear it and wishing I can be there while relieved I'm three thousand miles away at the same time. In addition, I spend nearly every waking moment crying, mourning the relationship I thought I had with Devon. It was the first time in my life I felt seen and understood, like I was exactly where I was meant to be—with Devon, exploring our dark desires.

Learning to let that go has been heartbreaking, and I'm not doing a great job of it, honestly. Most nights, I just lie awake, thinking about Devon—about what we had together in such a short amount of time, whether it was fake or not.

It was real to me.

Chapter 32
Obligations

THE FOLLOWING MONDAY, I START GETTING CALLS AND emails from editors of several prominent journals, asking me to freelance for them. Apparently, my name was mentioned as the only journalist who will be given access to certain members of the royal family as well as covering certain events related to them.

I'm completely stunned. Some of the names I see in these contacts are names that Devon showed me during that first meeting in his office...

It's an honor and, quite naturally, something that will put me in high demand. But I find myself hesitating to reply to any of them. I know Devon is behind this, and I feel weird about accepting anything from him, even if doing so would make a massive difference in my career.

On Tuesday, when I get home from a research session at the library, I sort through the mail on the table in the foyer and notice an envelope addressed to me in Devon's handwriting. I rip it open, heart in my throat. It's an invitation to a fundraising gala this Saturday for one of Devon's foundations.

I push out a breath and toss the invitation back down onto the table. "Thanks, but no, thanks."

There's no fucking way I'm attending that gala.

Meanwhile, my editor, Maura, contacts me about the follow-up meeting with her that I've been dreading. But it can no longer be avoided. When it happens, I very reluctantly admit that I'm empty-handed. And I have no good reason to explain why I need to drop Obscura from the now hollowed-out sex club story.

She is obviously less than pleased about it.

Her face clouds. "What have you been doing with all this time, then? I assigned you the straightforward sex club story. You were the one who pitched to me, saying you were on to some sketchy stuff going down at Obscura. Now you're saying you have nothing? Did someone shake you down or something?"

I stare at her wide-eyed. If only she knew. I open my mouth to take a breath, but before I can get a word in, she looks up from the notes on her desk and pins me down with a laser-sharp stare. "Maybe it was all that partying you were doing in Hawaii. If you didn't want to take this internship seriously, then why are you here?"

I take another deep breath as my heartbeat races. I'm irritated and also mortified that she thought I was blowing her off to go jet-set with the privileged on a tropical island.

Even if some of that was partly true for a little while, anyway. If Belize were an island, that is.

"I–I'm sorry. But as I got deeper into things, I found out that I was wrong. My hunch was totally off, and I couldn't find anything. However, I do have an angle that I can salvage from my research, and I don't think it would take me very long to write."

Maura's dark brows rise over still-skeptical eyes. "Oh? And what angle is that?"

"I, uh…I was thinking about making it a bit more personal. About a, um, a journey of sexual self-discovery."

She stares at me without blinking, but I see something in her eyes that gives me hope. "Tell me more."

I gesture with my hand. "I was thinking about…describing what it's like for a young person who's only ever been into vanilla sex to discover taking pleasure in dominance and submission, as a submissive."

She blows out a frustrated breath. "Oh, BDSM, that kind of thing was done to death when the *Fifty Shades of Grey* movies came out. That's well-tread ground."

"But…from a self-avowed feminist who actually found the idea of submission repulsive beforehand?"

She tilts her head and studies me, a spark of interest in her eyes, and I want to die from embarrassment. She's probably picturing me kneeling at my master's feet, hands behind my back with a collar on. Ugh.

"I like that. But you could go deeper and talk about what it means to be a feminist, a modern woman, and to also enjoy being a submissive if you look for a way to examine and explain that dichotomy."

We discuss the idea and brainstorm for another twenty minutes while I take careful notes before she assigns me a deadline two weeks away. And I try not to let it show on my face or body language how panic-stricken that short deadline makes me.

I've more than got my work cut out for me.

As I gather my notes and tablet and ready myself to leave Maura's office, she stops me again. "Oh, Gwen? One more thing, actually. It's the whole reason I called you in today, and I almost forgot."

She pulls out a copy of the gala invitation that I received in the mail a few days before. An invitation that I'm pretty certain comes from Devon.

"I was sent this copy of an invitation that was meant for you to the Everleigh Society Trust banquet. The letter accompanying it has given us exclusive coverage to their annual fundraising gala next week. It's quite an affair and usually covered in magazine spreads. Lots of stars and high-society folk. It's not the type of journalism you like to do, but your name was personally mentioned in the memo accompanying the invitation. I'll send Alex with you to take pictures and you cover the piece."

I blink, frozen in my tracks. "Uh, can someone else go?" I gesture to my arm full of notes as if to let the work of the story speak for itself. "I, uh, have a lot to—"

She makes a face. "Well, maybe if your name wasn't the one specifically mentioned. But it is, and I'm pretty sure that means you caught the eye of someone associated with the trust foundation. This would be a good in for us in the future so I'm going to have to insist. And yes, I know I just handed you a short deadline, but this is what being in the trenches is, Gwen. This is journalism. Deadlines, pressure. Multiple stories at once. You've got this. Trust in yourself."

I grit my teeth and bite back any reply I may have been thinking of. By sending a copy of that invite to my boss, Devon has now cornered me into going.

So that's what he wants, huh? A public confrontation with me at his very own gala?

Well, you know what they say, Lord Devon Howard of Everleigh… *Be careful what you wish for.*

CHAPTER 33
ACCOUNTABILITY

SATURDAY ARRIVES WAY TOO FAST. I'M STANDING IN front of the full-length mirror on the back of the bedroom door when Sam walks in.

Her excited gaze flicks over my plain black dress, and matching heels. "Oh, girl, you look amazing. Do you want me to curl your hair while you do your makeup?"

I flash her a tight smile. "Sure, thanks."

I'm not looking forward to this gala—or to seeing Devon again. I'm terrified at the idea of seeing him, actually. Terrified, because I know how easily I can fall right back into those steel-gray eyes.

About an hour later, Alex, our beat photographer, arrives looking like a snack—dark hair, neatly combed back from his chiseled features. He's so cute, and if I weren't still so emotionally wrecked from my relationship with Devon, then I might consider hitting on him tonight. But I'm not ready for that. So tonight, it'll just be awkward smiles and uncomfortable conversations about the weather. That's all I can handle right now.

He eyes me up and down with a wide smile. "Hey, Gwen. You look beautiful."

I return the smile. "Thanks. You clean up pretty nice yourself."

In LA traffic, it takes about an hour to get to the venue in Beverly Hills. After we drop the car off with the valet, we walk up to the beautiful art deco building. I suck in a breath and try to brace myself for the moment I see Devon again, but the second we step inside, I'm overwhelmed with the feeling that I'm going to throw up.

The ballroom is swarming with people, which is a relief. It'll be harder for Devon to single me out in a crowd like this—until I realize, when we receive our seating cards, that Alex and I are sitting at Devon's table.

Of course, we are. This is Devon's gala, and he would have arranged for me to sit near him. After all the trouble he's already taken to get me here, he wouldn't take the chance of missing me.

Fuck. I should have expected that. My mind races. Maybe I can swap out our cards with someone else's at another table? Bump them up to VIP?

Alex seems impressed by our table assignment and heads right to where we're supposed to be. I follow him, trailing like a dog being dragged to the vet.

When we get to the head table, we sit. A waiter shortly arrives with a bottle of wine in each hand, and I ask him to pour the white for me. Then I nearly gulp it down in one swallow and wonder how long it will take him to get back here. I should have thought to do some pre-game, but I was so nervous it didn't even occur to me. I'm nearly done with that first glass when I feel a presence behind me.

I know without looking…Lord Devon Howard has arrived.

And I know it's petty, but I lean over and whisper in Alex's ear. "Can you flag down a waiter and get me another glass of wine?" I ask, then add a loud giggle like I said something clever.

"Sure." Alex flashes a row of perfectly straight teeth. "I'll go hunt something down. White?"

"Yes, thank you," I say sweetly.

I hear a low growl behind me, and I know I've pissed Devon off. A thread of satisfaction snakes through me. Let him think I've already moved on. It's what he deserves.

Before Alex can even get up to grab my drink, I hear a familiar deep baritone. "Hello, Angel."

I stiffen instantly, unprepared for the effect his voice—and that nickname—has on me. Damn this guy and the hold he has on me he has. I slowly turn around, and look up, up, up, until my eyes meet his. "You don't get to call me that anymore."

He gestures with one hand on the back of my chair. "Take a walk with me," he says pointedly.

My God, always *commanding*. Do *this*. Do *that*. I guess that's what being worshiped by everyone will do. If only they knew his darkest secrets like I do—and the lengths he'll go to to get what he wants.

"No, thanks," I say, moving to turn back around.

Before I can completely blow him off, he reaches down and takes my hand. He tugs gently until I'm standing. "Please, Gwendolyn."

The sadness in his tone softens me a little, and I push out a breath. "Five minutes."

I follow him out of the ballroom to a terrace that overlooks a garden. The cool night air is fragrant—like rose and gardenia.

Devon leans against the wrought-iron railing and pulls in a deep breath. When his gaze catches mine, my heart jolts in my chest.

"Gwen, I brought you out here to apologize for everything that transpired between us—"

I shake my head and interrupt him. "Devon—"

He lifts a hand, stopping me. "I know an apology isn't enough—it doesn't even come close to what you deserve. That's why I've brought this." He pulls out a folded manila envelope from his inside jacket pocket. He opens it and pulls out the NDA I signed weeks ago. Then he shreds it, right there in front of me. "This was the only copy. I'm giving you leave to write whatever story you want. I won't stop you."

I watch as the pieces of the NDA float down to the ground. Then I look back up at him. "I don't believe you. Lord Devon Howard doesn't give up control like this. There's a catch. What is it?"

He pushes his hands into his pockets and glances down at the ground. He shakes his head. "No catch. I'm not telling you what to write. I'll give you whatever quotes you need for your story, whatever resources I have are at your disposal."

I blink. "Why? This doesn't fix things if that's what you're thinking. This doesn't make right of anything you did."

His steel-gray eyes return to lock with mine. There's true regret there, and something else. Deep sadness, I think. "I know that, Angel. I know it doesn't even come close."

I shrug, at a loss. "Then why? Why would you allow me to expose you?"

He pauses. "Because I love you, Gwendolyn."

The words are so unexpected that it's like he's punched me in the gut, and I struggle for breath, blinking. I must have heard him wrong. "I'm sorry, you *what?*"

He takes a step toward me, and reaches for my hands, pulling them up to his chest. "I love you, Gwendolyn Taylor—and I'm done telling you what to do." The sincerity in his tone guts me. "In fact, I've called a press conference for this evening, after the gala. I plan to confess everything in public, every dark deed—your kidnapping, the cover-up. Everything."

I pull back slightly to look at him. I'm so confused. "You'll go to jail."

He shifts on his feet and shrugs. "That is…a very real possibility. But I'm done hiding. It's time I take accountability for what I've done to you."

I glance away, off into the distance. This is probably just another manipulation—an attempt to get back into my good graces by pretending to be contrite. I should just call him on his bluff. What would he do then?

I glance back at him and shrug one shoulder. "Well, whatever. Do whatever you think you need to do. It's none of my business anymore."

He presses his lips together and nods once—accepting my decree with grace. "I can't apologize enough for what has transpired between us. If only we'd met under different circumstances, we might have known true happiness together."

For some reason, that last line about our missed opportunity at happiness hits me like a sharp knife to the chest. My heart aches because it's true. We could have been so happy if only he'd dealt with me honestly.

But what's done is done. There's no going back.

He reaches up and places a finger beneath my chin, lifting up my face. He studies me, his eyes brushing over every feature, as though he's trying to take in each detail and commit it to his memory. I can see the sadness in his eyes, and I half expect him to lean in and kiss me—I'm holding my breath, craving that soft press of his lips—but instead, he drops his hand and steps back.

"Goodbye, Angel." Then he turns on his heel and walks back into the ballroom without another word.

I stand in the crisp night air for a minute, in a haze. Confused. My emotions are all over the place—but grief is the most prominent feeling. The specter of loss has reached through my chest and taken hold of my heart, gripping tightly with a cold hand.

It takes me a few minutes to collect myself. When I finally walk back into the ballroom, I see that Alex is looking for me. He reaches out and brushes a firm hand down my arm. "Are you okay? You look like you've seen a ghost."

I flash him a fake smile. "I'm good, thanks. Did you ever find that glass of wine?"

"It's at the table, waiting for you," he assures me.

"Great," I say. "Let's keep them coming." I have a feeling I'm going to need *several* glasses of wine just to get through the night.

Alex laughs. "You got it."

CHAPTER 34
RECKONING

THE NIGHT PASSES IN A KIND OF BLUR. I WATCH AS DEVON moves around the room, shaking hands and laughing like he didn't just destroy my entire world. Again.

Damn, I'm so gullible. Out on the terrace, when he was apologizing—I hate to admit it, even to myself, but I *wanted* to believe him. The sadness in his eyes, the regret in his tone—he seemed so sincere.

Then he dropped those three little magic words as if to seal the deal, to win my silence forever. By telling me that he loved me, he could only count on me still having feelings for him, too. It was a trick to manipulate me, pure and simple.

This is why I should swear off men forever. I'm such a poor judge of character. Devon is a powerful man, and because he's powerful, he's also dangerous. I just need to remember that.

"Absolute power corrupts absolutely." Isn't that the famous quote?

I watch as Devon gives his speech, studying his body language instead of listening to the words about thanking donors and sharing his gratitude for the cause the foundation funds. I don't even pay close attention to his discussion of the progress he witnessed on the so-called Belize Project.

Instead, I study the way he carries himself. The tenseness in his shoulders, the way he grips the podium so tightly that his knuckles whiten. He's clearly nervous and tense but hiding it so well that only someone who knows him very well would be able to tell that.

And the entire time, I marvel at his presence and have no doubt that the reason he is where he is today, aside from his birthright, is because of his stature, charm and ability to command others to his cause. It's clear in talking to anyone who's worked with or for him, as I do casually when I ask around, even here at this banquet tonight, that a great deal think highly of him.

Film stars, TV journalists that I easily recognize and other prominent people of note jockey to shake his hand, and I watch this with my critical and mostly impartial journalist's eye.

None of this changes the fact that he's pissed me off with his manipulations. That he's easily pulled me in too. But I'm strong, and I'm now in resistance mode, even with every pang I feel, every desire where I want to be roped in yet again by him, feel his hands on my body, his body pressed to mine, his eyes gazing into mine. His mouth....

After the speech is over, across the room I catch the eye of one of the people lined up along the wall. She's not someone I've met—or so I think. But something about the way she stands and her eyes are very familiar to me.

It takes me far too long to realize with a shock that it's Jemma. But not in disguise. She's dressed as what I presume to be her real self. I wonder what her actual name is.

When it finally dawns on me who she is, I catch her eye again and smile. Her eyebrows arch high in her forehead and she returns the smile before her attention is called elsewhere.

It's nearly ten o'clock when the banquet ends, and the crowd has thinned out considerably. The glitterati of Los Angeles are moving on to their next destinations for the night—the after-parties or home gatherings or late-night exclusive restaurant visits.

But as I gather my things and give the room a sweep to ensure I won't be ambushed, I prepare to make my escape.

Just then, Alex sidles up to me. Oh, right, I all but forgot about him in the wake of Devon and his overwhelming presence and effect on me. He nods toward the entrance. "There's press outside. I asked around. Lord Devon Howard called them here for a special announcement. We should get out there so we can cover it too. I need to jockey for a good position to get some shots."

My gut drops, and I grow cold inside. Is it true? Is he going to announce to everyone all of his misdeeds? Is he going to turn himself in, to pay for his crimes, particularly those against me? Each beat of my heart inside my chest literally hurts as I follow Alex outside to where there is a metal podium with microphone and fellow members of the press gathered around it.

People are murmuring, wondering what the "special announcement" is that Lord Devon could have called a press conference for at literally the eleventh hour. A man stands nearby, adjusting stand lights, and photographers are readying their cameras as suddenly Devon appears at the podium.

"Ladies, gentlemen, I thank you for your attention in the matter that I'm about to discuss. I know it's late and you only found out about this conference from my release this morning. This is a serious matter, and I wish to be as open and forthcoming about the facts as I possibly can be."

He looks down at the surface of the podium, then his eyes jump up and search the crowd quickly until they find mine. We lock gazes, and the breath hisses out between my lips as I realize I have been holding it since the second I realized this press conference was a reality.

He licks his lips and stares into my eyes, and my throat tightens. I want to yell out and tell him to shut up. To not do this. Too many people depend on him. For jobs, for help. He's done so much good. And yes, he's done bad too. Against me. Don't I want him to pay?

He swallows, and his eyes flick away from me to stare straight ahead. He takes a deep breath. "I've tried to live a life of integrity, to do good in the world. As a man born of enormous privilege, I've always felt it my duty to give back and serve. I hope my works have left a good mark on this world. Unfortunately, I've done ill, too. Grave ill. And it's time that the price for my actions must be paid in full. This is why—"

Without another word, I shove aside the reporter standing in front of me and run at full speed the fifteen feet to the podium. By the time I get there, I nearly hit Devon with the full force of my sprint, jostling him. He reaches out a hand to steady me as a security guard closes in to whisk me away. But Devon stops him from doing that.

I blink up at him, and all I can do is shake my head. "*Don't*," I say in a hoarse whisper.

He frowns at me and briefly closes his eyes before opening them again. "I must, Angel."

Without another conscious thought, I turn to the podium, the mic and the clicking cameras, and the reporters holding out their phones to record. I stare into the light illuminating us and say. "Lord Devon Howard was about to announce that he's working on his memoirs. I–I was to be a silent partner in their creation, but he wanted to be open about it. I was hoping to stay anonymous, but I accept his generous acknowledgment and thank him for the opportunity to work with him."

I have no idea where any of that came from, and people start to ask questions. The presence at my side is stiff, and I can feel the shock emanating off him in waves. I answer the questions peppered at me. My name, my background. The nature of the work we'll be doing together…

I spontaneously answer all of them, not even aware of what I'm saying. Just bluffing through it.

After a few minutes, Devon takes control of the questioning and adds a few details here or there. He may be pissed that I've now publicly put him on the hook for an authorized biography, but it's better than facing jail time and public disgrace for kidnapping.

Not much later, the press crowd dissipates. Alex walks up to me, shaking his head in visible shock, and I feel Devon's hand settle possessively on my lower back in response to the photographer's approach. He hasn't forgotten that I'd been flirting with Alex earlier, and he wants me to know it.

I shrug away from Devon's touch and assure Alex that everything's true, that it was all a big secret and I haven't even told our editor yet. He smiles and congratulates me and asks me to put in a good word with our publisher for his photography. I promise him that I will and tell him not to worry about giving me a ride home.

I suspect that Devon and I will have a lot to say to each other before the night is through, so it's better that we're alone for this.

Chapter 35
Penance

As soon as Alex turns to go and other reporters, who seem to be lingering, appear to close in for follow-up questions, Devon takes a firm hold of my upper arm and leads me away with a nod and a wave to the others. He's got his phone out, and once we've made our way back into the building and through to the back door, a car is already waiting for us in the back loading area.

He doesn't wait for the driver to get out but whips open the door and tells me. "Get in, Angel...."

And knowing that this was where this night was going, probably since the first moment I even set foot on the premises, I do just that, ducking into the car and waiting as he slides in beside me.

When the car leaves the parking lot, he tells the driver to head to Pasadena, toward my house, then presses the button to lift the privacy barrier between him and us.

I've got my arms folded defensively over my chest and am sitting about as far away from him as I possibly can. And I'm not looking at him. I'm staring out the window, watching Los Angeles pass us by.

"Why did you do that?"

I swallow and suppress a shrug, finally just shaking my head. "I don't know. It just...happened. I thought about all the good things you've been doing, all the people you've helped, and I couldn't see you go to jail or even just be disgraced."

He takes in a breath and lets it out slowly. "Even after what I did to you? To forgive me like that is...you truly must be an angel."

I turn to him and pin him down hard with my stare. "No one said anything about me forgiving you. This had everything to do with all the people you've helped—and are helping—and not about you escaping the consequences of your actions."

He looks down, and his shoulders practically slump in defeat. "Indeed, I've lived a life where I've never much had to suffer consequences for my actions. But I have to admit that the thought of paying the price with a jail sentence or even a public outcry was almost a relief. As if in submitting to such punishment could scrub my soul of this..." He takes a shaky breath like he's barely able to get the words out. "This debilitating guilt and shame I feel."

I pause for a long moment, studying his bowed head. This doesn't feel like an act. This feels like true penance. He was ready to throw his life away at this press conference and likely accept an arrest sometime in the next few days.

I blink.

"You don't have to turn yourself in. There are other ways you can make up for what you did."

He seems to absorb that for a moment. "But no way to earn your forgiveness? I'd just as soon rot in jail, Gwendolyn."

"Live with the knowledge that you don't get to have me, then. That should be just as good."

"And yet, you want to work with me on a memoir…."

"I said that to the press because it was the only thing I could think of. You can just let it ride for now and then in six months or a year just announce that the project has been delayed."

He gently places a large hand on my upper arm. It's a firm but not a controlling touch. It's almost as if he wants to assure himself that I'm real, solid flesh sitting here. That he's finally having an honest and open conversation with me.

"There can be no excuse for what I've done, no matter the reason for my actions. I don't know how, but I do mean to earn your forgiveness, Gwendolyn. The memoir—"

I hold up a hand to stop him. "You can't buy me off with promises of connections and advances to my career. I won't be bribed."

He nods slowly. "Will you be loved?"

I frown. "What?"

"I've told you the truth, though I suspect you think it was a manipulation. I'm in love with you, and I don't want to buy you off. I want to love you. For the rest of my life."

I blink. Is he serious?

Chapter 36
Devil's Advocate

I DON'T SAY ANYTHING FOR THE REST OF THE CAR RIDE HOME, because I have no idea *what* to say. My emotions are all over the place. Happiness. Confusion. Anger. It's all warring inside me, and I suddenly feel lost.

When we pull up to Hill House, I move to open the door, but Devon reaches out and grabs my wrist, stopping me. Setting my jaw, I turn toward him, ready to tell him off, but the look in his eyes stops me cold—and melts me instantly.

His gaze is soft—and Devon is never soft—with pain in his gray eyes. "Say something, Angel."

I blink, fighting back the tears. The truth is, my heart aches at the thought of walking away from Devon forever. But what choice do I have? How could we possibly come back from what's happened?

I shake my head. "Everything is just so fucked up between us."

His grip tightens, and he tugs me around so I'm facing him. "Gwendolyn, I understand why you can't forgive me. But tell me you don't love me, and I'll leave you alone."

I swallow and glance away. I should say I don't love him, if only to end things between us once and for all. But my heart lurches at the thought of saying goodbye to him forever. Maybe I'm a coward, but I just can't do it.

"I'm exhausted," I say, finally. "I can't think about any of this until I get some sleep."

His hand drops, and he sits back. "Yes, of course." I can tell he wants to stop me. I can see the barely contained restraint in his beautiful face. This must be torture for him—allowing me to walk away. Giving up that beloved control.

He clears his throat. "I'll be heading to the East Coast on Monday for business, and I thought perhaps we could travel together, so you could see your mother."

I suck in a stuttering breath, remembering the last plane ride we took together. Heat blooms in my center, and I shift in my seat. I flash him a tight smile. "I'll think about it."

When I get inside the house and upstairs, Cassie is lying on my bed, watching something on her phone. She puts it down the second I walk through the door. "There you are!" she says, sitting up. "I saw what happened at the fundraiser. It was all over the news and social media."

"Yeah, crazy, right?" I laugh, but there's no amusement in my tone. I turn my back to Cassie. "Can you unzip me, please?"

She climbs off my bed and unzips my dress. "So, a memoir, eh?"

"Yeah, I don't think that's actually going to happen." I pause—what the hell? "It was just a cover for what really happened."

Cassie walks around so we're facing each other. "*What really happened?* Say what?"

I slink out of my shapewear and pull on a pair of sweatpants and a baby tee. I'm craving going to wash the makeup off my face but…I really feel the need to get this out to someone. There's no NDA anymore, after all. I can actually confide in a friend.

And I don't want to hide what happened between Devon and me anymore—especially from one of my best friends.

"Sit down. I have a ton of shit to catch you up on."

It's two in the morning when I've finally reached the end of my whole twisted story, and Cassie has both hands over her mouth like she's stifling a scream. When she finally lowers them, she clears her throat. "That is so fucking unreal," she repeats for the thirtieth time. "So, um, what happens next?"

I shrug one shoulder. "I go on with life. Study, get my degree. Write. Forget him."

God, it's all I'd ever wanted—an education, a good job—but somehow, without Devon to share it with, it feels…I don't know, empty.

"Okay, so, playing devil's advocate here—" At my grimace, she realizes her pun and makes a cringy face, then pushes on. "Aside from the whole kidnapping aspect, which, admittedly, was a huge fuck-up on his part…do you think he's a bad guy?"

I drop my head into my hands, then look up at Cassie. "Yeah, see that's the thing—during my time with him, I couldn't help but see the good in him. He's kind. He cares about other people. It's why he kidnapped me in the first place—to prevent my story from destroying his foundation's reputation."

Cassie nods knowingly. "And…you love him."

My heart lurches, and I suck in a sharp breath. "Is it that obvious?"

She lifts a brow. "You light up when you talk about him."

I gesture with my hand, as if grasping for something. "Maybe it's just...what do they call it again? That syndrome where captives fall in love with their kidnappers?"

"Stockholm syndrome," Cassie supplies.

"Yes, exactly. That one."

Cassie shrugs. "I mean, sure, maybe. I'm not a psychologist. But the kidnapping was for damage control. It wasn't something malevolent, and he treated you well. You believe he's a good guy. My opinion? I think it's love."

I suck in a breath. Cassie grabs my upper arm. "You should talk to him and tell him that, at least."

My mouth twists, and I nod absently, already imagining how a conversation like that would go. How would he respond? Would it be giving him false hope? Loving him was one thing, but could we ever be together?

"I don't know." I yawn loudly. "Maybe I'll text him sometime. He said he's going to the East Coast on Monday. He wants me to go with him so I can see my mom. I really want to see her, but I don't think I'm ready to travel with him."

Cassie yawns too, then gets up and walks to the door. Before she leaves, she points at me. "It's a long flight, and it will give you a chance to talk it out. Figure out your future. Life is short, Gwen. You can always give him another chance. Or you can blow what could be an amazing thing and move on and hope something comes along later. But if you don't give him that chance at least, you'll never know." Then she snaps the door closed, and I'm left to wonder if she might be right.

But I can barely keep that thought in my head for thirty seconds because I'm out the minute my head hits the pillow.

The next day, I war with myself back and forth on whether or not to take Devon up on his offer of a ride to New Jersey. I could fly myself, and I do desperately want to see my mom. She's recovering, slowly, but it keeps me up at night thinking about how close I came to losing her.

Which brings me back to what Cassie said last night. *Life is short. Give him another chance.*

I reach for my phone and type out a text to Devon before I can talk myself out of it.

What time do we leave tomorrow?

The new semester starts soon, and I've done no prep, even for the undergraduate course I'm going to be teaching. I really don't have the time to do this. A couple of days away can't hurt. That deadline from my editor, however, is another story. But I can bring my laptop with me and work on them while I travel.

My breath catches when I see the three dots pop up in the message window.

Devon's reply comes a few seconds later—almost as though he was watching his phone, waiting for me to text.

I'll pick you up at 8 a.m.

For the first time in a long time, I smile at the thought of seeing him again. I spend the rest of the day packing and texting my sister, letting her know I'll be there in the early afternoon tomorrow. And I hardly sleep at all that night, imagining all the things I want to say to Devon. In my imagination, I oscillate between slapping him, yelling at him, kissing him—and I end up tossing and turning until my alarm goes off at six-thirty. Then I pop out of bed like a lightning strike to get ready.

There's a knock on the front door at exactly eight o'clock.

With a deep breath, I open the door to reveal Devon—freshly shaven, in a white button-down shirt, and black jeans. He looks like an extra-yummy snack, and I'm suddenly very, *very* hungry.

I swallow and straighten my spine. *Be strong, Gwen. Don't fall into those gorgeous gray eyes again.*

Clearing my throat, I grab my bag and flash him a tight smile. "Right on time."

He reaches out. "Allow me to take your bag."

I hand him my bag, and we walk out to the town car that's waiting for us. Devon opens my door for me and moves around the back to put my bag in the trunk before joining me in the back seat.

The trip to the airport is long, silent, and filled with awkward tension. I wish I knew what to say—but I'm not brave enough to execute any of the scenarios I dreamed up last night. So I don't say anything. In the end, it's Devon who speaks first.

"Forgive me for saying this, but you look like you haven't slept."

I can hear the concern in his voice, and it softens me a little.

"I've had a lot on my mind." I glance over at him. "The term is about to start, and of course, I've been thinking about my mom. Thank you for inviting me along, by the way."

He smiles, and I get the sense he wants to lean over and kiss me, but he doesn't. His back is rigid, and his strong hands are laced together tightly in his lap like he's forcing himself to remain perfectly still.

When we reach the private jet, I draw in a deep breath. I can't help but remember our trip on this same plane to Belize. We spent the entire flight exploring each other's bodies, surrendering to the passion that crackled between us almost constantly.

This flight, instead of his staff being here with him, we are the only passengers aboard. This plane seems a little overkill for the two of us, but who am I to complain? It's better than commercial—even first class.

As we settle into our seats across from each other, Devon orders a coffee for me and tea for himself, then he glances over at me. "Once we're in the air, why don't you go back to the room and get some sleep?"

I suck in a breath—I am tired and that sounds heavenly, but there's no way I'm going anywhere near that bed. I'd be too tempted to invite him into it and pick up where we left off.

"You don't need to worry about me anymore," I say pointedly. "I'm not your responsibility."

He laughs a little and shakes his head. "Your well-being will always be on my mind, Angel."

I don't know why that simple statement pricks at my heart, but it does. Maybe it's because I know he's being sincere. After what happened between us, he could have just moved on. That would have been the easiest thing to do. But he hasn't. He still wants me.

We're silent for the rest of the trip. I do end up napping, but leaning with a pillow shoved between my head and the bulkhead rather than the bed. When I wake up, a soft wool blanket has been spread over me, and I awake just before landing, refreshed. When we land in New Jersey, the first thing I do is check my phone. My sister has already texted me with the address of the rehabilitation center where my mom is staying, so shortly thereafter, a car takes us straight there.

The second we pull up to the facility, my heart sinks. From the outside, it looks like a fancy spa. I frown. There must be a mistake. There's no way in hell we could afford a place like this. Probably not even a night. And while her health insurance is good, it's not nearly this good. There's no possible way.

"There's a mistake. She can't be here," I say out loud.

Devon looks up from his phone. "Well, let's see, shall we?"

The driver opens my door, and Devon slips out behind me. I give him a sharp look, and he holds his palms out innocently.

"Let's check with reception. Then I can walk you back and leave you to visit with your mum."

I'm not in the mood for an argument, and if it is a mistake after all, I'm going to need him to take me to the right place so I let him trail me up to the reception area where I check in by giving my mom's name.

With a helpful smile, the receptionist fills out two visitor tags with my mother's name on them. As we had a six-hour flight and a three-hour time change, it's rather late here, well after dinner. The receptionist warns us that we have less than an hour before visiting time is over.

Before I can turn to dismiss Devon, the receptionist is ushering us in the direction of her wing of the rehab center. I grit my teeth, hoping Devon will excuse himself.

Because, damn, I don't want my mom and sister to meet him. But I can't just tell him to shove off now in front of the receptionist. So I follow along and don't say anything. Hopefully, he'll dip out quickly.

We find my mother's room, and thankfully, she's up and about. But my sister has gone home for the evening, apparently.

Her eyes light up. "Oh, I was hoping you'd make it before visiting hours ended. Come here and give me a big hug."

With an irresistible smile, I go to her and accept her embrace as she squeezes me tight and presses a big kiss to my cheek. She looks so much better than the last time I saw her, though it pains my heart that, clearly, she still has a long way to go.

When I pull back, Mom's eyes are riveted on the tall handsome stranger standing just behind me. She arches her brow and smiles at him, almost batting her eyes.

"And who is this?"

I can see a dozen different speculations flicker across her features as her eyes snap quickly to me and then just as quickly back to Devon.

Well…this is going to take some splainin'.

Shit.

Chapter 37
Forgiveness

"**D**evon Howard at your service, madam." He grins, reaching out a hand to take hers, and I can all but hear my mom's heart flutter right out of her chest. Her eyelids are blinking so fast she could cool a room with those eyelashes.

Down, Mom. *Jeez.*

"And…how do you know my Gwen?"

"Gwendolyn and I met while she was working on a story for her job. She recently covered a benefit run in honor of a charitable foundation I work with. She's a very gifted writer."

I spear him with a shocked glance. I wasn't even aware that he'd read anything I'd written, though I have no reason to suppose he's lying. And my work is easy enough to find online.

After a few polite pleasantries, Devon discreetly checks his phone and excuses himself, telling me he'll be back to pick me up when visiting hours are over. Mom watches him leave with a wide-eyed stare, clearly still shocked.

"He talks like British royalty. He called you Gwendolyn. Who is he really?" Oh, God, if only she knew.

I quickly make up a story about how he's helping me with my story about his charitable foundation and offered to fly me out with him to the East Coast when he heard about my mom being so ill.

She shakes her head, marveling. "That's incredible. He's like Hugh Jackman in that movie when he played the duke who came through a portal from the past and had a romance with Meg Ryan." Leave it to mom to reference old rom-coms. And she's not wrong, really. He does remind me a little of the duke from *Kate & Leopold*. She shakes her head, marveling. "He's...a very impressive man."

"Yes, that he is." I cough discreetly as a way to change the subject, and Mom offers me a cup of water from her bedside pitcher. I sip at it, and before she can ask me any follow-up questions about "Duke Leopold," I pelt one at her. "So, Michelle told me that the police were here today."

She nods. "The man who hit me wants to take a plea, and though they don't really require it, they wanted a statement from me."

I frown. "He wants to take a plea? He should be locked up for a decade for what he did to you. Mowing you over in a crosswalk and then taking off. Disgusting jerk."

She blinks. "He's a kid. He was distracted and then got scared and panicked. If he got the full sentence, he wouldn't be out until he was practically thirty. I could never do that to someone."

My jaw drops. "What about what he did to you?"

Her brow furrows. "I'm okay. I'll heal."

"Mom—"

She holds up a hand. "There's a lot to be said in favor of mercy, Gwen. Of forgiveness. It serves me no good in my healing journey to carry anger and animosity toward this boy. He's nineteen years old. His attorney said he's written me three letters, but they can't send them to me for legal reasons until the matter is settled. He's apparently quite devastated and has been seeking counseling. I have no need to pile onto him. It wouldn't make me heal any faster. Life is too short to hold on to hate and anger. I choose to let it go and hope he changes his life."

I blink. We talk a little further about it, and the words roll around and around in my head. *Life is too short.* If anyone would know that lesson, she would, after what she's just gone through.

Life's too short. Cassie said that to me, too.

And you know what? They are both so right.

My mind is full of what my mother has told me, and emotions are swirling and swirling around in my chest. I have to blink back sudden tears when I give her a hug goodbye as visiting hours end. She puts a hand on my cheek and smiles up at me. "I worry about you. You seem sad."

My mouth turns up. "It's okay, Mom. I'm actually happier now that I've seen you. Be back tomorrow." And I kiss her.

Devon's car is waiting at the curb, and as soon as I walk through the front door, he pops out to hold the door open for me.

Without a word, I slip in.

As soon as Devon slides back into the car, shutting the door, I all but leap into his arms.

He lets out a gasp of surprise, and his strong arms come around me to hold me to him. "What is this?" he asks quietly, almost as if he's afraid of what the answer might be.

"Kiss me," I ask him hoarsely.

And he does. It's not passionate or suggestive. It's not meant to arouse, but it does tell me things. It tells me that he cares for me. That he loves me. When our mouths separate, he lets out a long breath.

"I don't dare to hope…" He trails off.

"You *should* dare. Life is too short to hold on to anger and hate. Especially…" I clear my throat when my voice falters. "Especially when it's blocking all the feelings of love."

He pauses, then reaches a hand up to my cheek. "Oh, my darling Angel. I do love you."

I tilt my head forward, resting it lightly against his chin. "And I love you."

His arms pull me closer to him, and the limo drives off into the night.

And I don't even care where it takes us. I just want his arms around me. For the rest of my life.

Chapter 38
Heaven

IT'S LATE FRIDAY A FEW WEEKS LATER WHEN I GET BACK TO Hill House after an arduous day of classes. I had to take an alternate route home because the paparazzi have been hounding me for weeks. It's gotten out that Devon and I are dating, and since then, I haven't known a moment's peace. They follow me everywhere—to class, to the coffee shop, to the grocery store...everywhere. But by far the strangest thing is seeing my face splashed all over the tabloids and shared everywhere on social media.

I drop off my bag in my bedroom, then head back downstairs to make myself some pasta for dinner. As I wait for the water to boil, I pull out my phone from my back pocket and text Devon. He's been in my thoughts all day.

Hey, babe. Just got done with class. What are you up to?

His reply comes almost immediately, and I smile. For such a busy, powerful man, he always makes time for me.

Working. Thinking about those pink, pouty lips and how best to put them to use the next time we're together.

He has such a dirty mind. I realize now just how fitting his Devil persona was at Obscura—he's positively wicked. I laugh and shake my head as I type out my response.

Well, you'll see these pink, pouty lips tomorrow.

Since making our relationship official, I've been spending the week here in Pasadena and the weekends with Devon at Exeter House. It's agony being away from him, but we've managed it well enough over the last few weeks.

Come see me tonight, is his reply. *I'll send a driver.*

I'm bone tired. This week has been hell. I swear my professors must have banded together and decided to pile as much work on me as possible. The thought of sitting through an hour or more of traffic isn't exactly appealing.

You can wait until tomorrow, I text back.

After scarfing down my dinner, I head upstairs and take a shower. As I'm brushing out my wet hair, my mind wanders to Devon. How amazing would it be to cuddle with him tonight? Curled up in the warm curve of his body is my favorite way to sleep these days.

I could invite him here, but with five other roommates, there's zero privacy. Plus, Devon's place comes with room service, so we can stay in bed all weekend if we want to.

By the time my hair is brushed out, I've decided on surprising Devon by driving out to Malibu tonight. I glance at my phone.

It's only seven o'clock. I can make it there by eight, then maybe I'll eat a salad while he eats a late dinner. I already know he hasn't eaten yet.

An hour later, I'm standing in front of Devon's penthouse door, punching in the security code. As I open the door, I try to be as quiet as possible. I slip my bag off my shoulder and remove my shoes in the foyer. Knowing Devon, he's probably in his office, still hard at work, so I head there first.

Without knocking, I push the door open. He's at his desk, head bowed over his laptop, typing something out. He doesn't even see me standing in the doorway. It reminds me of the first time I saw him sitting at the very same desk, back when I was a captive here. He was gorgeous then, and he's even more irresistible now.

It's crazy how far we've come since then. Weeks ago, after our reconciliation, I was shocked to realize *this* is where I'd been held captive. Here, in his penthouse at Exeter House. The men who'd kidnapped me had driven me around for hours, and I'd naturally assumed they'd taken me somewhere on the outskirts of LA, or even as far as Las Vegas.

I step into the room and close the door behind me, then I dip into a mockingly over-the-top curtsy, head bowed low. "Good evening, your royal hiney."

His head snaps up, and the second he sees me, he gets up and walks over to me. He comes to a stop and we lock gazes. Then he lifts my chin with the crook of his finger and studies me like he hasn't seen me in months. "You drove here yourself."

I laugh at the disapproval in his tone. "I can still drive and do things for myself."

Concern clouds his features. "The paparazzi can be dangerous. I'd feel better if you let me manage things. I know how they operate."

I brush his hand away and find the hem of my shirt, pulling it over my head. I'm not wearing a bra, so the second my shirt is off, his gaze falls to my breasts. Hunger flashes in his eyes, and I get pleasure from knowing that hunger is all for me, *and me alone.*

"I'm not here to talk about the paparazzi," I say. "Actually, I was hoping you could take a break from work."

The corners of his beautiful mouth lift up into a half-smile. "Oh, Angel. You know you have to earn everything you get here," he says, echoing his words to me when I was here in this office before.

I look up at him through my lashes. "What do you want?"

He chuckles. "You know what I want."

It's almost word for word what he said to me all those weeks ago when I was still a captive here. Back then, I was scared and unsure about what Devon had planned for me. But since then, he's risked everything for me, and I know he would do it all again in a heartbeat.

I twist and grab a beautiful decorative hourglass off the nearby bookshelf, holding it up to his gaze. Then I walk over to his desk, flip it over, and set it down. "You have *one* hour."

"That should be enough time for a few rounds, at least."

I arch a brow at him. "*One,*" I counter.

His eyes narrow. "*Three.*"

I bite my lip to keep from laughing. "Two rounds. Final offer. No safe word."

With a growl of approval, he snatches me up into his arms and carries me a few feet to his side of the huge desk. There, he sets me down roughly on the sleek slab of mahogany and captures my mouth in a hot kiss.

He devours me, drinking me in like a man dying of thirst. It's been five days since we've seen each other last, so maybe he is. Devon has a large appetite—one that I'm more than happy to satisfy.

Leaning back a little, I lift my leg and hook it around his hip. He's not the only one who's thirsty. I want him inside me. I've wanted him inside me for *days.*

Lifting my hips, I arch into him. His fingers dip beneath the hem of my skirt, and my panties until he finds my center. The tip of his finger brushes over my sensitive folds, teasing me.

We've been apart for so long I can barely stand it. My hands roam his chest, then smooth over his shoulders, where I dig in with my blunt nails through the fabric of his shirt.

I break the kiss, pulling back slightly. "Devon, I need you now. Please don't torment me."

His wicked mouth turns up into a self-satisfied smile. "Oh, now I *must* torment you." He trails kisses down my throat, to the tips of my breasts, down my ribs, until he reaches the waistband of my skirt.

He positions my legs so they're hooked over his shoulders, then he lifts the hem of my skirt and touches his mouth to my clit. The feel of his tongue is so intense, my body jerks the second his tongue makes contact with the swollen and throbbing bud. His warm tongue swirls around it, offering more torment than relief.

Whimpering, I allow my head to fall back as I'm engulfed in a flood of sensations. Then his tongue slips inside my channel as he sucks gently—and I swear, if I don't climax soon, I'm going to tear him apart with my teeth.

He breaks away. "*Christ*, Angel. You're so fucking wet. It's too much to bear," he grits out, and he hurriedly unzips his slacks. Pulling his cock out, he re-positions himself between my thighs, and with one thrust, he pushes deep inside me—his gaze locked with mine.

In this moment, we're joined together, existing as one.

One breath.

One heartbeat.

One soul.

He rocks his hips forward, stroking me on the inside, and I moan again. But he doesn't stop, doesn't hesitate—rocking his hips forward, he drives even deeper into me. Oh, God, it feels so good. He slams into my G-spot over and over, and I lift my hips, silently begging for more.

"*Fuck*, Gwendolyn," he pushes out through gritted teeth. "I'm going to come. I've been without you for too long."

"Yes, please," I breathe. "Come inside me."

Like a dam breaking, he comes hard and fast, growling my name as he pours himself into me. I break, too, giving myself to the violent orgasm that slams into me. I gasp as the hot, electric waves of pleasure wash over me, pulsing through my entire body. My head lolls to the side, and my eyes flutter closed. I'm completely spent.

Once our orgasms subside, he props himself up on his arms. We're still connected, but he pulls back even more and looks down at me in wonder. We stay like that for a minute while he brushes the side of his thumb down my cheek. "I never knew joy until I met you," he says softly. "I still can't believe you chose *me*—

the Devil, the worst of all men." He pauses for a heartbeat before continuing. "Are you happy?"

"Yes," I whisper, and I smile up at him. "I love you, Devon. As long as we're together, I'm happy."

"Good, because you are my everything, Gwendolyn, and I can't imagine my life without you in it."

My heart thuds against my ribs, close to bursting. "Then I guess it's a good thing I'm not going anywhere. You're stuck with me forever."

He smiles. "That sounds like a deal."

I nod, then lift myself up a little, glancing over his shoulder at the hourglass on the bookshelf. "Speaking of deals, though…that hourglass is only half gone. Didn't we agree on two rounds?"

He laughs. "I believe we did."

I bite my bottom lip. "Well, I'd hate to go back on my word. Should we, uh…head to the playroom?"

With a low chuckle, he grabs my chin and plants a gentle kiss on my lips. "God, I love you, Gwendolyn Taylor."

"The feeling is mutual, Lord Devon Howard of Everleigh."

And as he leans down to kiss me again, I can't help but feel like life with the Devil will be my own personal heaven.

CHAPTER 39
CASSIE

I CAN'T BELIEVE THE SHIT I GET MYSELF INTO. HONESTLY.

But that disbelief is right alongside the giddy feeling I have that my ship has finally come in. Last year, my dad died and my stepbrother Liam took everything—my dad's business, his money, *all* of it. He left me with nothing. The meager income I have is from the shitty part-time job I've managed to hold onto, or the occasional loan from my stepmom. With school and my mounting student loans, it's been impossible to keep myself afloat.

But that's all going to change. I've managed to land a lucrative job that will get me out of the financial nightmare I've been living in.

"Did you say four hundred dollars an hour? Just to sit in a chair at a gentleman's club and watch two people…fool around?" Avery stares at me wide-eyed, scandalized, her pale skin flushed crimson. She's so innocent, like a virginal medieval princess, heavy on the *virginal* part. It's not even a guess, either. She's readily admitted to the rest of us that she's as pure as the driven snow, completely untouched.

I shrug, pushing away feelings of self-consciousness. I already know Avery is going to judge me for this. "It's unconventional, but it pays the bills."

"*More* than just pays the bills, I'd bet." Gwen walks into the room, smiling. "But I can't imagine just sitting there, watching someone else get nailed. After a long night at work…you, ah, might need something to take the edge off, you know? There's a great online sex toy store. I'll send you the link."

If it's even possible, Avery's color deepens, and she looks even *more* scandalized than before, her pale blue eyes as wide as saucers. So I decide to spare her virginal sensibilities and drop the subject.

But a few hours later, Gwen accosts me while I'm in the bathroom brushing my teeth. She's got an overnight bag slung over her shoulder, which means she's headed out to Malibu to spend the weekend with her hot royal quillionare at Exeter House. Lucky bitch.

"I know you didn't want to say more in front of Avery because, you know, she's *Avery,* but I've got a few minutes before the car gets here. Tell me *all* the deets about this job and this guy."

I nod enthusiastically, then spit, rinse, and wipe my face. I glance toward the hallway behind her, and she pushes into the bathroom, shutting the door.

"C'mon. Spill it. You were at Obscura. Wild place, huh?" she says.

"Jeez, Gwen, I can't believe you didn't tell me about that place before!"

She laughs. "What happens at Obscura stays at Obscura. But now you're an employee. *And* you work for Ms. Lawrence. That's kinda wild. Such a small world."

I blink. "Well, it's a godsend is what it is. My bank account was on fumes."

She puts her bag down and leans against the door. "So what's your job, exactly? Just watching? Is that really all there is to it, or did you just not want to say anything in front of Avery?"

I shrug. "No, that's it. Really. I sit in a chair and watch the guy fuck his submissive. It's pretty straightforward."

"So they don't touch you? The guy doesn't ask you to touch his sub?"

I shake my head. "Nope. And it says in my contract that no one can touch me, or ask me to do anything I'm not comfortable with."

"Wow. That's a pretty sweet deal." Gwen pushes a breath out. "What's this guy's persona at Obscura? Maybe I've seen him there."

I wet a washcloth and use it to wash my face. "He goes by Hart at the club, and he wears a stag mask."

She straightens. "Oh! Is his sub a white bunny? Her name is…oh, God, what was it?"

"Willow," I supply.

"Yeah, that's the same guy! He's gorgeous. One of the few Americans I've run into there, actually. Most of the guys are British."

Wait, what?

"No, he's British, too. He has the most delicious accent, actually."

I hear that richly accented voice in my dreams. Hart's deep baritone wends through my body as I try to sleep. But every time I close my eyes, I see him—staring at me in that stag mask, his muscled torso flexing as he slides his cock into Willow.

And every night, I touch myself, imagining it's the stag's hand stroking me, coaxing me to climax. Sometimes, I have to come *twice* in the same night before I'm spent enough to fall asleep.

Gwen twists her head, confused. "Are you sure? I distinctly remember an *American* accent. It was noteworthy because it's so rare at Obscura. Especially for a founder."

"Wait, he's one of the founders of Obscura?" Now that's new information.

She shrugs. "Well, I'm assuming so. He was in one of the back halls of the founders-only area."

I purse my lips and shift the conversation back to Hart's changing accent. "Why would he have a different accent?"

She waves her hand dismissively. "I don't know. Maybe I just misheard. To be fair, he only said like…three words, and it was months ago. It's probably nothing."

I nod. "Ah, okay. Yeah. Maybe he just sounded American to you."

Gwen nods, but she doesn't look convinced. "Right. Exactly. Nothing to worry about."

I toss my wet washcloth over the lip of the tub and dry my face. "It's not like it matters anyway. My contract is only for a few weeks. And by then, I'll have a nice chunk of money that my wicked stepbrother can't touch."

"Yeah, fuck Liam," she says. "It's really too bad your brother is so damn hot. All the hot ones are evil." She points a finger at me. "*Don't* tell Devon I said that. He's really sensitive about his evilness. I mean, I love him, but he does have a fairly wide wicked streak."

We both laugh at that, and I swear not to say anything.

"There's just one thing I don't get," I say, "and maybe you can help me figure it out. Or maybe I'm just crazy, I don't know…"

Gwen nods, urging me to continue.

"When I'm in the room with Hart and Willow, he stares at me the whole time."

Gwen shakes her head. "*Stares* at you…how?"

I lean my hip against the sink and search for the best way to explain it. "Like when he's punishing her, he's looking at *me*. And it's not just looking, it's palpable. He's staring at me like he wants to *devour* me."

Gwen looks confused. "Wait, so while he's fucking Willow, he's staring at *you*?"

"Yeah," I say in a rush. "It's kind of hot, actually. Is that weird?"

My nipples tighten just remembering the look in his eyes beneath that feral stag mask. He's so damn hot, I can hardly catch my breath when I'm in his presence. It takes everything in me not to touch myself while he's fucking her.

"Uh, why do you think he's doing that? Is he watching for your reaction, maybe? Some guys really get off on that."

I shake my head. "No, see, that's the thing—I get the feeling he's fucking *her*, but he wants *me*."

Gwen shifts on her feet. "Huh. Why do you think he's so fixated on you?"

I shake my head. "I don't know."

I leave out what disturbs me most about this whole situation with Hart. When I'm in the same room with him, I get the unmistakable feeling he *knows* me. On a deep, intrinsic level. It's an odd notion, but the way he looks at me, and the way he makes me feel—I just get the sense that Hart is hiding something…and I'm afraid to find out what that something is…

BIOGRAPHY

Evelyn has been telling stories in her head for as long as she can remember. She lives on the west coast with her family, and a menagerie of pets. She loves lattes, all things Disney, gaming, and writing dark, wildly sexy stories that give readers all the feels.

Sign up for news and updates:
evelynaustinbooks.wixsite.com/my-site/newsletter

www.ingramcontent.com/pod-product-compliance
Lightning Source LLC
Chambersburg PA
CBHW021221310726
48971CB00006B/1644